ALL THAT WE ARE

ALL THAT WE ARE

Elizabeth Lord

This first world edition published 2010
in Great Britain and in the USA by
SEVERN HOUSE PUBLISHERS LTD of
9–15 High Street, Sutton, Surrey, England, SM1 1DF.
Trade paperback edition first published
in Great Britain and the USA 2011 by
SEVERN HOUSE PUBLISHERS LTD.

British Library Cataloguing in Publication Data

Lord, Elizabeth, 1928–
    All That We Are.
    1. Families – England – London – Fiction. 2. East End
    (London, England) – Social conditions – 20th century –
    Fiction. 3. Family-owned business enterprises – England –
    London – Fiction. 4. Domestic fiction.
    I. Title
    823.9'14–dc22

ISBN-13: 978-0-7278-6923-4   (cased)
ISBN-13: 978-1-84751-260-4   (trade paper)

Except where actual historical events and characters are being
described for the storyline of this novel, all situations in this
publication are fictitious and any resemblance to living persons
is purely coincidental.

All Severn House titles are printed on acid-free paper.

Severn House Publishers support The Forest Stewardship Council [FSC],
the leading international forest certification organisation. All our titles that
are printed on Greenpeace-approved FSC-certified paper carry the FSC logo.

Mixed Sources
Product group from well-managed
forests and other controlled sources
www.fsc.org Cert no. SA-COC-1565
© 1996 Forest Stewardship Council
FSC

Typeset by Palimpsest Book Production Ltd.,
Falkirk, Stirlingshire, Scotland.
Printed and bound in Great Britain by
MPG Books Ltd., Bodmin, Cornwall.

*In memory of my dear husband, Charlie, whose story
this is. And for our daughter, Clare, who suggested
I write it — thank you.*

PART ONE

PART ONE

One

The clothes post was looking very precarious, and no wonder after what her brother Neil had done to it as he came home drunk in the early hours.

Standing at the back door, Nora Taylor gave a wry smile. If nothing was done about mending that post it would probably collapse under the weight of Mum's current lot of washing. At this very moment she was working off her anger at having to do it again, all the time swearing under her breath in her London-Irish brogue.

Nora supposed she should offer to help but she knew she would only reap a sharp and hostile retort. Anyway, at twenty, with every neighbourhood boy taken by her slender figure and blue eyes accentuated by her dark hair, she could do without ruining her looks at a washtub. Let Maggie do it.

Eighteen months younger than herself, Maggie was usually the one expected to help with the washing. Ten-year-old Elsie would often be recruited as well. Rose, of course, being only six, wouldn't be called on for such heavy work, and certainly not fourteen-year-old George; boys not being expected to do any household chores – women's work.

As for Neil – that would have been unthinkable even though it had been his fault the clothes-line full of washing had been discovered lying on the ground earlier this morning. At twenty-three he should have known better than to behave as he'd done last night, barging in through the back gate like that, pretty drunk to the bargain.

The tiny backyard gate opened on to Slater Alley, though the house itself fronted on to Gough Street in Poplar. Backyards in London's East End were mostly concreted over, but Dad loved his bit of lawn even if it was more mud than grass with Mum moving up and down to hang out her endless washing.

The clothes post had always been a bit dodgy but Neil, heavily built and easily goaded into action had helped it on its way.

Coming home late after having seen a one-act drama called *The Ghost Sonata* at a small West End theatre with a few mates, he'd come in by the back gate and walked straight into Mum's line of sheets, shirts and underwear flapping like pale spectres in the drying winter night's breeze.

The eerie play still on his mind, and fortified by more than a few pints and chasers, as the sheets on the washing line lightly touched his face in the dark, like the pale spectres of all Hell's demons coming to get him, he'd wildly flung out his arms and torn the lot down before making a frantic run for the house and safety.

This morning he'd left for work sharper than usual without a word to Mum, who'd already gone off her rocker at finding all her hard labour from the day before strewn in the mud.

'It's that bloody post agin, that's what it is!' she'd raged at Dad, her brogue now mixed with Cockney after all these years living in London.

'If I've told yer once, yer lazy old divil, I've told yer umpteen times to fix it. Me working me 'ands to the bone scrubbing yer dirty clothes clean, ter find it all draped in the mud and 'avin' ter be done over again!'

That the other end of the clothes line had been ripped off the bolt on the house wall as well, didn't seem to strike her.

But last night Nora had heard the stifled cry of panic just below her bedroom window, followed by frantic scuffling. She had hopped out of bed while her sisters slept on and had crept to the window in time to see her brother's display of primitive terror. It was all she could do to stop herself bursting out laughing and waking up her sisters. She couldn't resist telling Neil, just before he left for work. Obviously trying to save face he mumbled something about the strange effect the play had had on him.

'Enough to give anyone a scare after that, blundering into something ghostly white you don't expect. Flapping all round yer face like that in the dark, you'd have felt the same as I did. It ain't no shame.'

'You'd better tell that to Mum,' she'd said, trying to hide a grin.

But she was glad he hadn't. This way she could blackmail him into handing over a few bob to keep quiet and not make him look a laughing stock and less than the man he saw himself to be.

Five shillings would buy the hat she had seen in that posh shop in Plaistow High Street, and a nice skirt and jacket to go with it to wear to the class of six-year-olds she taught at nearby St Saviour's infants' school.

She itched to tell Maggie about their brother's capers and share a good laugh, but Maggie would have then expected a share of the money too. Though Maggie was probably more taken up with the man she had met a few weeks ago, so she said. She said she'd first met him at one of those lectures she loved going to at a nearby public meeting hall around the beginning of December. Christmas had intervened but much to Nora's surprise she was still seeing him, though Nora was the only one she'd so far told and that only sketchily.

'He's ever so good looking and ever so mature,' was all she'd say.

A reluctance to say more not only revealed her feelings towards the man, but fear that Mum and Dad wouldn't approve before ever they met him – if it ever got that far.

Ten years ago any decent girl of only eighteen, and from a respectable family, would have definitely been discouraged from going off with friends, gallivanting and meeting young men just as she pleased, but this was 1910, if only January, and standards weren't what they had once been. Even so, Mum who had kept her strict Catholic faith, even though Dad and the rest of the family were Church of England, would be more than upset, especially as another small point Maggie had let drop in Nora's ear was that the man she'd met wasn't even a churchgoer. And there was one more thing.

'So what's his name?' she'd ventured at breakfast one day, keeping her voice to a whisper while their mother stood preparing porridge oats, Dad already gone off to the rag factory he owned having had his breakfast earlier.

'Mr Robert Titchnell,' Maggie whispered back, at last beginning to warm to her confiding in her sister.

'Mister!' Nora gasped quietly. 'You call him mister?'

'Shh,' Maggie warned as her mother's head turned. 'Tell you later.'

It wasn't until the evening as they were getting ready for bed that she said, gabbling it as if glad to get it off her chest, 'He's a widower. He's in his thirties and he has a son.'

Nora stopped combing out her long dark hair to turn horrified blue eyes on her sister. 'Widowed? With a son, and you're going to tell that to Mum?'

She saw Maggie's full lips begin to tremble. 'I don't know how I'm going to. I don't know what to do. She'll go right off her rocker, I know she will.'

'How old is this son?' was all Nora asked.

'Nearly nine, he told me. But please, Nora, don't tell a soul. If Mum knew she'd put a stop to it. I've fallen in love with him and I don't want to have anything happen to spoil it. Promise you'll say nothing to anyone.'

'I promise,' Nora said.

'You can be a proper bitch sometimes,' Maggie snapped as she tossed her honey-coloured tresses; her hazel eyes were like Dad's but now flashed in the way her mother's so often did.

'I told you about Robert in confidence and all you keep doing is dropping broad hints in front of them both.'

'Broad hints?' Nora repeated, trying to keep her face straight as the pair of them undressed for bed this Friday night.

All evening Maggie had been giving her looks. According to Maggie it seemed that almost every word she'd spoken to their parents, as the family sat hugging the fire against the February draughts from under doors and window frames, had apparently been loaded with connotation.

With the two younger girls, Elsie and Rose, in bed, everyone had been preoccupied with their own pursuits as usual, saying little to each other. Nearing the end of her penny novelette, Nora wanted only to see how the final page would pan out, though already guessing that the willowy heroine would marry the man she loved. Maggie and fourteen-year-old George had been engrossed in an ongoing jigsaw puzzle of a Scottish castle. Neil was out as usual, either with mates or some girl or other. Tall and handsome, he apparently had endless female admirers.

In his wooden armchair by the fire, Dad dozed, braces dangling, collar off, feet propped on the fender just far enough from the fire for the soles of his boots not to steam, his pipe lying in one limp hand, the tobacco in the bowl long since burned away and tapped out.

Only Mum, sewing at the big table by the light of an elaborate oil lamp pulled nearer to her from the centre of the table, had things to say, asking how her two eldest daughters' day had gone.

'So then, how'd yer teaching go today?' she had asked Nora without looking up from her sewing. 'Little ones caused yer no trouble?'

'They never cause me trouble,' Nora had said absently, her gaze concentrated on her book. 'They wouldn't dare.'

She meant that. Her children were well behaved. If one stepped out of line, a quick look from her soon brought the child to heel, failing that a quick slap to the back of the head always did the trick.

'And what about you, Maggie?' Mum glanced up at her. 'You was a mite late coming home to tea. Was your bus late? It's been snowing well and it don't take much to make buses late. Or was you kept late at work?'

'No. We closed on time,' Maggie replied absently, her mind on the piece she was trying to fit into the jigsaw puzzle.

Maggie was employed by what Mum saw as befitting a young lady, a small haberdashery in Commercial Road. Deep down, she didn't approve of young ladies going out to work. She'd have preferred to see her stay at home like the young daughters of the upper classes did. She considered this family to be middle class at least, having come up in the world since her parents came over from Ireland bringing their humble rag-picking trade with them.

Their small business brought in good money and their children spoke moderately well which was how Nora had become an infant school teacher and the family held its head high among those of humbler means.

'Why so late then getting home?' Mum queried, still sewing away.

She could have sent out her mending to a nearby seamstress but felt she could make a better job of it herself. It was the same with her washing, certain no washerwoman could, in her estimation, bring it up as clean and sparkling white as she did. At least they had a cleaning woman who came in daily to sweep, dust, polish, wash the outside windows and sills, whiten the doorstep and black-lead the grate, and a young girl as a maid-cum-cook.

Before Maggie could reply to her mother's questioning, Nora had burst out without thinking, 'Probably some young man,' immediately wanting to bite her lip as the look Maggie shot at her had been enough to kill.

Mum's blue eyes had lifted sharply from her sewing to take in both girls. 'What young man?'

Her tone had been full of suspicion and realizing her error, Nora said hastily, 'Just a thought, that's all.'

Mum's glare had concentrated itself on Maggie. '*Is* there a young man?' she questioned. 'Yer mind yerself young lady, because I'm not having you gallivanting with the sort o' roughs we've around these parts. Me an' yer father need to meet whoever it is to see what he's like.'

Compelled to lie for her sister, Nora cut in, 'I didn't mean anything by what I said, Mum. It was just a remark. I expect it was more like one of her girl friends talking to her so long who made her late. Isn't that so, Maggie?'

'Yes . . . Yes, of course,' came the hasty response and Mum had seemed satisfied enough, but Maggie's eyes had continued to dart fire in Nora's direction and now she was bringing it up again as they got ready for bed, Rose and Elsie already fast asleep in their own bed.

'If you ever drop another hint like that, I'll kill you!' she hissed as she dragged her warm, white winceyette nightgown over her head, having sluiced her face and combed out her long hair from the ribbon that had held it back off her face.

In the act of unpinning her own hair from where it had been dressed full and wide on top of her head, the dark strands falling heavily about her shoulders to reach her waist in a glossy cascade, she turned on her sister.

'Why? I didn't mean to do any damage,' she whispered so as not to disturb the two younger girls huddled together in their narrow bed.

'You know full well you did,' Maggie hissed back. 'You did it on purpose.'

'I didn't do it on purpose. Honestly.'

'Honestly or not, what matters is that you've got Mum thinking. And I hate you!'

Nora shrugged. Her sister was always hating someone or something.

Shivering in the cold as she too struggled gratefully into her own thick night gown, anxious to get into bed and warm up, she sought to calm things down.

'You'll have to bring him home sooner or later to meet everyone,' she said gently. 'How long are you going to wait? That's if you're both serious.'

Maggie seemed to wilt a little. 'We are! He says I'm the right person for him and he's certainly becoming more . . . well, intent.'

Nora looked at her, her blue eyes widening. 'He hasn't . . . I mean, you haven't . . .?'

'Of course not!' Shocked by the unspoken implication, she looked just like their mother as she glared back. 'How can you think such a thing? We've only been going out since just before Christmas, and only a couple of times a week when he takes me to the music hall. Mum still thinks I'm out with friends. And now you've almost spoiled everything for me. I wish I'd never told you.'

'It wasn't intentional,' Nora said, genuinely sorry. 'But you are going to have to introduce him to them eventually. And what I said wasn't meant to be horrid. I promise I'll really watch my tongue in future.'

She herself was dying to see what this man looked like. All she could visualize of this widower was someone a little boring, maybe suitable to Maggie's somewhat staid nature, perhaps not as good looking as she made out, though, like herself, Maggie was fussy about looks and presentation, both in herself and in anyone she might one day decide to go steady with. Was this the one?

Well, in time, they would see, Nora told herself as, with Maggie having partway forgiven her, they snuggled up together in the bed for warmth in the freezing bedroom, burying their faces under blankets and eiderdown.

Two

This Sunday morning Nora sat on their bed watching Maggie getting herself ready to go out. Maggie had told her mother it was with a girlfriend, though in truth it was her Robert.

Nora was still the only one she'd told, here in their bedroom, the only place they could share confidences, the rest of the house always full of people and Mum's ears sharp as a bat's.

This morning, Mum had gone to Mass as usual and Dad was down the pub with a few mates. Neil was out with one of his many girl friends, Nora guessed. But the younger children were in, their mother forbidding them to play in the street on Sundays, and young ears soon carry tales as Mum often said. So the bedroom was the best place.

'Don't you think it's time you told Mum and Dad about this Robert of yours?' asked Nora continuing to watch her sister dressing. 'You'll have to tell them soon. After all, it's been nearly three months. It must be getting serious.'

Maggie's hazel eyes were wide with anxiety as she paused in getting into the skirt of her smart Sunday costume, pleated to the calf to flare out about her ankles to go with a tailored bolero over a high-buttoned blouse.

'The moment Mum knows more about him she'll try and put a stop to it, I know she will. You know what she's like.'

Nora knew exactly. Mum was not the easiest person in the world to get around if it didn't suit, and this person Maggie had found would certainly not suit the moment she revealed him to be a man in his thirties – fifteen years older than her daughter – and a widower with an eight-year-old son at that.

'She'll go barmy, even though he does have his own business. It might have helped if he was Catholic. But he isn't.'

'Neither is Dad but Mum married him.'

'Yes, but Robert don't even bother to go to church, any church.'

'Nor do Dad.'

Maggie pouted, unconvinced as she finished buttoning up her skirt.

'But she stuck to her Catholic faith despite him insisting on us all being christened Church of England. They must have had lots of rows about it, but he stuck to his guns and who knows, perhaps he'll stand up for me.'

Nora smirked knowingly. 'What, against her? It's years since he ever got his way against her. He gave up arguing with her long ago.'

Sticking to his Protestant guns had probably been the last time he'd ever stood up to her, that and the naming of his children. Only Neil the first born had been given a good Irish name as she saw it, but when she'd wanted good old Irish names for the others he would have none of that either.

'Good old London names fer the rest of our kids,' he was supposed to have told her firmly.

And so it had been. But after that it seemed he must have lost the will to fight her. As far back as Nora could remember she'd always have the last say. It seemed he'd long ago wearied of arguments which she usually won by the simple means of wearing a person down. Mum could wear mountains down to pebbles when she had a mind. Nora just hoped she wouldn't try wearing down this present mountain of Maggie's, leaving her distraught.

'Still, you can't keep on meeting in secret,' she said. 'I'm sure Dad will be on your side if this Robert is as respectable and mature as you say.'

Maggie gave a despondent shrug as she went over to the mirror to add a last touch to her hair, piled into a Pompadour style to make her look older.

'All Dad wants is a quiet life. I just have to hope he won't take her side just to keep the peace. Sometimes I hate her!'

'Don't say that,' Nora came to her mother's defence. 'She can be a bit of a tyrant at times but she's brought us all up properly. And it's because of her that Dad's business thrives like it does. She's so good at figures. She keeps his books in order marvellously with a strict eye on the overheads. It leaves him free to get on with the rest of his business like selecting the best stuff from the rag and bone men that come here and overseeing his sorters.'

'That's about all he does,' Maggie pouted, patting her hair in place.

'He does much more than that,' Nora retorted, now needing to stand up for her Dad in turn. 'He deals with all the big clothing manufacturers which she can't do, that being a man's job.'

'I know, but if she says bark, he jolly well barks, and if she says don't bark, he shuts up like a trapdoor. And if she's going to be against me seeing Robert, then I just hope Dad will be on my side at least.'

'I hope so too,' Nora agreed. 'But you know how Mum can be if she wants her own way. And another thing, Maggie, has this Robert, who none of us has set eyes on yet, gone as far as talking seriously of marriage, before ever being introduced to us, even before asking for Dad's consent?'

Maggie drew herself upright and turned from the mirror, all ready now to leave. 'He has asked me to marry him, yes, and we both know he needs to speak to Dad first, but I want to bide my time just a little longer before telling Dad about it and see if he can talk Mum round about Robert coming to tea one Sunday. Then we'll see what happens.'

With that, she snatched up the beige parasol and natty little beige hat that went with her cream-coloured costume and stalked out of the room.

Until now Maggie hadn't replied one way or the other to Robert's references to engagement and marriage. It was flattering and thrilling to know that a mature man of good standing should think of her as worthy. She was in love, but with Nora's warnings ringing in her ears she had become torn between defiance and fear of being too ready to say the word.

'We've known each other for such a short time,' she told him. 'And there's our age difference, me still eighteen and you thirty-three. What if my parents don't agree to it? You've still to meet them and I can't really say anything about it to them without you speaking to them formally first. As old as you are, my love, you've still got to speak to my father for his permission.'

He burst out laughing. 'Me? Old?' But she didn't laugh with him.

'I meant mature, Robert. I meant that although I'll be nineteen next month, my father might still consider me too young to marry. What if he says no? What do I do then? I mean, it was only a few months back my mother was still insisting on my hair being tied back in a ribbon like all young girls. And now I have to tell them that someone wants to marry me. I'm so scared my father will refuse his consent.'

'So *you* aren't against it,' Robert said, taking her drawn out and garbled reply as a positive rather than negative response.

Maggie in her best costume, waist pulled in tight as she could get it, blouse fashionably pouched to give the current look of a fine figure of a woman, her hair in a well styled bouffant, waited on tenterhooks for Robert's arrival.

Four weeks had gone by and now she was sure. Robert was the man for her and a few days ago she had at last said yes to him.

The dining room table was set for high tea. Sally their maid hovered in the kitchen awaiting her orders. In the parlour Mum was sitting on the edge of her armchair where she would receive their visitor, Dad standing behind her. The rest of the family had been banished upstairs until called, leaving just herself and her parents to greet their guest. Nora was still out with her friends but Neil had not long come in from seeing his, and had been asked to retreat upstairs until formalities were over then to come down to tea.

Hoping her mother wouldn't see how pent up she was, Maggie sat by the bay window risking furtive peeps through its heavy lace curtains and the broad leaves of the aspidistra on the small table in the bay. From here she'd be the first to see the motor cab draw up to the curb. She just hoped she would contain herself properly when it did.

She'd avoided as many of her parents' questions as she could about Robert, even today, going only as far as saying how good looking he was, how caring and considerate, that his scrap metal business was a thriving one, still not revealing his age only to say he was a fraction older than her.

It wasn't exactly a lie, just a small distortion, but she could see from the set of her mother's lips that she was far from satisfied with such a scant description. She looked slightly bewildered too, as far as that woman could ever be bewildered.

Maggie wished now that she'd been more forthcoming much earlier on, not been such a coward, and by now they would have been prepared. Though perhaps not Mum. Looking across at her, Maggie realized that it had been a mistake not to have told them earlier. The longer she had left it the worse it had got. And now, despite all her efforts her mother was still reading something unsavoury into a relationship by it having been kept secret for so long.

When she had finally told them a few days ago of wanting to bring Robert here to see them as quite out of the blue he'd asked her to marry him, Mum's reaction had been typical.

'Marry you? Who is this person? And what d'you mean, you've bin seeing this person for several months? Someone none of us know and you not tellin' us? What's so unsavoury about it that you've bin frightened to tell us, havin' ter keep it secret from me an' yer father 'till now? What've you an' him bin up to, girl? If you've got yerself . . .?'

The rest of the suspicion had been cut off, too dreadful a thought to put into words. Maggie had leapt instantly and violently to her own defence.

'Mum! How could you think such a thing of your own daughter?'

'Well, what's a body to think when yer bloddy spring something like this on me an' yer dad? We've bought you up ter be a good Christian girl. If yer stupid father had agreed to letting you be baptized into the Faith this sort of trouble would niver happen.'

'What trouble!' she'd retaliated, angered and deeply hurt by such uncalled-for accusation. 'Mum, me and Robert have done nothing wrong!'

'I believe her, Moira,' her father had cut in, suddenly forceful. 'She wouldn't think for a moment of doing anythink wrong. Not our daughter.'

The firmness of his tone had modified hers for once. 'Orright, but she should've told us before now, not spring it on us of bringing someone home. So now we must see him and judge for ourselves if he's right for her. We'll have to ask him to come for Sunday tea – the quicker the better. Then we can see for ourselves. She should have told us earlier so she should.'

Since then Mum had done nothing but probe, appalled at

what had been slowly and reluctantly extracted that he was in fact a widower which had put her against him instantly. Maggie had at least managed to avoid mentioning just how much older he was than herself and certainly nothing about his having a son, just telling her that he was financially sound and in business like themselves.

The fact that his business was akin to theirs, turning scrap material into something profitable seemed to satisfy her to a point. The rest would speak for itself when she met him. And hopefully all that would be for her father's ears first as it should be, at least paving the way before her mother got in her forceful two penny-worth as to his unsuitability as a husband to her daughter when she discovered him to be considerably older than she had been led to believe.

Beyond the window the busy Manor Road resounded to the endless racket of wheels and motorized vehicles that had recently begun to take over from the horse. But nothing had drawn up. Then she saw it, the cab moving out from the flow of traffic to pull up at the curb, Robert alighting and paying off the cabbie. She saw him turn towards the front gate as the vehicle pulled jerkily away into the traffic. Her attentiveness however alerted her parents, her mother's back snapping even straighter than it had been as her father went to take up a position with his back to the fireplace.

Seeing it, Maggie felt her heart had all but stopped. Already she knew the outcome. Dad would heed his wife and refuse to give his consent, aware that his life would become a misery if he didn't. Then what? Would she have the courage to defy them? Could she bring herself to run away with Robert, marrying in secret, fleeing with him to Gretna Green, lying about her age, perhaps never see her parents or her family again, disgraced, disowned?

Such possibilities and consequences rearing up inside her she felt sick as she heard the bell ring, Sally's footsteps hurrying on the tiled hallway floor, the door being opened, Robert's deep-toned announcement followed by Sally's high voice bidding him enter.

There came a brief silence while he divested himself of his overcoat, scarf and hat, Sally no doubt taking a time to hang them on the hall stand for him. Then the parlour door opened and Sally was announcing, 'Sir, Madam, Mr Robert Titchnell.'

As she withdrew, Maggie resisted the temptation to run to him but their eyes met for a calming second before he looked towards her father to offer a small nod of the head, first to him then to her mother.

He looked so handsome, so in control of himself as he came briskly across the room, a hand extended towards her father, not at all put out by his hosts' wary expressions in seeing a mature rather than a young man.

'How d'you do, sir?' Robert said cordially as her father took the offered hand. 'It's good of you to consent to see me. I'm much obliged.'

Maggie had never seen him look so relaxed and hoped he wasn't going to overdo it, but her father seemed impressed.

'You're welcome,' was all he said, but friendly enough she felt.

Robert nodded and smiled then turned to the hostess. 'And thank you too, Mrs Taylor. I trust you are well.'

Mum's tight, answering smile, however was as chill and rigid as ice as she inclined her head in a poor imitation of queenly dignity, Mum not given to graciousness or grace. 'Very well, oi'm sure,' she said icily in her London-Irish brogue and Maggie found herself hard put to control a nervous giggle.

Robert held out towards her a flat, blue box he'd been holding at his side. 'I wasn't sure what to bring, Mrs Taylor. I hope you like chocolates.'

And what could she do but nod her thanks, finding herself bound to accept them out of politeness, and although the stiff smile remained, perhaps it wasn't quite so frozen.

'Well, introductions done,' Dad said briskly, never a one to stand on ceremony for long, 'let's get the business bit over before we have tea. Your letter said you wanted to have a chat with me about you an' Maggie, so what if us two go into the back room.'

Called the back room, next to the kitchen with the parlour and dining room on opposite sides of the hallway at the front of the house, it was where Dad liked to retreat whenever Mum's petty displeasures got the better of his good nature.

Through the wall between the parlour and the back room Maggie could hear only the low murmur of their voices in conversation but then came her Dad's high chuckle. It was going far smoother than she'd dared hope.

It also went quicker than she'd expected and before long Robert and her father were back with broad grins on their faces, much to Mum's grim disapproval as far as Maggie could see.

Even so, her joy was immediate and almost unbounded, Mum for once having had no say in this matter, being men's business to a certain extent. But Maggie knew it wouldn't be the last she'd hear of it, Mum's opinion on the unsuitability of this man as her daughter's prospective husband not altered in the slightest. Once her mind was made up little would change it. It wouldn't matter that Dad had approved of this match Maggie knew the future was already set to be far from a serene one. But it didn't matter – Robert was now hers and it wouldn't be long before the wedding date was set. She'd never felt so happy in all her life.

'Well,' Dad stated amiably. 'What about tea. Where're the others? Let's call 'em all down.'

Three

Five thirty. She should have been home by five for tea to meet their guest but she'd got carried away wandering with friends along Regents Canal in bright February sunshine. Despite the chill they'd been chatting with some young men they knew and the afternoon had simply flown by. Bursting into the house she was just in time to see her Mum already ushering everyone into the dining room and by her sharp, blue-eyed glare, knew she was in her bad books as she hurriedly took off her jacket, outdoor boots and hat.

Slipping into her house-shoes propped against the hallstand rail, she smoothed her hair with her hand and went into the room as discretely as she could to take her place at the table with its snow-white cloth and best china. The rest of the family, already seated, watched her in silence. Nora tightened her lips that had been about to offer them all a smile of apology.

Her mother had glared at her in silence but it was Dad who made her feel the most uncomfortable with his effort at a disarming introduction, 'Oh, Robert, and this is my eldest daughter Nora. A bit late I'm afraid. But then she always is!' Then to her: 'But now you're 'ere, Nora, this is Mr Robert Titchnell, now your sister's intended being as just before you came in I 'ad a talk with and been more than 'appy to give my consent for the two of them to get married.'

As Nora acknowledged the introduction she glimpsed the look that passed between her parents, her father with a warning gaze while her mother's lips tightened stubbornly. But Maggie's intended had given a warm smile and a polite 'How d'you do?'

Nora's answering smile unfortunately became somewhat lost in that second of discomposure, her reply sharper than she'd have liked in having been taken off guard by the look on her mother's face.

He must have thought her churlish for he didn't once glance her way after that, in the same way as he seemed to avoid her

mother's eyes whose expression had remained one of stiff disapproval of this whirlwind match, an expression that didn't change
throughout the whole meal.

Annoyed with herself and wanting to make up for it, Nora
was aware of her own eyes being drawn to the man time and
time again, willing him to look her way so she could offer him
a smile to convey that she did not share her mother's attitude.
But he'd seemed too caught up between sporadic conversation
with her Dad and attending to what Maggie was saying to notice.

It left her cursing herself for not having come home sooner
and able to meet him on a more convivial note, but of course
then she'd had little interest in this person her sister had found.
Now, as teatime progressed, her opinion began to change rapidly
until all she wanted was to catch his eye, and not just to compensate for her mother's frigid behaviour towards him. It was only
towards the end of the meal that she caught his glance enough to
give him another smile this time far more friendly.

To her consternation he returned it with such a deal of warmth
that she felt her cheeks glow. From then on it seemed that each
time she glanced in his direction those blue eyes were looking
back at her. Such an intense blue they were too. Unaccountably
they made her glow with pleasure until she caught her mother's
eyes trained on her with a look that immediately straightened
her lips.

Alone in her bedroom Nora sat listening in the dark to her
mother's voice as it rang clear through the house; clear through
the neighbourhood it seemed. That voice could probably be heard
a mile away when she got her dander up.

'No, you ain't goin' ter marry him and that's flat, no matter
what yer father says. What was you thinking of? The man's near
fifteen years older than you. When you're fifty he'll be sixty-five.
Sixty-five! Ten years older than yer dad is now an' be fit fer nothing
but be nursed. Is that what yer want? Yer could even already be
a widow. No, I ain't having it! I'm sorry but I ain't!'

'But . . .' came Maggie's tearful wail but her mother wasn't
listening.

'Now we find he's got an eight-year-old son.'

'There's a woman looks after him. He hires her . . .'

'I don't care, I don't! What I care about is are yer really and truly ready to take on some other woman's child? And you only eighteen—'

'I'll be nineteen next month.'

'What's a month!' the raised voice persisted. 'No, I won't allow it! Besides yer've hardly known him but a few months, *a few months*, girl, not hardly time enough to know what he's like, him all charm this afternoon and you all dewy-eyed. No, you don't know, so you can put a stop to it now. Find someone yer own age.'

Nora heard her father's deep voice break through the tirade. 'You must admit, Moira love, he might make a more stable 'usband than some young—'

'That's right, you take her side!' was the shrill interruption, 'just as you always do. I'm not listening to you, Jack! I shouldn't have listened when you insisted our children be brought up Church of England. I said it was wrong at the time, so I did, but you *would* have your way. And now look, not one bit of respect in any of 'em! The nuns would've made certain they learned to respect their parents. But you . . .'

As the tirade tailed off, her mother too beside herself to find more to say, Nora couldn't help a smile. Dad insisting all those years ago on his kids being baptized in his own religion, not that he'd ever been involved with his own religion one bit, was probably the one and only time he'd ever won an argument with her.

She bringing that up time after time over the years, he'd no doubt learned to keep his opinions to himself for the sake of peace and quiet. But today at least in the matter of his daughter's future happiness he was trying to have his say, though Nora already guessed that it wasn't going to wash with Mum.

Her smile faded as Neil's broad-shouldered figure passed by the open bedroom door. Catching sight of her expression he paused to grin at her.

'She's really 'aving a go, ain't she?'

He seemed to have forgotten her small attempt at blackmail several weeks ago when he'd challenged her, telling her quite amiably to go to hell.

With no heart or courage to further her attempts she'd let it drop but a week later he bought her a lovely warm woolly scarf.

'Peace offering,' he'd said jovially, and even though she already had two, a black one and a fawn one, this was white and she'd accepted it gratefully.

'Poor old Maggie,' he said now. 'I don't think she stands earthy up against Mum.'

'But she's in love. She should fight for him.'

'Too bad, once Mum digs her heels in. But you can't blame her, she only wants what's best for her daughters and you must admit she's right. This bloke Robert is a bit long in the tooth for an eighteen-year-old.'

'Nineteen come next month!' Nora echoed her sister's words and Neil's grin widened.

'That's as may be, but we don't know anything about him. We've only met him the once and all we know of him is only what he's told us about himself. We don't know what he's told Maggie and I still think Mum's right.'

'Mum's always right!' Nora retorted and heard her brother's deep chuckle as he continued on his way to his room he shared with his fourteen-year-old brother, no doubt to get all spruced up to go out for the evening, he hardly ever home, a man needing no one's permission to go off with mates looking for girls, and who knows, Nora thought wickedly, probably even looking to get more than just their company.

Nora was left wondering that when he finally found someone that he fancied to marry, no one would question him, forbid him, and she suddenly felt so sorry for Maggie.

There'd been no need to be. It seemed her sister suddenly found a spark of rebellion no one thought her capable of. It was now April and even though Robert had never been asked back by her parents since that Sunday tea in February, whenever he brought her home after an evening together, she'd defiantly bring him in for a cup of cocoa before he went home, taking him through to the kitchen without asking by-your-leave from her mother, or even glancing into the room where Mum and the family gathered.

And what could Mum say without showing herself up by telling a mature man of means, a polite and dignified man, that he was to leave her house as she might have done a young, un-welcome, cub of a lad?

It wasn't easy to tell him to his face that he was forbidden to court her daughter without making a fool of herself, especially with Dad having been all for the match in the first place. His argument that in good families many a young daughter would be married off to an older man cut no ice with her.

Arguments would wax fast and furious between them over it. Dad did his best to stand up for the girl but Nora guessed that given enough time Mum would wear him down. When she got her teeth into anything it was like being gripped by the fangs of a ruthless bulldog.

At the porch to Maggie's front door, Robert moved away from their embrace, not too sharply he hoped. They'd spent the afternoon on the Serpentine in the warm, late April sunshine although it had turned cold towards evening.

'I don't think I should come in this evening, Maggie,' he said as gently as he could. Even so he saw her frown.

'But you always come in.'

'I know, darling, but not tonight.'

'Why not?' Her tone sharp, he felt he needed to soften his words.

'To tell you the truth, darling, I always feel a bit uncomfortable about it, and . . .'

'You've never said so before,' she cut in, annoyance beginning to ring more positively in her voice.

'I didn't like to hurt your feelings, my sweet, but I can't keep invading your mother's home like this. It's not as if she is inviting me.'

'It's me who invites you, not her. It's my home too.'

'I know, but from the beginning I've felt that she doesn't approve of me that much.'

He'd spoken several times before of the fact that having been invited to Sunday tea that first time, the invitation had never been repeated, but Maggie had always pooh-poohed his concern. After a while he had let the matter drop but it didn't make him feel any less uneasy. Now at last he had to come out with it with a little more certainty but knew that he'd angered Maggie.

'I don't care whether she approves of you or not!' she flared. 'I'm your fiancée and if I want to invite you home for a goodnight cup of cocoa I shall. And she can carry on and say what she likes. Before long I'll be your wife and there's not a thing she can say or do about it, so there!'

'There is everything she can do about it,' he reminded as he remained standing away from her. 'You're still under age, my dear.'

'I'll be nineteen soon,' she challenged and he smiled.

'It still leaves two years before you're twenty-one. Although she hasn't said it to my face her attitude alone shows she's dead against us marrying.'

'But my Dad isn't. And so long as he says we can marry there's little she can do about it.'

'But you can't cause trouble in your family. If we do marry . . .'

'*If* we do?' Maggie broke out in alarm. 'What d'you mean, *if we do*? Are you trying to say you don't want to marry me?'

'I didn't mean it to sound that way,' he hurried. 'I meant what if she is so against it she refuses to go to her own daughter's wedding? That would be terrible and you'll always remember how it felt. I don't want to be the cause of such a rift. I only have your happiness at heart.'

She didn't answer. She merely stood there looking at him and he could see in the meagre glow of the nearby street lamp that tears were coursing down her cheeks.

'Don't you love me any more, Robert?' came the faint, tremulous question finally.

'Of course I do!' was all he could find to say.

Seconds later she was in his arms, throwing herself at him with a little cry. He caught her and held her to him to protect her, as much from the thoughts going through his head as from the chilly March night air.

'Of course I do,' he said again though he didn't kiss her to cement the statement, adding only, 'But I think it better not to come in quite so often. It only adds to how your mother obviously feels about me. Perhaps we should let a little more time pass too before we talk of wedding arrangements, even perhaps leave buying the engagement ring a while – give your mother more time to come round to the idea of accepting me into your family.'

'What difference is that going to make?' Maggie sighed, pouting.

'Be patient just a little while longer, darling, that's all. Believe me I do understand a little how she feels. But I think we should say goodnight before your parents wonder what we're up to out here. They must have heard our voices. I'll pick you up next Saturday, darling, OK?'

His kiss was brief though he allowed a small hesitation in parting just to reassure her that he was being sincere. Then with her gazing bleakly after him, he walked away, turning once to wave at her as he continued on to seek a taxicab in the main road as he always did.

Four

'You staying in again?' Her mother's tone was almost peevish as Nora came into the room to sit by the table, nicely dressed but no intention of going out.

'You always went out Saturday nights, Nora. Now yer niver do. You ain't under the weather are yer? Something wrong with yer is there?'

'No, I'm fine,' Nora said as she glanced up at the clock on the mantle shelf. 'I just don't feel like bothering tonight.'

Her mother put aside the invoices she'd been studying to glare at her. 'How many weeks it been? It's not healthy. Teaching in school all week, yer should be out in the fresh air so yer should. What about yer friends?'

'I see them on Sunday afternoons. It's just the weather has been so miserable these last few Saturdays,' Nora evaded.

'That never stopped yer before, no matter what the weather. And don't tell me you'd not go out looking for the young fellers on Saturday nights, so yer did.'

Nora knew Mum disapproved of the modern girl who seldom sought permission to meet young men, not that she'd met anyone she fancied so far. And she'd turned twenty-one just before Christmas, now had the key of the door as they say, so Mum's disapproval of young men now fell on deaf ears.

When she didn't reply, all Mum could do was mutter, 'You an' Maggie, the two of yers will be the death o' me,' as she returned to checking invoices.

Dad, sitting by the fire staring into it, hadn't even stirred. Now he looked up at Nora, made a face in Mum's direction and grinned. Nora grinned in reply but he wouldn't know the true reason why.

These last few weeks she'd made a point of being at home when Maggie brought Robert back for his evening cocoa. Tonight as usual she had her eye on the clock. It would be another couple of hours before Maggie and Robert came in; Maggie always with

Elizabeth Lord

a defiant bearing, Robert following her awkwardly as though imagining himself an interloper.

'I've made a point,' she'd said, 'of letting Mum see that we don't need her invitations to tea – or not – thank you very much! I think Robert's glad. On Sunday's he just brings me to the end of the road and waits for me to go indoors safely before leaving. Mum can say what she likes, I don't care!'

But Nora cared, tortured by images of them locked in each other's arms, shielded from other eyes in some dark corner before coming home. She too at some time or other had been locked in the arms of one or two of the young men she knew though Mum would have had a fit had she known. But it wasn't the same, she wanted to be in love and so far she'd never felt that way, not in the way Maggie obviously felt judging by the light in her eyes and that distracted smile hovering on her lips when she spoke of her Robert.

From the porch came the faint sound of voices. Nora grew instantly alert. It was she who would open the door to them, Mum not moving an inch as if there's been no knock at all and Dad merely giving a grunt under his breath leaving Nora to go.

Minutes ticked by, the muffled conversation had died away but no knock came. Nora waited. The voices began again, slightly louder, somehow more urgent. Then again silence. The silence went on, leaving Nora's heart to race, conjuring up a vision of the two savouring a long and ardent kiss.

There came a faint rap of the knocker. Nora hurried to answer it, a ready smile on her lips for Robert but Maggie was alone. Before she could ask where he was, Maggie let out a sob and threw herself into Nora's arms.

'He's gone! Said he'd rather not come in. I don't know what's got into him. I don't know what made him leave like that. I must have upset him, but I don't know what. He wouldn't say.'

Quickly Nora drew her, gabbling wildly through a flood of tears, into the hallway, closing the door with as little noise as possible, but already her mother's quick ears had caught something amiss. She was in the hallway like a cat after a mouse, her eyes cold, trained on the weeping girl.

'What's going on? What's wrong? What's the pair of yers been up to? What's he done to yer?'

For reply Maggie gave a shrill cry and tearing herself from Nora's arms fled upstairs as fast as her tight, ankle-length suit would allow. Her mother stared after her. 'If them two have . . .' She broke off, no doubt daring not to voice such a thought. 'But no, likely he's just broke off with her so he has.'

Her tone was almost hopeful but Nora felt a pang of regret – for herself as well as for her sister. If Mum's words proved true she would never see Robert Titchnell again. She found herself praying it was only a row and they would soon make up, Robert again being there in the kitchen on Saturday nights for her to feast her eyes on him if only in passing. Even so, her heart seemed to have sunk down into her very boots that this might not be.

Extracting herself from the armchair where she had been engrossed in a book from the library, Nora went to answer the knock on the door.

Sunday morning, Mum had gone to Mass taking little Rose with her. She'd done this now for several Sundays on the trot. Nora secretly suspected she had it in mind to convert her youngest to her faith. Rose being only six could easily be persuaded and with Dad being so set against such a thing, Mum's next best bet was quietly taking the child off with her whenever he went down the pub on Sunday mornings. He was down the pub right now, taking Neil with him or rather Neil was down the pub taking Dad with *him*.

This morning Elsie had gone off to a friend's house, so had George. Maggie was also out with a friend. Nora was entirely alone in the house revelling in a bit of peace and quiet for once if only for an hour or so. The place was usually so noisy and chaotic with squabbling kids, Mum's piercing voice adding to it all, that until this moment the silence had felt like a little bit of heaven. She should have known it couldn't last.

With lips set in readiness to tell the caller they didn't want anything he was selling, Nora yanked open the door, then gasped, a smile instantly replacing the scowl.

'Robert! What're you doing here? Maggie's out.'

Quickly she wiped the smile from her face, replacing it with a look of concern. 'She's out with some girlfriend or other.'

'Oh,' he said slowly as if contemplating what next to do, then seemed to recover himself, lowering his head a fraction but his eyes not leaving her face.

'Well . . . it's . . . well, it's you I've come to see,' he faltered.

She was taken aback a little. 'Me?'

'Well, yes. I need to talk to you, about Maggie, but only if you're on your own. I thought it being Sunday her mother might be at her church and I know your father goes for a drink on Sunday mornings – Maggie said. But if you're not, then I won't bother.'

'No, I'm on my own. Why do you need to talk to me about her for?' she asked, disturbed that her heart had begun to beat too fast, too heavily.

He hesitated, looked back at the street as if fearing one of the family might appear unexpectedly, then he said almost urgently, 'Would you mind if I came in for a moment? I promise not to keep you too long.'

Nora stepped back, her heart racing even faster. She had never been alone with him before. What on earth did he want to talk to her about and what on earth would she find to say to him?

'You'd best come in for a moment then,' she said, trying to sound suitably reluctant.

Leading him through to the kitchen, neither the parlour nor the back room seeming to be the right place at this minute, she too had begun to feel edgy lest her family came in on them, or at least her mother. She could only guess what her mother's reaction would be if she came in on her alone with Maggie's fiancé and Maggie nowhere to be seen.

In the kitchen she turned to face him. 'So then, what did you want to see me about?' she asked, no smile on her face this time, her brow creased by the uneasiness inside her.

He stood with his hat held between the fingers of his hands, twiddling it round and round by its brim. 'I . . . I don't quite know how to begin,' he faltered, then taking a deep breath grew more precise.

'It's to do with Maggie. We all know your mother doesn't approve of me as her suitor and I'm beginning to feel the strain of it. The truth is I like Maggie. I like her very much and for a time I thought I was in love with her but now I no longer feel that way enough to continue our relationship. Not that I have ever conducted myself improperly!' he added quickly. 'I've nothing but respect for her but I can't think how to tell her that I cannot love her as she would like me to.'

'And you want me to tell her,' Nora said sharply and a little unkindly.

Was this all he'd come for? Yet a certain excitement had begun to grow. If he didn't love Maggie, did he perhaps have feelings for her instead? It was a selfish thought but she couldn't help it.

'No, I am not looking for a go-between,' he was saying with some dignity. 'I'm merely wondering how to go about it, what I should say to her.'

Was that all? Nora's moments of excitement waned but she put on a bright smile. 'Well, I think it's up to you, Robert, to find the words. No one can do it for you.'

'I suppose not.' He stared down at the hat he was still toying with. 'It will hurt her badly. It could take a while for her to come to terms with it and I don't think she'll ever want to see me again.'

'I shouldn't think so.'

'The sad part is I'll probably never see you again either.'

He hadn't looked up but his voice betrayed him and Nora experienced a leap of anticipation as she fought to appear calm.

'Probably,' she said as casually as she could. 'Although it would be a pity to lose touch with you entirely, and you never know, by keeping in touch with me, you and Maggie might get together again.' Why had she said that?

But he shrugged. 'I doubt it. In a way I suppose I was looking for a companion. I've been very lonely since I lost my wife but that doesn't give one cause to expect any young lady to take her place. I realize now, one has to be very much in love to remarry.'

He now looked directly at Nora. 'However, I don't enjoy being alone. I need companionship. I was wondering . . . Please forgive me but would it be audacious for me to ask if you would . . . I feel you and I . . . What I mean is that if I were to keep in touch, with you I mean, sort of friendship. I'm sure as time went on you and I might . . .'

His voice trailed off in confusion, looking away, leaving the two of them standing facing each other in silence, neither one looking at the other.

'What do you say?' he prompted at last, his eyes still averted.

'And what about Maggie?' she countered before she could stop herself. She was saying all the wrong things.

'Ah. Maggie.' He sighed deeply, his shoulders lifting briefly.

Nora waited, holding her breath, aware how cruelly she was behaving towards her sister by this taut anticipation that was making itself felt deep in her stomach, but he remained silent.

'And when she finds out,' she burst out at last, more to still the sense of guilt than fill the silence. 'You're going to have to tell her how you feel.'

Robert was chewing at his lip. 'I feel bad about that, of course.'

It sounded so cold-hearted to Nora's ear that she drew in a horrified breath. He noticed immediately, contrition written all over his face.

'I didn't intend that to sound as it did,' he hurried on. 'I do feel bad but it would be wrong to continue lying to her. As I've said, I like her very much. She's a wonderful girl, but not for me. I've lost sleep these last two weeks for thinking about how to tell her.'

He stopped and moved closer. 'I know by the way you look at me, Nora, that you've taken quite a shine to me more than you admit. And I have to admit in all honesty that I have . . . well, I need to say it, that I have lost my heart . . .'

Nora cut short the rest of what he was going to say by turning to glance at the clock on the mantle shelf, her voice bright and urgent.

'Oh, look! It's nearly eleven. Mum and Rose will be home from Mass soon. Or Maggie might walk in on us any minute. I don't think they'll be pleased to catch us here alone together.'

Robert pulled himself up sharply. He looked suddenly taller than she had imagined. 'Then I had better go,' he said tersely. 'Sorry I bothered you.'

'No!' she blurted. 'I'm glad you came. I'd like to see you again – to talk about Maggie,' she ended and saw him relax.

'If you wish,' he said.

'But you mustn't come here.'

'No, of course not.'

'Where then?' There was a sense of panic, of urgency, of needing to throw caution and niceties to the wind. Her heart was thumping like a drum, her chest had filled with a sense of danger and of wrongdoing but this feeling of haste overrode it all.

She clasped her hands to her throat as he seemed to hesitate, as if he was wavering. But he was only thinking. 'Outside the main entrance to Liverpool Street Station,' he said at last. 'Tomorrow evening? Seven o'clock?'

'Yes,' she breathed.

'And we can discuss at greater length what I ought to do about your sister.'

'Yes,' she said again, certain that his last words were only an excuse to see her for herself but daring not to put too much reliance on it lest she had in fact read too much into things.

She tried not to think of Maggie and what she might be doing to her as she let Robert out.

Five

Sitting on the bed, Nora tried to stem that small feeling of guilt with Maggie pouring out her heart in between stifled sobs and choked whimpers that caught in her throat again and again.

'I don't know how it all went wrong. I've written several times asking but he don't reply. I don't know what else to do . . .'

The last plea wrung itself from her but Nora had no answer to give. When she'd first met with Robert two weeks ago he'd begun by talking about Maggie and the difficulties that would be raised by his continuing with her.

'I don't want to be unkind,' he'd said. 'She's a sweet girl. I did think at first that it was her I wanted but giving it serious thought, I know it would have ended in disaster. The longer I put it off the worse it's going to be.'

She had sympathized but his next words had sent tiny darts of joy through her heart.

'I've known it for some time now and all because of you, Nora. Every time I came into your house, there you were. I could hardly take my eyes off you. I felt so disloyal at times but my regard for you became so strong that I really felt I should go mad if I didn't tell you.'

Coming to the end he had hesitated, then asked if she felt the same about him. She had nodded and he had given a great sigh as if of relief.

When he asked if he could kiss her, she'd hardly nodded her consent than his lips had found hers, tentatively, gently to start with then finding it willingly returned, his kiss had become firmer and positive. For her it grew into a magical moment. This was the man she knew she had waited for, why she had spurned all those hopeful lads who'd looked to court her.

What she hadn't considered with that first wonderful kiss was that she would immediately entangle herself in a web of intrigue. She could tell no one without causing such a fearful uproar, ruining the bond that had always been between her and her sister.

Thoughts of Dad's embarrassment before this sudden and unsettling change of daughters made her cringe. Even the contemplation of her brother Neil treating her to one of his oblique looks of amused disapproval at which he could be so good, made her squirm.

Aware that something had gone wrong between Maggie and Robert, Mum was going around the house with satisfied smiles, pooh-poohing her daughter's heartbroken sighs and prolonged sniffles.

'You don't know how lucky you are, so you don't!' she said, totally unsympathetically while Dad looked on bewildered.

'I can't understand the man,' he mused. 'He came 'ere to this very 'ouse, looking for my permission for 'im to marry me daughter, and there's me agreeing. Now it's over just like that. She says they ain't 'ad a row, only that he just seems to have gone off 'er. It beats me.'

It was making it even harder to reveal the truth especially with Mum saying flatly, 'I guessed it'd happen, so I did. Sooner or later, and it's just as well it was sooner than later. All I pray now is that we've seen the last of that one. In time, God willing, she'll get over it and meet a nice boy of her own age, so she will, and I for one will put me hands together.'

When Dad had suggested toning down her rejoicing for the sake of poor Maggie's feelings, she turned on him.

'And you! Didn't yer stop to think he'd see in time she was too young for him, him with a nine-year-old boy and a wife hardly dead in her grave. She's better off without that one if you ask me and I'll tell her so too.'

Telling her so wasn't making matters any easier for Maggie.

'I'll never get over him!' Maggie was saying. 'I've never said anything to upset him. I'll even go to Mass with Mum and pray then maybe he'd come back. Perhaps it's just a hiccup of some sort. But how can he be so cruel?'

'If you think he's cruel, maybe like Mum says, you've had a lucky escape,' Nora tried to soothe, at the same time grabbing at opportunities.

But her own situation made matters all the more precarious and the thought of finally having to tell the truth had started to haunt her. Maggie herself had kept her association with Robert a secret for quite a while and when she had finally revealed all, the fat had truly been in the fire.

Now it was her turn to hold secrets. When eventually she did admit the truth, how much more fat would be in that same fire?

'I shall have to tell them soon,' Nora murmured as she and Robert left the restaurant where they'd had supper after having gone to see a comedy play at the Vaudeville Theatre in the Strand.

Walking arm in arm along the Victoria Embankment, the fading twilight still glowing off the water of the Thames, Nora clung lovingly to the arm, still feeling his tender kisses lingering on her lips as they'd stood half hidden and dwarfed by the obelisk of Cleopatra's Needle.

Robert had asked her if she would marry him and she had said yes, the laughter remaining from watching the comedy play swept away, the seriousness of that wonderful moment all that mattered.

It was June and they'd been meeting in secret for three months even if only once or twice a week. She dared not let it become more lest someone in the family began to become suspicious.

'I hate all this subterfuge,' she murmured now. 'It's starting to weigh on me.' She felt the arm she was holding tightened against hers.

'Then I think it's time you told them, Nora. I should be there with you when you do but it could make things worse, the two of us barging in on them with our news. It could cause a serious row.'

'It'll cause a row anyway,' she said glumly but felt his arm tightened still more. In the dark she sensed him smiling gently.

'I've a feeling it won't be too bad. What I'll do is come home with you when you've made up your mind to tell them. I'll wait outside for you to open the door to me the moment you need me and we'll face them together.'

But it took a further two weeks for her to come to the decision. It came about due to a fit of temper from Maggie. It was when Mum suddenly asked one evening if any young lad had yet taken her eye and Dad chiming in saying something about it being best to let sleeping dogs lie, that Maggie suddenly flared up.

Jumping up from where she had been reading a magazine, she

yelled: 'Why can't you let things rest, Mum? It's all over. It's been over for months. I hate him and I don't ever want to see him again.'

Her mother's face was a picture of shock in the light of the oil lamp under which she was darning a hole in one of Dad's socks, holding the wool firm over a wooden darning mushroom.

'I'd no intention of bringing anything up, Maggie,' she said sharply. 'All I meant was whether by now you've met anyone nice enough to take your eye.'

'I know what you meant,' was the retort. 'You still think I'm seeing Robert in secret.'

The sock and wooden mushroom went flying across the room, falling into the empty fire grate, Dad sitting nearby ducking just in time to miss contact with his temple.

Mum was on her feet, her blue eyes glaring at her daughter. 'Yer managed to keep it secret from us before. Don't forget, lying tongues find themselves being ripped out in Hell, so they do.'

Nora had been gazing from the window at the last faint translucent green of evening. Interrupted by the hubbub, she moved to her sister's defence.

'Maggie hasn't been seeing him.' It came out without thought and suddenly she found all eyes being trained to her. But it was her mother who spoke.

'How would you know?'

'I just . . . Well, I just know, that's all,' Nora stammered, fighting to amend the stupid, careless statement she'd come out with.

'How do you know? What's Maggie told you?' her mother shot back. 'Is there something the two of yers not been telling me . . . me an' yer Dad?' she added as an afterthought.

'No,' said Nora defensively, but Maggie had started glaring at her.

'Yes, why would you say something like that?'

'Because . . .' Nora chewed her lip. Was this the right time to confess? Would there be a more opportune time? Whenever, there was bound to be an uproar. She'd have to face it eventually.

'Because I've spoken to him.'

'You've spoken to him?' Her mother and sister echoed the words together. 'When?' Maggie added feebly.

'It was one evening last week – Saturday.' She was fumbling over the words. 'We met and we chatted.'

'You chatted to him?' Maggie looked as if she was about to leap on her and throttle her. Nora jumped to her own defense.

'Well, you don't see him any more. You and he have parted company.'

'And you've jumped in!'

'No . . .'

She could see Maggie was about to explode, tears springing to her eyes. But Mum was there before her. 'You've been seeing him then? You've been meeting him?'

Nora nodded.

'How long?' came the hard question but Maggie with an anguished shriek fled from the room, her slippered feet padding up the stairs in a rush followed by a trail of sobbing.

Mum's eyes hadn't even bothered to follow her daughter's flight. Trained on Nora, the coldness in them seemed to melt a little.

'How long?' she repeated and again, 'How long then have the two of yers been seeing each other?'

'We've not been seeing each other,' Nora began but knew that trying to prevaricate would be just silly.

'A few weeks,' she lied, her mind running fast. 'I happened by chance to run into him as I was coming home from the school and we got chatting. He apologized for upsetting Maggie and the unkind way he'd behaved towards her as her family might see it. He said the truth was that his feelings for her had cooled and it was only right that he did the proper thing and nipped it in the bud before he ended up hurting her too badly.'

She dared not add that Robert's cooling off had been partly the fault of her mother in turning against him.

'He's a good man really, Mum,' she ended lamely, at a loss to interpret that odd warm gleam in her mother's eyes.

'So it had nothing to do with him fancying you over your sister?'

The discerning remark made Nora cringe inwardly. At any moment now her mother would pounce. It had all gone wrong. She should have waited a while longer. Forbidden to see him what should she do? But to her surprise her mother now began to smile.

'Why did you feel you needed to keep this to yerself then?' she said quietly while Dad turning in his chair was listening intently.

'I thought you'd stop me seeing him. I know Maggie's upset.'

'Time Maggie got over it. She's too young to marry someone of thirty-something. But you're older and the years between him and you, don't count so much. He's got a good business and can no doubt keep a wife in comfort, and as you say he's a good man, that I knew from the start, but not for yer sister.'

She paused for breath then went on somewhat charily, 'So, is he serious?'

'I think so,' Nora said, heartening a little.

'You think so. Either you're sure or you're not.'

It was mildly said and Nora's heart lifted, in fact began to sail with hope and relief. Her mother was approving of it. Now she could be honest.

'I am sure. He says he loves me and I love him. But how can you be so nice about him when you were so . . . awful to him when he was with Maggie?'

'That no longer matters. I'll deal with yer sister. But wait until you have a proposal of marriage before getting too excited. And be good. You know what I mean when I say be good. Our Lord won't smile on a young girl standing before Him in shame on her very wedding day.'

She took a deep breath, disguising a yawn. 'Now I'm off to bed. I think it best you sleep on the sofa tonight, love. I don't want ter be woken in the small hours by you and your sister screaming at each other.'

As she marched out of the room, Nora looked at her father but he had already turned away, for some reason making her triumphant heart sink with a thought that after agreeing to give his younger daughter to this man he could feel somehow betrayed.

Just as well then that she hadn't admitted yet having already been proposed marriage to. That could come later, after Dad had got used to the change of daughters in marriage. One thing she did know, in time Maggie would find herself a nice boy and marry him and forget all about Robert.

Six

Maggie hadn't got over it as Nora had so confidently thought. Her animosity towards her was total and persistent, even to her refusal to have Nora sleep beside her in the bed they'd shared all their lives.

When Nora had tried to reason with her the furious row that ensued compelled Mum to arrange to have a single bed put up in the corner of the parlour, with moderate privacy attained by a curtain pulled across the narrow alcove.

It was totally inconvenient of course in a room most of the family used in the evenings. It meant her having to wait until everyone else retired before she could go to bed.

The very act of retrieving anything from the wardrobe or the chest of drawers they still had to share would start Maggie off so much that whatever Nora needed had to be got only after she had left the room.

With Mum constantly raging at Maggie, invariably resulting in Maggie breaking down in tears, accusing her sister of betrayal, it would turn into a screaming match and Nora would find herself being blamed for having started it whether she had or not.

More wearing was the interminable sulking. If they met in any room in the house, Maggie would instantly stalk out leaving whatever she had been doing. She'd even refused to be at the same meal table as Nora, which was almost every day if she wasn't meeting Robert, and would refuse to come down until finally Mum had to let her have her meals in the bedroom or have Nora eat in the kitchen.

Nora felt herself being slowly worn down by it all, her Mum no less, she voicing her feelings loud enough to be heard across any military parade ground.

'I've just about had enough of it all, so I have!' she broke into a tirade after two more months of it. 'The pair of yers will drive me to a bloddy insane asylum. I could even put up with the two of yers bickering but ignoring each other loik neither of yer exists is wearing me down until I go mad. Either you start to mend yer differences or this wedding, Nora, will have to be brought forward. I see no other way out.'

The mention of wedding had only served to exacerbate Maggie's wretchedness and she'd fled from the room in floods of tears that could be heard going on and on without break through the bedroom door after it had slammed with a resounding crash that shook the house.

'It's not me,' Nora protested. 'I'm willing to bury the hatchet. It's her. She just won't give up. She knows Robert doesn't want her so why keep on?'

'I don't care!' was the irascible reply, 'I can't take much more of this. Yer dad does nothing. He sits and looks lost by it all. Neil's no help. He just walks out. I feel I'm on me own and as far as I'm concerned, for the sake of peace, the sooner you're off and married the better, fer me, for all of us!'

It was the first time she'd truly felt the undercurrent of resentment in her mother that her association with Robert had caused. Until now she'd been so sure Mum was one hundred per cent on her side. Now it felt she was practically ordering her from her home.

The wedding had originally been planned for June, exactly a year after Robert had proposed, Mum seeming so enthusiastic about it, snorting at Maggie when she endeavoured to get her on her side with her weeping and grizzling. Now all that had suddenly changed.

'I can't wait to get out of that house,' she told Robert on the Saturday afternoon. 'I'm sick of Maggie's sulking and now my mother's starting on me almost saying I'm to blame. This afternoon she told me the quicker I was out of the house the better for all the family. It's so unfair!'

It was unfair. She'd not stolen Robert from Maggie, it was he who'd tired of her and she felt no compunction in having fallen in love with him. She told him this now and had him enfold her in his arms in the peace and quiet of his bedroom with which she was now so very familiar.

She would stay at his home in Stratford at weekends though never overnight. Mum would have gone for her with a broom had she not come home until morning, sure she'd have been up to something, Dad supporting her silently, being Dad. Even being out too late could bring a harsh glare of suspicion to her eyes and concern to his, he saying nothing of course, Mum quite adequate at making herself plain enough for the both of them.

But did anyone need to stay overnight to be *up to something* as Mum would put it? Such things can take place any time and Nora now knew as much of Robert as he of her, just as if already married. She was sure of his care of her as anyone need be and told him so as they lay quiet and content in each other's arms on this sunny March afternoon.

'But I still can't wait for when I'll truly be your wife,' she whispered and gazing at those handsome, mature features, eyes closed as if in sleep, she saw the neatly clipped moustache move slightly to a slow smile.

'Not in my wildest dreams,' he murmured, 'did I imagine I'd ever be happy again but I am, totally, and all because of you, my lovely darling.' And turning towards her he kissed her long and ardently, his arms enfolding her to him.

Robert was beaming as he helped Nora into his Vauxhall. He would always wait for her at the end of her road, sensitive to her sister's reactions should she see him draw up. She felt so proud sitting in this grand vehicle, the only one she had ever ridden in. Her father still used public transport, his little factory only just round the corner to his home and he too old-fashioned now to teach himself to drive a motorcar. 'Waste of money,' he would say.

Even Robert hadn't thought much of them when he'd first met Maggie, just over a year ago now, and had preferred taxi-cabs, but with the blocks and cobbles of roads being torn up with smoother bitumen being laid, there were far more motor-cars than horses to be seen now. Anyone who wanted to be with the times and had the money now had a motorcar. This Vauxhall was Robert's first, bought just eight weeks ago and Nora never failed to feel like a queen every time she climbed into it.

'I've some very good news for you, my love,' he said the moment she settled herself next to him, the motor running but not yet moving off. 'I've managed to bring our wedding forward by two months to the sixth of April.'

Nora, gasping in surprise, opened her mouth to speak but he gave her no time. 'It means a bit of a rush of course getting everything sorted out in time but we can do it if we . . .'

It was she who interrupted this time. 'But that only gives us two more weeks. My wedding gown's not finished and my cousin Mabel's bridesmaid's dress hasn't even been started on.'

That statement made her heart sink. She'd always intended Maggie as her chief bridesmaid when she married. Now there was only her eleven-year-old cousin, her mother's sister Aunt Minnie's girl. Maggie was now voicing a downright refusal to even be present at her sister's wedding, which hurt Nora more than she would ever admit as she now shrugged off the feeling.

'There are so many arrangements yet to be done,' she went on. 'All the food for the wedding breakfast to be sorted out, and our honeymoon hasn't even been properly booked yet.'

They'd decided to spend the honeymoon near Lulworth Cove in the heart of the rolling Dorset countryside, peaceful, quiet, away from the buzz of any city. For weeks she'd thought of nothing else but strolling hand in hand as his wife along the winding country lanes, on her third finger a wide, golden wedding band nestling against the lovely five diamond engagement ring she'd been wearing these past few months. But two weeks! It gave no time to sort everything out as she hoped, a rushed wedding, having to book a hotel at short notice, get the train tickets and reserve a compartment for the two of them.

'It can't all be done in such a short time,' she said, growing ever more worried.

He was still beaming at her. 'I thought you couldn't wait to get out of the family home and be my wife. It's what you wanted.'

'I do. But not at the expense of having to . . .'

He didn't wait for her to finish. 'And I've got even better news for you. We may not be going to Dorset because I've something far more special in mind for my wife. I've had a stroke of luck, darling. If it works out we shall spend our honeymoon on an ocean voyage – to New York.'

He passed over her frown of disbelief. 'We can spend a week there then sail back home. A business chum of mine knows someone who's booked a couple of tickets, not first class but near enough. His wife has fallen ill apparently and they can't go so he's offering them at a reduced price to my chum. But he can't go either so he offered them to me and I jumped at the chance. It's for the maiden voyage of that new ship Titanic just over two weeks from now. I had to move before he gave them to someone else, hence a need to bring the wedding forward. But I told him to hold on to the tickets because I felt I should ask you first, and if you said no . . .'

Nora's anxiety vanished like a tiny summer cloud. Did he need to ask? 'Me say no? Oh yes, yes! Darling, I can't believe it!'

She threw herself at him so hard in excitement it was a good thing the vehicle hadn't yet begun to move and cause an accident. As he laughed she began beleaguering him with one question after another. 'When will you get them? How long has he had them? How long will he hold them? What if he thinks you don't want them and gives them to someone else?'

'Hold on!' he chuckled. 'It was only a couple of days ago.'

'A couple of days! Why did you wait so long to ask me?'

'I haven't seen you for a couple of days.'

'But you could have come round and told me.'

Immediately she stopped, realizing he wouldn't show himself at the house for the sake of her sister's peace of mind. 'You could have sent a note.'

He was still laughing at her. 'By the time you got it and wrote back to me, I would be here myself, as I am now.'

He was being silly. There were three or four mails a day. She'd have got his note a couple of hours after he'd posted it and could have written back the same day. He'd have got it early next morning and given her reply to his friend straight away. She knew he had a telephone in his scrap yard office but her father didn't and he couldn't contact her that way.

Robert was saying, 'I shall get them first thing tomorrow morning, my love.'

'What if they're gone by then, someone else snapping them up?'

She was near to distress, excited, but still unable to believe such a wonderful prospect as a sea voyage could ever be happening to her, she who'd never even been to the seaside, not even to Southend. Her parents could of course have afforded the fare but had always been so tied up in their rag business. She and her friends were too occupied enjoying life round here to go traipsing off to places like Southend, all that travelling there and back.

Going on honeymoon all the way to Dorset had had her so excited – a real adventure, and with the man she loved, one who could easily afford to go all that way off, booking a hotel, reserving a special compartment just for the two of them. But now there came this wonderful news.

'You must see him this evening. Tell him yes, yes.'

Grinning still, Robert had extricated himself from her arms to release the brake having let the car's engine run all this time to save having to use the crank handle to start it up.

'It'll be too late this evening. He might have gone out by then, or gone to bed because it'll be late by the time we leave the Palladium.'

He had booked seats at the Palladium ages ago, a huge theatre with the largest seating capacity in the whole of London, opened two years ago in Argyll Street in Soho and even now usually always booked to capacity.

Tonight there was a variety bill. She'd been looking forward to it for ages. Now it had taken second place to this new exciting news of his and it was an effort to make herself look eager for tonight's outing. Perhaps Robert understood, leaning over and kissing her before drawing away from the kerb.

'I promise, my love, I'll make certain to see him first thing tomorrow morning, all right?'

'Yes,' she breathed and settled into her seat while he negotiated their way between the building evening traffic.

In her uncomfortable single bed in the parlour shielded by the curtain across the alcove, she couldn't sleep for thinking of the wonderful voyage she was about to have. What should have been a lovely evening enjoying those variety acts had dimmed beside what she was going to enjoy on board a great liner out on the Atlantic, entertainment, dances, fine food, rubbing shoulders with illustrious passengers, women in their fine dresses and sparkling jewels. She would need lots of nice clothes not to feel dowdy. But this evening Robert had promised to buy her a veritable wardrobe of dresses and accessories.

'Nothing too good for my beautiful wife,' he'd said this evening. 'I can afford it, my love. You'll knock them all into a cocked hat.'

She hoped so.

The next day, she met Robert at the end of the road, her excitement still intact. But Robert wasn't smiling as he kissed her and helped her into the passenger seat, he sinking back into the driving seat as she settled beside him, his expression glum, almost terrible to see.

'I'm so sorry, darling,' he began then stopped, turning off the engine.

'What about? Whatever's wrong?' Nora cried, expecting to be told of a death in his family.

'It's about our honeymoon, darling.'

'What about it?' His expression was beginning to frighten her though she didn't know why.

'It's off,' he said simply.

'What d'you mean, off?' Now she was really frightened. Was he having a sudden change of mind about their relationship?

'You were right, my love, I should have snapped up those tickets as soon as they were offered to me. The bloke who had the tickets because the other one's wife was ill, had second thoughts. He apparently talked it over with his wife who was a bit scared of going on a sea voyage and told her that the ship was a great modern liner and had been guaranteed unsinkable by good authority and probably wouldn't even rock in an Atlantic gale, and she was persuaded. So he kept the tickets – said he was sorry. I'm so sorry too, my darling. You were so excited. I've let you down. I feel a rotten so-and-so.'

Why, she didn't know, but the loss of those tickets came almost as a relief in comparison to what she had felt a moment ago. 'Never mind, my love,' she said eventually. 'It was a nice idea, but we still have Dorset, and I've never seen Dorset.'

He was looking at her. 'Aren't you disappointed?'

'Well, yes, but what's the good of crying over spilled milk?'

'You're not upset with me, darling – not at all?'

'No. We'll keep to our first arrangements,' she said firmly and as he somewhat shamefaced agreed, she felt a flood of relief, half surprised by it but glad.

'I love you,' he said as he took her in his arms. 'I love you more than you can imagine. Let's go and find a nice place for lunch, somewhere near Epping and put it all behind us.'

'Yes, let's,' she said readily.

Seven

Life had wound down. With nothing to rush for any more she could look forward to taking things slowly preparing for a June wedding. The only fly left in the ointment now was Maggie.

Maggie still hadn't found a boy friend much less a fiancé. It was as though she deliberately needed an excuse to make Nora squirm, almost at the expense of her own happiness. It was stupid; her bitterness against Nora not diminished one inch even after all this time.

'The wedding can go on without me,' she announced over and over just in case the first statement hadn't sunk in, usually ending, 'I'd be dead before I set foot anywhere near your wedding!'

Nora hoped that as time went on she'd change her mind though deep in her heart of hearts she knew that would never happen.

'Oh Robert!' she whispered as she lay in his arms. 'It's so . . . awful!'

He was holding her tightly. 'I know. It's shaken me to the core too.'

She'd gone there immediately on hearing the news, running the length of Gough Street to Upper North Street to find a taxi the quicker to get to him.

'To think it could have been us,' she wept, 'or one of us. It could have been you? They said it was unsinkable. All those poor people! We could have been on it.'

'But we weren't,' he consoled in an effort to rally her. 'We couldn't get the tickets anyway. We didn't know it then but we were so lucky.'

'That's what I mean,' she wept against his chest. 'Lucky, while all those poor people weren't. Hundreds and hundreds drowned in that bitter ice cold sea. It must have been dreadful!'

Once again he held her away from him, more sternly this time. 'Now look,' he said. 'None of it had anything to do with you, with us, it happened, that's all. We *were* lucky. Call it providence but don't start blaming yourself.'

She knew he was right but she couldn't get it out of her mind that they could have both drowned, or he could have and she left to mourn him. In the privacy of her single bed, her mind would conjure up thoughts of losing him that felt almost real, reducing her to tears of imagined anguish.

The papers were reporting there had been survivors but she was sure Robert would not have been one of them, unbearable almost as the disbelief that they'd escaped that fate by the skin of their teeth. But she told her family none of this, leaving them to wonder why she was looking ever more drawn. Maybe she *was* making herself ill thinking about it because every morning she'd wake up feeling vaguely sick. This morning she really had been sick, getting to the kitchen sink just in time to stop bringing up last night's supper all over Mum's well scrubbed kitchen lino. Bending over the sink heaving, she didn't see her mother enter.

'What's all this then?' The sharp voice made her almost jump out of her skin, twisting round mid vomit so that the last of it fouled her nightie.

Giving her no time to answer, her mother went on, 'How long has this been going on, you being sick?'

'Only a few seconds,' replied Nora, misinterpreting the question. 'I just come over all sick.'

'I don't mean now.' There was no sympathy in the tone, no asking why she had suffered the attack, if she felt better now, what she might have been eating to cause it. 'I mean how many mornings.'

'It was only this morning. I'm sorry.'

Why was she apologizing? She couldn't help being sick. She felt a little angry – typical of Mum to start giving her a telling off for something she couldn't help, more annoyed at having her clean sink messed up.

'You've been feeling sick before this?' her mother was saying slowly.

'No . . . well, yes, these last few days I've felt queasy. But it's the first time I've been properly sick.'

There was a moment's pause. Nora touched her lips with the back of her hand searching for any dregs her retching may have left there. She was dying for a drink of water to clear the nasty taste from her mouth.

When her mother spoke it was again in that same slow tone. 'When was it the last time you remember seeing your monthlies?'

Realizing now what her mother was getting at, anger rose again in her breast. She lifted her head defiantly. 'They should be any day now.'

Her mother didn't look convinced. 'And the last one?'

'It has nothing to do with you when, Mum,' Nora flared. 'You know I've never been that regular. I don't count them!'

'Then I think it time you started to, my girl.'

With that, her mother turned and went back into the passage in the direction of the parlour, that door closing quietly, leaving Nora staring at the empty space where her mother had stood.

She'd spoken as if not one bit surprised and it set Nora thinking. She hadn't seen her last monthlies as Mum called them but had thought little about it, too happy in love to notice much else than her own happiness, and because she had never been that regular so had never bothered to count. But Mum would know by the square pieces of towelling a girl used at such times. These were left to soak in the covered pail of salt water under the sink in the outhouse, waiting to be boiled clean for next time. When dry they'd be vigorously ironed to get them as soft as possible before putting away. Harsh towelling could chafe a leg quite miserably after a while.

Mum sometimes sent her washing out to be done by a hired woman. But these squares of towelling were too personal for outsider's eyes so Mum did them, and she'd know quick enough who had, or had not, seen their monthly cycle.

The thought that had now been planted in Nora's mind had her heart plummeting into her very stomach even as she told herself she could be wrong. Knowing little about the facts of life as with most girls her age with mothers usually too embarrassed to explain such things to their daughters, she was ignorant of most of it.

She remembered at fourteen, seeing the spotting of dark red on her linen, going to Mum in a panic, thinking she'd injured herself in some way to have her mother say offhandedly, 'Oh, it's nothing to worry about. It just means you've become a woman, so yer have.' With that she had walked off from her bewildered daughter to begin cutting an old towel into smaller squares, showing her how to fold and pin each end to a bit of linen around her waist, she still with no idea of what it was all about.

She remembered when Maggie in her turn had been in the same state of panic being given the same instructions and told it was quite natural. It had been left to Nora to explain a few more details which she'd learned since becoming a woman, also thinking to hint that love making without protection could be quite risky.

Pity she hadn't followed her own advice. She and Robert had been most careful except for those couple of times. It hadn't really registered then but now came as a shock, her only thought being to go to him and hope he could tell her what she should do.

Far from being shocked, Robert couldn't have looked happier.

'But we're not married,' she burst out, surprised by having him clasp her joyfully to him in his motorcar.

'But soon to be.' He said brightly. 'We'll have been married months by the time it's born and who's going to criticize – if you *are* in the condition you think you are.'

It was wonderful to hear and when her next monthly again failed to arrive it no longer worried her, in fact she even felt excited and able to shrug off her mother's disparaging looks. May, her wedding day three weeks from now, why worry about her condition now? She looked as slim-wasted as ever she had. Her wedding dress, almost finished, still fitted perfectly. No one would even suspect she was carrying seeing her moving down the aisle on the arm of her father, he with no idea of her condition, Mum, thankfully, having kept her thoughts from everyone of the family.

The three weeks were flying by, she and three small brides-maids with their final fittings; behind her the knowledge that Maggie would definitely not now be a chief bridesmaid, her two other sisters, Elsie now just fourteen and Rose eight, would be in her place and Aunt Minnie's girl, her eleven-year-old cousin, Dora. In fact it seemed better to have children, all of them excited but hopefully able to conduct themselves properly. She'd suggested Robert's son Richard as pageboy but he'd been against it. 'Better not,' he said wisely.

Despite being gloriously happy as her wedding drew nearer, she would have been even more so had Maggie been part of it.

But Maggie refused even to look at her and it seemed as if she never would again, not even bearing to be in the same room, just as if some impenetrable barrier had been lowered between them. She'd never have believed it of Maggie but after so many tries to break that barrier only to have each attempt thrown back in her face, she had steeled herself against making any more attempts. But sometimes it hurt so much that she would dissolve into tears in her lonely bed for thinking about it.

To think that once they had been such close friends, confiding in each other, supporting each other against Mum's tirades, cuddling up together in the big bed upstairs while giggling over something quite idiotic – all that was gone.

Nora stood in the front room gazing from the window. Mum and the rest of the family and other relatives, aunts and uncles and cousins had gone on ahead, her three small bridesmaids too. The wedding car would arrive any moment now. Standing here in her wedding dress, she stared at the world beyond the curtained window, letting it become glazed and fuzzy before her eyes, turning away only as Dad's voice came to her from the doorway.

'All set, love?'

She nodded without turning.

'Car shouldn't be long now.'

Again she nodded, still not turning round, not wanting him to see the glistening of tears in her eyes and start asking questions, start trying to reassure her that everything would be all right, trying to give comfort. To the very last minute she thought Maggie would have relented, would have turned up to get into the car with the rest.

What she wanted to do was to pull the bridal veil over her face to conceal what should have been a joyful face, but all the neighbours waiting outside their doors would want to see her smiling. She glanced down at her wedding bouquet, a trailing of sweet smelling lilies and carnations and green fern. Her white gloved hands were gripping it far too tightly. She should be happy. She was about to enjoy a wonderful married life. Relaxing her hands she lifted her head and forced a bright smile to her lips. She *was* happy!

As if in reply to that thought, Dad's voice came again.

'Car's here!'

'Yes,' she said, seeing it too and turned, eyes glistening not with tears but quiet serenity. This was her day! Blow Maggie. In fact Maggie was her own worst enemy and she wasn't going to let Maggie spoil her day.

The chauffeur had got out to stand by the open door of a grand, open-topped, silver Rolls Royce motor, Dad having spared no expense for this his first daughter's wedding. Dad looked quite odd all got up in his new dark suit, stiff colour, stiff cuffs, dark tie and immaculate waistcoat buttoned over his slight paunch, his treasured gold hunter watch peeping from one of the pockets, the gold chain looped across to the other, that she gave a little giggle and instantly felt much better.

'That's the spirit!' he said as if he already knew that she'd grieved the absence of her sister, and crooking his arm for her to hold, conducted her to the front door and the Rolls with its chauffeur waiting to assist her into the splendid vehicle and help adjust the train of her white satin gown for her.

The only pause they'd made was for Dad to close his house door, turn the key in the lock and pocket the key.

'Right!' he said succinctly as he got in beside her. 'Here we go, love.'

The wedding was a high Church of England one in an effort to satisfy her mother, who finally condescended to enter the place if with a certain amount of reservation, which she'd made known to everyone in no uncertain terms.

She now sat in the front pew, her Catholic prayer book clasped tightly to her breast as if shielding her from some heathen god, her expression tight and immovable. Dad would join her after completing his duty of giving away the bride and perhaps bring about a relaxing of those tight features.

Moving slowly down the aisle on his arm, Nora wasn't interested in her mother's sentiments, instead found herself scanning the congregation from under her veil, her family and friends on one side, Robert's slightly smaller gathering on the other. But the main face she looked for wasn't there as far as she could tell from the sea of faces following her progress to the slow, dignified strains of *Here Comes the Bride*.

Even as she joined Robert who, moving to stand beside her, gave her an encouraging as well as an appreciative smile, he immaculate in grey frock coat, single-breasted waistcoat and matching trousers, and she returning his smile, her mind was more on the missed face in the congregation. Maybe she could have missed it. But no, Maggie hadn't intended to come.

All she could think of as the priest began on their wedding vows was that hers was the first wedding in her immediate family and Maggie might by some miracle have changed her mind if only for their sake.

Early this morning she'd gone out, to see a friend, so Mum said. Nora still in her best underclothes saw her hurrying down the stairs to the front door, making no secret of it, in the simple, somewhat drab beige one-piece barrel-shaped day dress she wore for casual with its wide scalloped collar and long plain sleeves gathered into cuffs, ordinary brown shoes and that large but only slightly adorned hat she would put on when popping out.

Unable to stop herself, Nora had called her name as she reached the front door. There had been the slightest of pauses before she continued on walking, closing the door behind her, leaving Nora with a heaving heart and close to tears.

'I shouldn't take no notice of her if I was you,' Mum had said. 'I've tried talking to her, so I have, but it makes no difference, so you're going to have to make the best of it. One day when she finds herself a nice young man, she'll come round, so she will.'

Nora found her mind jerked back to the present and their priest's opening words, 'Dearly beloved, we are gathered together here in the sight of God and in the face of this congregation . . .' From then on she thought no more but the entire ritual of matrimony seemed to pass like a dream and suddenly she was Robert's wife, they were receiving holy Communion, having agreed to it for the sake of her mother's peace of mind.

That done, they were led to the vestry to sign the marriage register, emerging to triumphant organ music, the congregation following them out into brilliant sunshine, photos being taken, then on to the reception. Not one moment did she think any more about her sister, her only goal now to be away and off on their Dorset honeymoon. If she thought at all about her it was to vow not to let it worry her any more. She was married. She was Robert's wife, the wife of a man in the scrap metal business – one far more lucrative than her parents' trade. She'd come up in the world, a ready made mother to Robert's young son and soon to be a mother in her own right. She could hardly wait for their baby to be born. Life was sweet.

Eight

There were voices coming from the parlour. Maggie heard them the moment Neil opened the door to her knock.

This Sunday afternoon she'd spent with a few friends watching a large suffragette demonstration in Hyde Park, all parading round holding huge colourful banners, blowing trumpets and banging drums, shouting their message through megaphones, voices distorted, and all in boiling August sunshine. The crowds watching had been enormous adding to the heat and now she was ready for her tea in the cool parlour.

She'd never had any wish to join them. Why should she? The idea of women needing the vote didn't interest her but it had to be admitted that their demonstrations and rallies were enjoyable to watch, the antics they got up to. One of her friends though, Lila, had been quite moved by the colour and excitement and despite what Maggie and their other two friends had said, had gone over to one of the tables that had been set up and had signed to become a member.

It just goes to show, Maggie thought as Neil let her in, just how easily a body can be mesmerized by a parade into doing something silly like that. Now the voices from the parlour took her mind away from that thought.

'Who's that in there?' she queried as she took off her hat and gloves.

Neil was looking down at her. He was nibbling his lip. 'People I don't think you'll want to see.'

Just then a man's voice came, followed by a small burst of female laughter at some quip he'd evidently made. Maggie recognized the voice immediately and the laughter too.

'What're they doing here!' she demanded of her brother.

Giving him no time to answer she blindly pushed past him and fled up the stairs, yelling as she went a frenzied gabble of words:

'Make them leave! Tell them to go! They're not wanted here!'

By the time she reached her room she was in a flood of tears, the bedroom door crashing behind her enough to shake the whole house. Moments later her tears had subsided. What were they saying about her down there in the parlour?

Taking a deep, shuddering breath, she pulled herself together with an effort and crept back to the door, opening it silently. She could imagine the four people, her parents, Nora and Robert, sitting in the parlour shocked, their cups of tea held rigid in their hands.

She heard Neil go into the room. 'I didn't know what to say to her,' she heard him say wretchedly.

'You shouldn't have said anything,' his mother shot at him.

'And have her coming straight in here and finding out?' he countered.

There came no reply from Mum but it sounded as though she had turned to the two guests. 'I did warn yer both it was best not to come. I knew this might happen.'

Nora's voice came in a sudden angry gush. 'You mean I'm not allowed to visit my own parents now?'

'Not while she's in this frame of mood.'

'It's been over two months since the wedding. It's about time she got over this? Me and Robert are married now and there's nothing she can do about it so what's the point her carrying on like that?'

Listening carefully, Maggie heard her father give a little cough. She could imagine him studying his words in his mind as he leaned forward to replace his cup and saucer on the white afternoon tablecloth Mum used for visitors on a Sunday. When he spoke his voice was measured and soothing, typical of Dad. 'I do think she needs a bit more time yet.'

He was given no chance to continue as Nora burst out, 'Time! How much time does she need to come to her stupid senses! I didn't take Robert away from her. They'd already parted company before we began going out together. I don't know why she blames me.'

'Even so,' Mum chimed in, her voice high and harsh as ever. 'The way things are it might be best for yers both to say 'bye fer now and maybe it'd be best we come to you – for a while anyways. We don't go out much together, me an' yer dad, and it'd make a nice change for us.'

In all this Robert hadn't said a word, but Nora's voice was full of hurt. 'How can you think of her feelings over mine, Mum? Well, if that's how it is, me and Robert won't come here again messing up your quiet life.'

'Don't talk like that, Nora,' Dad's voice came shakily pleading.

'I'll say it as it is, Dad,' was the harsh reply. 'I'm sure I don't want to be the cause of family strife. But she's the one causing trouble, not us.'

There came subtle sounds of people standing up.

'It's best we go now, Mum. Thanks for the tea. Sorry about all this but Maggie's the one to blame, not me.' There was a pause, then, 'By the way, what we came to tell you is I'm pregnant. By the end of the year you'll be grandparents. By then I just hope the situation's changed because I wouldn't want you never to see your first grandchild. And if my own sister who I've loved and felt close to all my life, still can't even look me in the face, then I'm sure I want nothing to do with her.'

The words tore into Maggie's breast and she hurriedly closed the door to deaden the sound of the sob that escaped her lips before she could stop it.

It took weeks to get what should have been a pleasant Sunday afternoon tea out of her head. She'd so expected to be clasped in her mother's arms as she revealed that they would soon be first-time grandparents and see her Dad shake Robert's hand in hearty congratulations. Trust Maggie to spoil it.

She hadn't expected Mum to be all that surprised by her news of course. Mum had noted all the signs well before her daughter's marriage. Dad's expression, however, would have been full of surprise but after being put ill at ease by Maggie's disruptive arrival and the ugly words it had raised, he'd been given no chance to express his joy.

The whole purpose of coming to see them had been to announce her news to them but she herself had ruined it all by letting the situation take over, she the injured one, leaping up saying what she had, departing as if they were all her enemies. If only she could have those moments over again, how much better she'd have handled it.

'You've got to stop brooding over it,' Robert told her.

She knew that. She knew too that their relationship was suffering. She was being snappy with him and he didn't deserve that. He was the kindest, most thoughtful person she had ever met and she was so lucky.

'You've got to put it out of your head, love. Letting yourself get down in the dumps like this, you can't be doing the baby any good, and for what?'

That brought her up sharp. If she harmed the baby, Maggie's revenge would be complete. His words made sense. She must put her right out of her head, think of her own future, the future of their first child together, make Robert happy and be a good wife to him.

Even so it took nigh two months to get over it completely. Mum and Dad coming over to visit almost every Saturday evening was a tremendous help. As Christmas drew closer she had more to busy her than bothering about Maggie. Maggie was her own worst enemy, no doubt still going on about it all, upsetting Mum no doubt, but so long as Nora knew nothing about it – Mum never said and she didn't ask – Maggie could do what she liked.

Waddling around their big Victorian house in Stratford, she found enough to occupy her. True, now a mother-to-be with her own pursuits and occupations, she'd tended to lose touch with many of her old friends. Most days Robert was at his scrap metal yard in Stepney but she had made some new and pleasant friends among her neighbours, all of them living in similar fine Victorian houses like hers, a few with young children therefore sharing a like interest. They'd have tea and cake in each other's homes, discuss babies, fashions and husbands. Occasionally she and one of them, usually Gladys, fast becoming her best friend, would go off to the West End to window shop, though more likely coming home laden with nice purchases. Gladys was around thirty with two children, both looked after by a nanny, was wife of a successful businessman like Nora and money came easy.

Nora of course no longer taught, married now, no respectable married woman expected to earn a living, her husband providing all her needs.

Robert had a cook general and a young housemaid so there was no need for her to worry about household duties, her only real responsibility now being a stepmother to young Richard.

To her mind he'd been somewhat spoiled but she having been used to teaching and controlling young children she soon let him know where he stood with her. At first he resented it a little but on the whole they got on well enough though most of the time he was at school, much of the rest taken up doing homework before going to bed, so they really only met over family meals.

He was a good looking boy, very like his father, but unlike his father had a tendency to laziness. When she tried to motivate him into stirring himself a little more, Robert would take his side saying he was still only a child. It was probably the only time they were at odds.

'If Robert would only stay out of it, I could do something with that child,' she'd told Neil the last time he'd come to visit, which he often did.

She felt at ease confiding in him whereas her parents might read more into any tiny complaint, quite normal with any marriage, to have it get back to Maggie who'd immediately savour a sadistic satisfaction that the marriage wasn't all it seemed. But with Neil, she felt completely safe.

Neil was bringing a young lady with him these days. Her name was Emily. She was tall and willowy, and Nora swore that her waist could not be much above sixteen inches so that her long skirts draped beautifully. Unlike Neil still dressing as he pleased and damn what people thought, she was highly fashionable, and instead of high-necked blouses hers had more up-to-date rounded necklines and flat collars. She looked so trim that Nora was painfully conscious of her own expanding stomach even though she'd noticed Emily regarding it with some longing.

'When Neil and I are married, I hope to start a family straight away, just like you,' she said when they came this November Saturday afternoon, at which Neil fidgeted as Nora and Robert turned enquiring eyes on him.

'Yes, well . . . we're planning to get engaged in a couple of weeks but don't tell Mum and Dad yet. I've not introduced her as my intended yet though we've been going out together ever since last March.'

He'd kept that quiet. 'Why haven't you told them?' Nora queried as she poured them a cup of tea.

He gave a wry grin as he stared out of the heavily lace-curtained window at the damp November sky. Emily fidgeted uncomfortably.

'As soon as I do, Maggie'll start throwing one of her tantrums and I know what she'll say: "*Everyone's getting married except me!*"' He mimicked a high female voice then grew serious. 'She still goes on about you, y'know. Won't let it rest. I won't go into detail but according to her you're practically the devil 'imself, snatching *her* Robert from under her very nose, snapping your fingers at her, living it up as a well-off business man's wife, that sort of thing. If you ask me, I'm sure she's going a bit off her trolley!'

Nora didn't want to discuss her sister. 'I know that as soon as you tell Mum and Dad your good news they'll be tickled pink,' she told him. 'And who cares what a certain other person says or thinks.'

That was a good lesson for herself to remember as well.

Two Sunday's later an excited Neil and Emily came to say that Mum and Dad *were* over the moon and the wedding would be next March.

She couldn't resist it. 'And what did Maggie have to say about it when she was told?'

There was a short silence. She could see Robert waving a stealthy but frantic hand at her to say no more. Then Neil said awkwardly:

'Well, I might as well be truthful, Sis. She said she'd only come if you and Robert don't. I'm not saying no more than that.'

It was a strained Sunday tea, Maggie's attitude weighing most upon their minds while they made an effort to stick to small talk and for once Nora was glad when it was time for them to leave.

'I'm *not* going to miss my own brother's wedding!' she burst out defiantly the moment she'd closed the door on her visitors. 'I refuse to be deprived of attending just because she's vindictive enough to stay away if I am there. What kind of person has she turned into? Thank God you didn't marry her, Robert. What sort of life would you have had with her?'

He moved towards her to gently lay the calming tip of one finger on her lips.

'I married you. That's all that matters,' he said softly. 'I married you because I love you. And I always will love you, so no more about her, eh? Let's leave the clearing up 'till the morning and go to bed.'

He put his arm about her waist and led her upstairs. 'Monday tomorrow, a new week, work to do – we ought to have an early night.'

Nora smiled her agreement and clung to him, knowing it wouldn't be that early a night as he put it.

As the days shortened towards winter Maggie didn't seem to be moping as much as she had. She had taken to going out more often seeing friends while her mother regarded her with an expression of mixed relief and satisfaction to see her enjoying herself once again.

Among her friends were plenty of young men. And she was pretty and shapely, had a happy outlook when she wanted. There was no lack of admirers, just that she had wasted half a year or more moping around, her head filled with nothing but thoughts of getting back at her sister. Well, this was one way and she intended to work hard at it.

So far none of the young men she knew met her standards, though one face among them insisted on pulling her gaze. He was the brother of one of her less close girlfriends. He was twenty-one, tall, slim, good looking in a sensuous, careless sort of way that had all the girls after him.

His name was Donald Lea though everyone called him Donny Lea. He was neither wealthy nor learned like Robert. He worked as a casual labourer, if and when he felt like it, so it seemed. His father too was hardly ever in work and his mother took in washing. There was a horde of kids. They lived in the slums. Being constantly in and out of work didn't seem to worry him but he was good company, usually the centre of attention with an ever ready store of good jokes and tall tales.

True, he liked his beer but was quite able to hold his liquor. And he could stand up for himself very well when a situation called for it – unlike Robert, always the self-controlled gentleman who would never have dreamed of having a stand-up argument with anyone.

Robert, Maggie told herself, would have turned out quite a bore in time and she almost pitied Nora her eagerness in becoming his wife. Even so, she could never forgive her for taking him away from her. That would always stick in her memory and it was from a still lingering sense of sheer resentment that as Christmas loomed she took up Donny Lea's light-hearted invitation to go out for a Christmas meal with him.

Nine

Hard to believe it was already March. She and Donny had been seeing each other for almost three months. He'd never gone steady with anyone before her. Maybe – and Maggie had to smile at her own whimsy – because he was hardly ever in work, always short of cash and most girls looked for young men who could at least spend out a little on them. Of course female eyes would be turned by his handsome features and flippant attitude but any attraction soon dwindled when there was no money to back it up, though he didn't seem to care. But having fallen head over heels for him she was happy to pay for small treats for them both out of the allowance Dad now gave her, she having turned twenty-one. Being in love, it pleased her to help Donny.

But there was always Mum. When she learned of his background she had immediately put her foot down. 'Yer can pack that one up as soon as yer loik. You was brought up to better things.'

Maggie's protest was harsh and virulent, thinking of the Robert business. 'You're not taking this one from me!' she said. 'We love each other and this time you're not going to part us. He might be a bit below the standards you set—' She was given no chance to finish.

'A *bit* below! He's virtually walking in a tunnel, so he is, and I won't have rubbish like that keeping company with a daughter of mine. So you know what he can do.'

She had said a lot more, but Maggie had thrown a fit each time, bringing up all the old sores: how Mum had let Nora take her Robert away from her and not done a thing about it. How she had stood by and watched her suffer, turning a deaf ear to her sobs, and now when she had found herself a young man and found honest love, her mother was prepared to break that up too when she should have done more to break up the union between Nora and the man Nora had stolen from her.

Dad had defended Donny. 'It's not easy finding steady work

labouring and with feckless parents what probably don't care how he does. If Maggie and 'im are serious about each other, I can give him a job working in our factory. If he proves a good worker I'd give 'im a decent wage, enough to keep her in decent enough circumstances.'

'That's it, make a fool of yerself,' Moira raged at him. 'If she brought home a tramp I reckon you'd kiss his backside for him so yer would. Didn't I have enough trouble sorting out all that blessed bother between her and Nora over Robert? I can't keep on sorting out daughters' problems.'

'So long as she's 'appy,' he said passively, forcing an explosive puff of aggravation from his wife and a sarcastic quip.

'Well in that case we'll let her bring home whoever she loiks, then! I've other things to think of than worryin' meself about her troubles.'

There was Nora's baby for one, a beautiful little girl born on the tenth of January after two days of labour with Nora growing so weak that she began to fear for both her and baby. Finally out had popped a most adorable baby girl, no marks, clean as a whistle and sturdy as they come. Fortunately everyone saw January as the correct date for the birth. Only she knew the true date when Nora had become pregnant and intended to keep it that way. Nothing to be gained by bringing shame on the family, was there.

Christened Elsie after Nora's second youngest sister and Moira after her herself, she still felt just a little put out that hers had not been the baby's first name after all the worry she'd gone through for Nora's wellbeing over the length of the labour. More disappointing was the parents having wanted the baby to be christened Church of England despite her hopes that Nora would soften to her wish for it to be the Catholic faith. She was just glad to be a doting grandmother – the only one, being that both Robert's parents were dead.

She'd taken it on herself to be on hand any time, catching one of the busy, morning workers' buses to Stratford on most days to be there to take the pressure off the new mother and to coo over and cuddle the dear little scrap, her first grandchild, not coming home until late afternoon.

Everything seemed to be coming at once – the christening, Neil's wedding, then Maggie's engagement to this Donny fellow despite Moira's intense dislike of him, no ring as yet, he being unable to afford one but there had been an engagement party, against all her mother's objections to it.

The worst of it was that Nora and Robert were not invited. Then later her refusal to attend her own little niece's christening no matter how much Moira had argued with her. An innocent child who'd done *her* no harm.

Even more upsetting was the nastiness at Neil's wedding, caused solely by Maggie. Forced to bow to her mother's demand that she be there, she had placed herself in the very back pew of the church as far from her older sister as she could. Sitting there holding tightly to the hand of that ne'er-do-well fiancé of hers, she had refused to come and sit at the front with the family and so hurting and angering Neil and embarrassing the bride.

At the wedding breakfast at the house, she'd taken herself off to her bedroom leaving a bewildered Donny downstairs, Moira having put her foot down against his going up there to be with her, causing a scene with herself and Maggie before the guests – all so as not to have any truck with Nora.

It was so ridiculous and hurtful for the newly-weds as to put a damper on the entire celebrations. And just when she thought things couldn't get worse, there was Maggie's downright refusal to have her sister and her little family to her and Donny's wedding this following April.

Seeing no end to this enmity and fearing it could last the rest of their lives, Moira could have wept bitter tears had she been that kind of woman.

Nora's face shone as she looked at Robert across the Sunday breakfast table.

'Darling, I think you should know. I've been sick several mornings. I'm afraid it means we'll be having another addition in a few months time.'

He hadn't looked up from his newspaper. Maybe he hadn't heard. She smiled tolerantly and prepared to rephrase her news more gently. After all, Elsie's little sister Nora had only been born early this January, conceiving so soon after their first child having been quite a shock. It was also a girl, called Nora after herself and Margaret after Robert's late mother.

Now she'd fallen yet again far too quickly, all due to her milk having dried up in just a few months, leaving her open to conception, and to Robert being an all too affectionate a man in bed – not that it wasn't wonderful being so loved, and he hadn't been at all surprised or put out by a second child arriving so close after the first.

But maybe he might not be so pleased this time. On the other hand if it were a boy how could he not be pleased? She just hoped it would be a boy for his sake, and now was the time to tell him of her condition while Richard was still in bed on this Sunday morning and not pricking his young ears up and opening his mouth with embarrassing questions.

It had made her feel embarrassed enough during her first pregnancy having him, a mere stepchild, watching her swelling stomach, asking in all innocence why it had got so large and was she ill. She'd told him offhandedly that this happened to ladies after they married and not to bother his small head about it. But it had been awkward.

Last time when he'd smirked at her condition, coming up to thirteen, putting two and two together, no doubt having picked up bits and pieces of the facts of life from school mates, she'd scolded him quite harshly, as a result almost making an enemy of him. But he'd been over the moon at the second baby, a proud brother to his two little sisters. Now she was pregnant again, preferring to tell his father with Richard out of the way, in case he smirked now with even greater knowledge from boys how babies were made.

Repeating her news made Robert look up from his copy of *The Times* but there was no smile on his face, only a look of deep concern.

'I'm sorry, I was reading what it says here,' was all he said.

Nora's happy expression vanished. 'Haven't you heard a word, Robert? I said we're having another baby. It could be a boy, just what you wanted.'

He had been thrilled by the birth of both his daughters, stating that a father isn't a proper man until he's had a daughter to love and protect as she grows up. But all fathers want a son, she thought now.

At her words he appeared to cast off the sombre look with some effort.

'Darling, of course I'm pleased and it doesn't matter what it is, it's wonderful and I didn't mean to look so down. It's just this.' He tapped the newspaper. 'It's not good. I think I'd better read it out to you.'

All her own joy faded as she listened in growing dismay to the news that early this morning Britain had declared war on Germany.

Over the last month the British public had been reading casually of the series of squabbles in Europe after the assassination in Bosnia at the end of June of the Archduke Franz Ferdinand, heir to the Austro-Hungarian throne. But this had all been in Europe and most British readers had turned to more interesting news, their thoughts on the troubles much nearer home in Ireland. Then yesterday the British Government said it would stand by the 1839 Treaty of London guaranteeing Belgian's neutrality – sticking its nose in where it shouldn't as some people put it – but late last night Germany had thumbed its own nose at the Treaty, marching into Belgium as a convenient back door to France. So what seemed to have been a mere run of trivial European squabbles had escalated so fast it took the breath away. Britain was at war. So stupid, ran the thought through Nora's head. And it had ruined her happy news.

But hardly had the morning advanced a few more hours when there arose a surge of national pride, with throngs of enthusiastic young men filling the streets in eagerness to enlist and show Germany that no one thumbs its nose at Britain and expects to get away with it.

Over the evening meal, Nora gazed across at Robert with imploring eyes. 'You won't think of joining up, will you? Not with a third baby on the way.'

He looked at her in surprise, then laughed.

'My dear God, Nora, do you really think I would? I've a business to run. What would happen to that if I joined up? And what would happen to you with three children to take care of all alone? No my sweet, let them who want to run off to fight do so. Most of them won't be married, just young and looking for excitement and adventure. Don't be silly, darling, I wouldn't dream of leaving you in your condition.'

With that he got up from his chair and came round the table

to kneel beside her, take her in his arms and plant a long, tender kiss on her brow.

'Silly girl,' he murmured lovingly.

It was February. Despite every certainty that with Britain involved it would all be over by Christmas, the war was still going on. No one had experienced any other war like it. The Boer War and South Africa had been half a world away. This one was far too close, something new – war at sea, Royal Navy ships, even merchant shipping sunk by German mines in the North Sea and elsewhere with terrifying loss of life, sometimes only 30 miles off the British coast.

Robert's business involving scrap metal had so far kept him out of the war, being that such a commodity could be melted down to help make weapons of war. Nora was so deeply grateful for it that it almost hurt, and prayed she might be allowed to go on being grateful.

She sat now gazing down at her beautiful baby, yet another girl born just a month ago. They'd named her Eileen after one of Robert's sisters.

He'd insisted on their second baby being named Nora after herself while she had added Margaret for his dead mother, rewarded by seeing him humbly pleased, but also for her own sister, in a way hanging on to the close ties they'd both once had for each other. But apparently when told, for she'd not attended the christening, Maggie had shrugged and said, 'I don't care, she can call it what she likes, I'm not interested.'

It was so silly continuing this obsessive vendetta of hers. Maggie not inviting her to her wedding still hurt, so she shrugged off not being asked to her first baby's christening. But it was a boy while she'd still not yet given Robert a son for all his joy of their three daughters.

What did hurt was her naming the child John with all the intention of calling him Jack after their father, obviously knowing that she'd hoped to give her own son that name, when she had one. It was so obvious. For all Maggie was now married with a little family, she still smouldered over the past; deliberately going out of her way to do her sister out of that pleasure.

Even so, she'd given little Eileen the second name of Margaret not only for Robert's mother but for her sister too, making sure the message reached to her that she could be generous even if Maggie wasn't.

With three healthy daughters now she sat in her comfortable nursing chair enjoying the strong pull on her breast as the baby sucked – a strong one for which she gave thanks.

Two-year-old Elsie was in her highchair playing with a spoon. When this one finished feeding she would put her down to give Elsie something to eat. Little Nora was still asleep in her cot but would be awake very soon whimpering for her bottle. It was putting a strain on her but Robert, bless him, noting the pressure she was under was at this very minute arranging to hire a proper nanny to help.

'What's the good of money if not to take some of the weight off you? I need my wife to enjoy more time for herself – she deserves it.'

He'd laughed, cuddling her to him when some days ago she had broken down in tears somehow feeling quite weak. Within two days a new face had come to share their home, a young woman by the name of Amy Lane whose husband had died at the Front back in the autumn.

With no children from the marriage she had been doing war work in an ordnance factory, hating the harsh conditions and living alone had leapt at the offer of work that was far nicer with accommodation to boot, if only a single room at the top of the large Stratford house.

Quite content with a modest wage she'd be doing small tasks around the house as well as taking care of Elsie and little Nora. This way it left their mother more time to concentrate on feeding baby Eileen in the hope that her milk would last longer this time.

Though she still hoped to have more children until she could produce a boy, she did feel she needed a rest for at least a couple of years before falling again.

Ten

Four years and war was still dragging on. Three years back her brother Neil, being Neil, answering the call for more men, had volunteered with the full blessing of his wife Emily. Even today Nora couldn't believe how she could have been so willing. Poor Emily, it wasn't fair!

In her eyes it had put Maggie's husband to shame, hanging back for a whole year until conscription forced him. Even then he'd tried to worm out of it, his excuse that his wife had just given birth – a girl they had named Dora after his mother – and he couldn't leave her. It cut no ice with the authorities in desperate need of men, married or single.

She worried for Maggie but not for him, hearing that he'd proved an unreliable employee, always with some excuse for not turning up for work where he was supposed to help Dad oversee the sorting of rags, shoes and other waste clobber. With Neil no longer there to help and his few workers doing military service, Dad was finding it hard to keep going, though Nora felt that he'd not miss his son-in-law's absence that much for what it was worth.

Maggie left with a small son and a new baby, Nora wanted to help but it was best not to interfere. And she had her own problems at the time when even Robert began to feel almost obliged to respond to the call for more men. She'd begged him at the time to think of her and his children. 'You've not been called up! You're married,' she told him angrily. 'Leave it at that.'

Yet despite arguments, usually ending up with her in tears, he'd been acutely aware of eyes turning accusingly to any of military age still in civilian clothing and to the endless posters crying out: 'Women of Britain Say – GO!'

She'd been so relieved when he came back from the recruiting office to say he'd been refused, their examination revealing a slight heart condition – not serious but enough for him not to be accepted – and that his business was of more use to the country by supplying the government with whatever scrap metal he bought for melting down to go towards the making of munitions.

It had been such a relief. Later he said he was sorry for putting her through such anxiety especially after she told him a little later that she was pregnant again. She'd clung to him in tears of relief and forgiveness yet felt it was hard to forget what had seemed a total lack of consideration for her. But all that faded when in April 1916 their fourth baby turned out to be a son.

'I'd like to call him Charles. It's my father's second name,' she'd said, trying to ignore the small voice in her head that said she was really getting back at her sister who'd got in with Dad's first name, Jack, for her baby. 'And I want his second name Robert, after you, darling,' she'd added.

Four children in four years, all healthy and strong, it made her feel she'd achieved something special – a boy at last and still with his father at home. Even later with the war going badly and conscription, including those formerly rejected as unfit, he was still at home. She felt so fortunate, even went with her mother to Mass one Sunday morning to cement her thanks.

Maybe it hadn't been the right thing to do. Or maybe she had felt too self-satisfied, for not long after that it seemed that *someone up there* decided to pour cold water on her contentment. During the carnage that was the Somme, her brother Neil was killed. Knocked for six, she'd spent a long time, it seemed, in a strange sort of waking coma, the world feeling unreal.

Even now two years later she could not quite recall how the days had passed or anything she had done at that time. Neil had been her favourite brother. She'd had little to do with her young brother George, he just sixteen when she'd married. At eighteen he'd volunteered, was an instructor corporal in England training others to fight. But Neil, for all his gentle tormenting, had always been the one nearest to her heart, the one who, when serious, would give her good advice, one whom she felt she could turn to in a crisis. Losing him had almost ripped her heart out.

Mum was never quite the same afterwards, her old aggressive spirit vanishing overnight. Oddly she found herself missing the mother as she had known her.

Sometimes she'd talk of Neil as though he were still here,

causing Nora to burst out in frustration: 'Neil's dead, Mum! He won't be coming back!' But it never seemed to penetrate.

Other times she'd speak of going to visit him at the cemetery next to her church. Unable to fathom her strange thinking, Nora would repeatedly find herself becoming angry, unable to help herself saying: 'Mum, Neil isn't there. He's buried in France! We don't know where he is.'

Where once Mum would have met her outspokenness with a sharp reminder to watch her p's and q's, she would merely smile as if she alone knew exactly where he was.

Realizing she was never going to get through to her no matter what, she had ceased trying to reason with her even when Mum began attending Mass often twice a day saying she would probably see Neil while she was there.

Dad let her get on with it. Always a man of few words, he'd grown even more silent these days. He seldom went to his yard, his elderly foreman left in charge. Though the moment Mum started talking of Neil he would get up from his chair and leave the house, usually to go to his work and sit brooding in his untidy little office there.

The house had become a lonely place, Nora's younger sisters, Rose now twelve, off with school friends whenever possible, Elsie at sixteen now working in a factory making military clothing forever out with her friends too. Even Neil's widow, Emily, no longer visited. After losing him she'd gone back to her parents, unable to cope with her mother-in-law's incessant references to him as if he were still alive.

The day the telegram came, her father had sat by the fireplace staring silently at the unlit coals, Robert seated beside him puffing one cigarette after another as usual, not knowing what to say, while Mum had rambled on and on about how the Good Lord would soon be seeing her eldest son safely home.

Two years later, Nora was still trying to make her understand that he was buried somewhere in France; where it might be, they'd never know.

Although she was a lot more rational these days, she felt that her mother still saw him as still being here in this world. It was best not to contradict or question. It had taken a time to realize how Mum felt, and it stayed with her too – not knowing where

Neil was buried or if he was buried at all but perhaps blown to bits. The telegram hadn't said he was missing believed killed, but dead, and later one or two possessions had been sent back so there must have been a body, but how much of a body? It made her go cold thinking about it and she'd come to understand why Mum needed to blot it out of her mind, needing to live with something that felt more comfortable. She wasn't insane, it was her way of dealing with the unthinkable, but she was changed.

The war was over.

They'd been expecting it for months after years of stalemate, setback, bits of ground gained and lost again, so many times clutching at hope only to lose heart with never any end in sight and so much loss of life that it froze the blood.

There'd never been a war like this one; brought to the very doorstep of civilians, Londoners bombed by Zeppelin and aeroplane that nightly droned overhead to bring fear of a bomb falling on their home or frantic cheering when a Zeppelin or aeroplane got shot down in flames. Now it was over.

For weeks Nora like everyone else had been devouring every snippet of good news the papers carried; of allied gains, enemy lines overrun, pushed back and demoralized; every account of each piece of ground won being followed as avidly as some might follow football results.

When news of an armistice came, Nora was in the middle of giving two-and-a-half-year-old Charlie his breakfast, a bit late, he having slept on until gone ten thirty. Hearing all the bells of London starting to peal, she read instantly what they were telling her. Sweeping him into her arms she hurried to the door to be met by such an uproar of cheering and singing, the road already full of dancing revellers that she could hardly hear herself laughing.

A man prancing by grabbed her and Charlie, giving them a hug and planting a huge smacking kiss first on her cheek, then on the child's, before dancing on, leaving her giggling, though Charlie had begun to bawl his little eyes out at having a stranger kiss him so violently.

When Robert came rushing home she told him about it making him burst out laughing.

★   ★   ★

Nora nibbled at her lip as she felt little Nora Margaret's brow for the fourth time in as many minutes. The five year old had woken up this morning after a somewhat disturbed sleep complaining of having had funny dreams as she called them. She was still in bed, listless and fretful.

'I feel all achy, all over,' she said miserably in her childish way.

She'd been somewhat out of sorts for most of yesterday though not able to explain just how she felt except that her head was painful when she raised her eyes. But this morning she was definitely running a temperature, her mother cringing from what was going through her mind as she left her to hurry downstairs.

'Robert, before you go, I think you ought to get a doctor to look at our Nora,' she said as he came to kiss her cheek bye-bye before leaving for his business.

He paused as he reached for his overcoat and trilby, his son Richard already standing by the front door waiting for him, at seventeen now working with his dad.

'Is she that much under the weather then?'

Last night Robert had slept through her having to get up several times to answer the child's whimpers and soothe her back to sleep. She had not wanted to disturb him, not really feeling too concerned being that little Nora had fallen asleep again quickly enough but this morning finding her hot and feverish, alarm bells began to ring in her head.

'I really think she needs a doctor,' she said in answer to Robert's question. 'She's really feverish. It could be the 'flu.'

Influenza had reached epidemic proportions in other parts of the world and was reported to have reached Britain just over a year ago. But people still caught up with the progress of the Great War, as it was now being called, thought little of it.

Peace, now three months old, had brought its own troubles: growing unemployment, thousands of servicemen returning to find no job for them; food shortages as bad as ever they had been in the war, while thousands of families were in grief for their lost loved ones. Ten million men were reported to have been killed by the war's end, three quarters of a million in Britain alone – a whole generation wiped out.

But influenza, called the Spanish flu, was said to be claiming two thousand or more victims a week in London alone, schools closed and council workers spraying disinfectant around the thoroughfares. Little Nora, complaining of what looked very much like the flu, was scaring the life out of her mother.

'Robert, forget work, just get the doctor!' she almost shouted as she heard her daughter's moan from upstairs. 'I think she might have it!'

In the darkened bedroom, Nora sat silent unable to find strength enough even to acknowledge those who crept up to offer their condolences.

Robert and her mother were downstairs in the parlour trying to deal with those still arriving. The children were upstairs being cared for by Amy Lane. The hallway filled with flowers and wreaths, the funereal smell of them wafting up the stairs, pervading the room in which Nora sat, and seemed to cling to her clothes.

She became vaguely aware of someone kneeling beside her, someone speaking to her, a woman, but she didn't recognize the voice.

She remembered Dad had been in a little while ago. He'd taken her hands and she had felt their roughness on her own. He had muttered her name in a broken tone, no doubt thinking of his own son gone from him, never having fully recovered from the loss.

The woman kneeling beside her was talking gently to her though she couldn't place it. She just wished she would go away, whoever she was. All she wanted was to be left in this room with its drawn curtains to continue to drift in this ocean of nothingness, letting it surround her, emptying her mind, her very soul.

She thought she'd said, 'Please, go away,' but realized she hadn't spoken. It was as if she were standing outside herself watching this thing that was supposed to be her.

'I had to come,' the voice said quietly and gently. 'I needed to.'

When Nora made no reply, the voice spoke again, still in a whisper. 'Nora – it's Maggie.'

The spoken name shook her for a second or two in disbelief, then suddenly everything seemed to explode inside her head and she found herself falling forward into her sister's arms, felt them come about her as a welter of sobs was torn from her.

There were no words except those that were now ripping silently through her mind, words said years ago – wicked, horrid words spoken in anger and accusation, then in the bitter, lonely silence of resentment and enmity. Now her sister was crouching in front of her, her arms about her, and she crying her heart out on her sister's shoulder as she couldn't have done with anyone else.

How long they remained this way, Nora couldn't have said. It may not have been as long as it felt but slowly, as the weeping subsided, and Maggie straightened up from her crouching position, Nora sank back in her chair, strangely exhausted.

Maggie was holding her hand, her other hand coming to cover it. Until then no words except those first few whispered ones had passed between them. Now Maggie spoke again, her voice still low, 'I'm so sorry.'

Whether it was in commiseration for her loss, or whether it was regret for all those years neither had spoken to the other, Nora had no idea, too lost in grief to care.

Since the passing of her beloved little girl, was it only days ago, she'd been incapable of feeling anything but emptiness. Now the words brought a tiny spark of rancour to stir in her and before she could stop herself she heard herself saying harshly, 'Sorry for what?'

Maggie's whispered reply was almost inaudible. 'For your loss – and for mine. For throwing away what we had. For all those wasted years. I'm sorry.'

Nora didn't reply but the words had dragged her mind back into the world, forcing her at last to face the death of her child; an almost unbearable pain but more proper and natural than the void into which she had been allowing herself to sink.

Something else she felt – relief, like a great gate suddenly opening. Her sister was here kneeling beside her. Her sister's hand was on hers. She could feel the warmth of it on her cold one. The need to respond took hold hardly without her having to think about it.

'I'm sorry too,' she managed to say.

All these years, an exchange of two small words, two words of healing; could it really make a difference? She found herself wanting it to so much, as she let Maggie help her up from the chair. With her sister holding her arm, she allowed herself to be guided down the stairs to the hushed and stilted conversation of those waiting below.

It was Maggie who helped her on with her warm black coat,

her black gloves and hat with its heavy veil. It was Maggie who stood beside her with Robert on the other side, both supporting her as the tiny coffin was borne from the house to the waiting hearse, helping her into the following car, aware now of the world around her, of her mother crying into a black-edged handkerchief, Dad seated silently beside her.

In the church and at the graveside it was Maggie again who stood close to her, one hand under her elbow, the grip tightening as she shivered, the day dull and cold though the sleet had held off until later.

The mourners coming away from the sad little grave, she again let herself be helped back into the car. Tears fell unseen behind her veil at seeing no hearse now proceeding them – little Nora was gone, she would never sit at the meal table again, never come laughing into her arms, never to be sung to sleep or woken in the morning with a kiss.

Robert was holding her hand. She heard him ask quietly, 'You all right, darling?'

She nodded but couldn't shake off the sweet but awful thoughts; felt she would never do so as long as she lived. Then she felt Maggie take her free hand in both of hers in such a grip it almost hurt, and somehow that gesture swept away the painful memories to bring fresh and far more acceptable ones, ones she could cope with.

Her brother George had come home, having spent his war at Aldershot, and her mother arranged a small celebration for his homecoming; Mum didn't talk about Neil as much as she once did, seeming in some ways to be returning to her old self. Nora had no idea how Maggie's husband had fared in the War, Mum still somewhat confused at the time to talk much about him or Maggie, and Nora hadn't asked or wanted to know.

She had truly believed that any hope of reconciliation would never happen – not so long as they lived. Now here was Maggie sitting beside her, holding her hand in both hers with such a grip of love and comfort she would never have known possible even as near as a few days ago.

Nora lifted her head. She would never forget her darling little daughter, but for the sake of her other children, Robert, and all those she loved, she had to face the future and learn to move on. Also she had a feeling that she could be pregnant again.

Eleven

Life was definitely stirring inside her. She'd guessed herself to have been just under two months when poor little Nora was buried, so she would now be just over three months, but there had been no time to think on it.

To her relief none of her other three contracted the flu, nor had Robert or herself, though she spent weeks in dread of it with spring bringing an ever growing number of deaths. Then both Maggie's little ones went down with it, Nora finding herself compelled to give help after the rift there'd been between them, all the time fearing that she might be bringing trouble back to her own family.

Both children recovered, but just as Nora was offering up her thanks Maggie herself caught it. She spent days praying it wouldn't take her sister, not after they having made up for all those wasted years. But as she lay ill and feverish it seemed to Nora at times that God was refusing to listen. But it seemed God had a change of mind, for the fever finally broke and Maggie began slowly to recover.

1919 wasn't turning out to be the land fit for heroes it had been promised to be, with growing unemployment and strikes breaking out. On the other hand both Robert and Dad's businesses were picking up. Wives and mothers trying to keep their family going would look for a few extra pennies handed to them by rag and bone men for old clothes worn beyond repair, or utensils fallen apart. They in turn looked to sell on whatever they collected to people like Dad and Robert, even at low prices.

Dad had vowed not to re-employ Maggie's husband after coming out of the forces until Maggie begged him almost on her knees, she fallen pregnant hardly had Donny come home and still carrying despite having had the flu.

'What can yer do? He's family.' Dad implored Moira who had been against taking him on again.

'Yer'll have the same old trouble with that one,' she'd warned flatly but he wasn't as hard-hearted as she.

'I could at least give 'im another try. Being in the forces he might of changed. If he ain't then I'll just 'ave to sack 'im again.'

'That's easier said than done. And upset yer daughter twice!'

'It's a chance I'm willing ter take. As I said, it's family and I can't see me own daughter destitute, now can I?'

'Be it on yer own head then,' she said. 'If he starts ter come his old malarkey again, don't come to me with yer moans. Remember I'm doing yer books again for yer so I think I've got some say in the matter, so I have. But if that's what yer want, then you get on with it!'

Nora was relieved, having visions of Dad refusing Donny employment, he coming to them for a job instead and what could Robert have said in that case? She didn't trust Donny as far as she could have thrown him, but would have felt bound to help her sister, making up for all those years of bitterness.

Nora sat in Maggie's tiny front room, both of them with their stomachs well distended, both due to give birth within weeks of each other.

Around them the children played, Maggie appearing to have little control over her two boisterous ones. Unlike Nora, there was not the remotest chance of her affording a nanny.

'Not on what Dad pays my Donny. It hardly keeps him and me, much less these two, and now with this one coming . . . I can hardly make ends meet as it is. Perhaps you could have a word with him.'

It was embarrassing being asked that. 'At least your Donny's got a job,' she pointed out. 'Unemployment's getting worse and worse, and all these strikes, it's a wonder anyone can keep body and soul together.'

'Your Robert don't do too bad though, does he.' It sounded faintly more of an accusation than a question. Nora bit back a retort.

'Nor does Dad,' she reminded.

'It'd be nice if he was a bit more generous, give Donny a bit of a pay rise maybe,' came the acid response. Again Nora curbed her tongue.

It was too easy to start a row with Maggie these days. She'd mellowed over the years, though she could still seem able to find one thing or another to be bitter over, and today it was what their father paid his son-in-law. It was wiser not to say Donny didn't warrant a rise in pay. Despite having been in the forces, which would have led one to imagine he had bucked up his wits a bit, he remained the same good-for-nothing waster, always with some excuse or other not to turn up for work, instead looking for some easy pay-out.

When she went to see Mum she would sit hearing her going on about Donny's hopeless punctuality and slapdash timekeeping.

'Spending his weekend drinking with his cronies,' she'd say. 'Then come Monday too much the worse for drink to get himself to work.' Once she started there was never any stopping her.

All this Nora held in her mind as she listened to Maggie's tale of not having enough to scrape together even to put clothes on the children's backs and how she had to scour the second hand market stalls for clothes.

She knew that the moment she dared offer help, not money of course, but a few kid's clothes, some garment she no longer wore, or maybe a few groceries, Maggie's face would tighten, her head go up, her tone grow acid. It did now as, unable to resist the need to help, Nora found the offer spurned.

'Thanks, but I've not sunk yet to taking charity!' the reply cold.

'I didn't mean it that way,' Nora said but Maggie wasn't listening.

'Because you and your husband are doing all right, there's no need to come the lady of the manor with your handouts.'

'I wasn't!'

'. . . showing off with your money and your fine clothes.'

'I'm not! And if you'd not gone silly over someone like Donny Lea you might have married someone else and be better off yourself now,' Nora shot back at her, anger getting the better of her.

Maggie's eyes widened. 'I would of done if you hadn't pinched Robert off me!'

There it was, hovering in the background, ever waiting to spring. Nora took a deep breath and stood up. 'I'm sorry, Maggie, I'm going to have to go. It's getting late.'

She almost began to say she was sorry about marrying Robert, but that would be going too far. She wasn't sorry. She'd not stolen him off her sister. He'd rejected her sister and that hadn't been her fault. But the old sore had still not healed underneath its fading scar.

By the time she got into her coat and hat, things had calmed. Maggie coming to the door with her as if no harsh word had passed between them, she kissed her on the cheek and said in a small voice, 'I didn't mean what I said, Nora.'

'I know,' Nora said, returning the sisterly kiss.

'It's just that I'm under so much stress. I think Donny's sending me slightly potty. I never know where I am with him. He comes home so drunk, starts flinging his arms about – he's shouting and letting his fists fly and sometimes one's caught me by accident. I know he don't mean it and he's always sorry after, but I worry about the kids and this baby. I really wish I wasn't having it.'

'Don't say that!' Nora cried, catching her sister to her in an effort to give her a big comforting cuddle. But Maggie pushed her away.

'What else can I say? I mean how are we ever going to afford this one? I'm going off my head worrying about it.'

'Have you talked to Mum about it all?'

'No. She'll go mad. She'll go and have a busting row with him.'

That was true. Mum was beginning to be her old self again as the years moved on, even to regaining that quick temper of hers.

'Perhaps it would do some good, knock some sense into him,' Nora advised, confident of Mum's ability to sort things out once and for all.

'He'll only take it out on me,' was Maggie's reply. Her voice sounded small, tinged with fear and it was then for the first time that Nora realized Donny's fists hadn't always landed by accident.

Not knowing quite what to say she merely said, 'You should still tell Mum,' before hurrying away. But she knew Maggie wouldn't say anything about it to their mother, even though she was sure one sharp word from Mum would stop Maggie's husband in his tracks.

The telephone was ringing. Robert had installed the instrument in the house only a few weeks ago. Nora was still unused to it and she cautiously lifted the earpiece off its hook, holding the stem between thumb and finger, and put it to her ear.

'Hullo?'

'That you, Nora?' The voice at the other end sounded un-familiar.

'Yes. Who is it?'

'It's yer dad.' His voice sounded tense. 'Thought I'd best tell yer soon as I could. Quicker than coming round. Didn't want to bother Robert and 'im 'aving ter telephone yer. It's just yer mum's not well, not at all well. I think you ought ter come round if yer can. I know yer've only got a month ter go before you 'ave the baby, but if yer can make it 'ere . . .' It was the most she had heard her father say in one go for ages and she was instantly alarmed.

'Yes, I'll come round. Of course I'll come,' she cut in quickly.

'How ill is she?' she burst out, her mind flying to Spanish flu which was still rife. Dad's anxious voice mirrored that thought.

'I think it must be the flu. She went down with it a couple of days ago and it's got worse, 'er tossing an' turning and she's all 'ot and feverish an' coughing a lot too. Says 'er chest 'urts when she coughs and I don't like the way she's breathing, sort of short and fast and she bringing up lots of green phlegm and it looks like streaks of blood in it too. I'm really worried, love!'

'Haven't you called the doctor?' Nora almost yelled into the mouthpiece. She knew Mum had had a nasty cough but attributed it to just a bit of a summer cold, certainly not flu. The symptoms Dad described didn't exactly sound like flu either. But she was still worried.

'I done that,' Dad was saying. 'But 'e can't come out fer an hour or so because 'is surgery is crowded with ill people.'

He and Mum had never stretched to paying for a private doctor, she maintaining they were a healthy family with no cause to throw good money away on one they seldom needed to call out. Going to the surgery was good enough. Dad let it go at that, too busy with his scrap business to argue.

'An hour or so!' Nora now blazed. 'That's not right. I'm getting our own doctor out to her. I'll be round as soon as I can.'

She hung the receiver back on its hook, fumbling so that she had to find the hook twice before it caught. Then immediately lifted it again and dialled the telephone exchange, giving her family doctor's number.

Quickly she explained the symptoms to him, saying she was prepared to meet any extra fee asked for attending someone not his patient, grateful to have him say he would go immediately to the address she'd given. He would probably charge a handsome sum for his trouble but she didn't mind. He was a good doctor and knew they could afford it.

He'd already arrived by the time she got there, having used his car while she had delayed her arrival by telephoning Robert and waiting for him to come and drive her there. Even as they came into the bedroom, Doctor Martin was at the bedside, holding Mum's wrist, a thermometer in her mouth.

Releasing the wrist and withdrawing the thermometer he glanced at it and shook it down, turning to smile at the new arrivals as they entered, then directing his attention to the sick woman's husband.

His face had grown serious. 'I'm afraid your wife has pneumonia. You say she complained of cough and chest pains. How long has this been?'

'I ain't sure – a week per'aps.'

'And you say you never thought to call a doctor?'

'She said it was just a summer chill and she didn't want to go and see no doctor. She wouldn't 'ave that it could be the flu and didn't want ter go sitting around other people what might 'ave it and catch it from them.'

'You should have insisted she went.'

'You don't know my wife, doctor,' was the reply accompanied by a brief, sad smile.

'Shouldn't she be taken to hospital, Doctor Martin?' asked Nora.

'Hospitals are overcrowded still with flu patients. She is probably better off here at home under medical supervision. I shall call in tomorrow.'

He was already writing out a prescription which he handed to Nora rather than her father, whose smile had faded.

'Take this to the chemist straight away,' he continued. 'She must finish all the medicine. Keep her warm, plenty of water to drink, she will probably not want to eat but if she does, she can have some thin soup.'

He turned to Nora, smiling, glancing at her pronounced bulge. 'Not long now, my dear. We'll see you very soon I expect. And don't worry about your mother, she's in good hands, you just take care of yourself, my dear.'

She had been told not to worry, but worry came like some dark spectre as, despite all Doctor Martin's reassurances, Mum grew progressively worse.

Nora spent all her time with her, her three children in the care of their new nanny Miss Edith Riley, a forty-year-old spinster, Amy Lane having left to remarry. Richard, at seventeen, could look after himself.

Throughout the week Mum's house was full of people, Nora's sisters Rose and Elsie, Maggie and her two kids, Dad fearing to go to work as his wife seemed to be worsening despite the doctor's visits, her brother George and his fiancé, Irene, they hoping to marry early next year. Even Mum's sister Nellie had come down to see her, and one or two neighbours had popped in to offer help. But at this moment the bedroom was empty for once.

Nora sat by her, holding the hot hand that seemed to have no life in it. Her mother was apparently sleeping, the medicine she'd been given helping to stem much of the restlessness. She became aware her mother's eyes were open and she was looking at her.

'How're you feeling, Mum?' she whispered.

The eyes half closed in response then opened again, but not looking at her. She seemed almost to be looking past her. Her lips were moving and a small, quiet, somehow distant, but surprisingly clear voice spoke.

'I feel . . . well enough. It'll be nice ter see my Neil again.'

She had obviously gone back to what she had been when they'd lost Neil. Alarmed, Nora leaned towards her. 'Mum, Neil's . . .'

Mum's quiet voice interrupted her, still sounding distant, as if she was talking to someone else, yet clear as a bell. 'I've had enough of this life, so I have.'

'Don't say that, Mum,' Nora whispered urgently. 'You're going to get better.'

She believed that implicitly. To her ears Mum's harsh and difficult breathing had eased slightly. Soon she would be up and about again.

But her mother's voice, weak though it was, held a tiny ring of that old intractableness of hers. 'It'll be good to see Neil again.'

She gave a dry little cough, turned her head slightly away and closed her eyes. When she opened them again they held a far away look and an odd gleam of elation. Her voice came hoarsely but strong: 'It's lovely. He's with our little Nora. They're so happy. Our Lord is with them, so He is, and please God, I'll be with them again, soon please.'

The long speech seemed to take it out of her and she closed her eyes again. For some time Nora sat holding her hand thinking how peaceful she looked asleep but hating the content of what she'd heard.

Robert came into the room. 'How is she?' he whispered.

'Sleeping,' she whispered back. 'Her breathing seems a bit easier.'

He put a gentle hand on her shoulder. 'Perhaps we'd best leave her to it. You've been up here a long time. You must be tired. Let someone else, your dad maybe, come up and sit with her.'

Nora nodded and releasing her mother's hand got up and followed him out, closing the door quietly.

Dad went upstairs to take her place, coming down later to say that he didn't want to disturb her too much. She had woken up and looked at him. He tried to speak to her but she made no response, merely closing her eyes again and seemed to be sleeping.

She never woke up and a few hours later, Mum, who had never done anything quietly in her life, slipped silently away.

Twelve

It broke her heart going into labour two weeks early and unable to be at the funeral.

'I've got to be there,' she kept shouting between bouts of pain, as the baby struggled to get into the world. 'I've got to be there – she's my Mum!'

How could her mother be buried with her not being there?

If only the baby could be got out in time, she could have herself carried to the church if need be, so as to be at the grave-side so that Mum wouldn't be alone.

She must have babbled this aloud in the height of her labour for she was aware of the attending midwife saying, 'Your mother is not alone. All her family are there.'

'But not me! Not me!'

'You just concentrate on delivering this baby,' she vaguely heard as she lay gasping. 'Your mother would want it to be born without mishap, now wouldn't she?'

But her mother had lain in the ground twenty-five hours before the baby finally arrived, its somewhat feeble cries at being projected from a warm womb hardly loud enough for Robert to hear, as he paced the living room until finally summoned upstairs to see his wife and their new child.

Death and birth – all jumbled together in Nora's head as she lay, the little scrap nestled in its shawl in her arms looking so tiny. And when Robert came in to look at her and then his new daughter, saying quietly, 'She looks like your mum,' the signifi-cance of death and birth hit her like a sledgehammer and she burst into an all-engulfing flood of tears.

Robert stood by until the tears had subsided before bending to kiss her forehead. Then after gently kissing the baby he gazed into Nora's eyes.

'What shall we call her?'

There was no need to think about it. 'I want to call her Moira, after mum.'

Seeing no reason to disagree, he gazed again at his new daughter's tiny screwed up features. 'She seems so much tinier than our others were,' he remarked. 'Is she?'

Nora also gazed at the baby's little face half hidden by its smothering woollen shawl, the scrawny little limbs seeming not to want to move against the restricting material.

'She's only six pound and a few ounces,' she said, but the midwife who'd come back into the room with a cup of tea for the mother butted in.

'Not to worry, she'll put on weight quickly enough in a few days.'

But Nora already knew this one was not strong like the others. She seemed not to have any zest in her and when put to the breast a few minutes before Robert came in, the midwife helping her, she didn't seem to want to bother to suckle, and even when she finally did it was very half-hearted.

What worried her was that when Doctor Martin had arrived to examine her and the baby, she had noticed a grave expression pass briefly over his round features as he put a stethoscope to the little chest.

Seconds later he had given her a kindly smile, assuring her that she was doing very well.

'And my baby?' she'd queried. 'She looks very small.'

'Yes,' was all he'd said, but moments later asked, 'When do you plan to have her christened, my dear?'

'Why?' she'd asked quickly.

'I think it would be good to have it soon.'

'Why?'

'It's always best for a child to be baptized as soon as possible after birth as a sign of admission into the Christian church.'

'Is there something wrong with her?' Nora had burst out.

He hesitated then said, 'The heart beat is a little weak perhaps. It will no doubt get stronger but to be on the safe side it would be wise to have her baptized, my dear. You mustn't worry. The heart could gain strength as time progresses. Birth is a very great trauma for the child.'

'But it never happened to my others!'

'Every child is different,' he'd said, then telling her not to worry overmuch, had left as Robert came up.

'I think we ought to have her baptized very soon,' she said.

She still felt almost too drained to stand when some days later the small assembly gathered about the font in the Stratford church.

Maggie and Rose had readily agreed to be the child's godmothers, her brother George consenting to be a godfather, Robert against Donny acting in that capacity with his unhealthy attitude to life.

Nora held on to Robert while Maggie passed the tiny thing over to the vicar officiating. She'd struggled with the idea of having her baby baptized in the Catholic faith in honour of her mother, knowing it would have made the woman so happy. Yet it felt too much like blasphemy in a' way and she had finally resisted the temptation. Hardly a week later, little Moira was in hospital, the medical staff doing all they could to save the tiny life but with no success.

Nora felt nothing as the tiny coffin was lowered into the ground to join her grandmother in heaven. As she saw it, it was as if Mum needed to have the little one with her.

'It's like yer mum's got a proper little family up there with 'er,' Dad said sadly, still immersed in his own keen sense of loss and loneliness as he stood with his four daughters and remaining son.

It had been an eventful eighteen months since losing Mum. Nora still hadn't felt able to shake off the regret in not having been present at Mum's funeral; sometimes it felt as if it would be with her for the rest of her life, even though so much had happened since.

Last April, George had got married to a girl named Irene who lived in the next road to his. She was two years older than him. It was happening a lot; with so many young men lost in the Great War a young man older than the girl had become hard to find.

They were now living with Dad for the time being. Since losing Mum he had become a lost soul, forever saying as how he missed her, even for her sharp tongue. He would reminisce continuously on how she had sometimes practically driven him to drink cold tea, as he put it, or at least had often driven him out of the house to drink something stronger at times, he seeing it wiser to shut up and let her get on with it rather than argue with her, arguments she would invariably win.

'I got no one to get my goat now,' he'd say, his Cockney terms more sad than whimsical these days. 'Yer mum was a proper caution at times.'

George took over the rent of the house after he and Irene married. He was also handling Dad's business, Dad no longer much interested in it or in anything it seemed. It had always been expected that both his sons would become partners in the business in time, but with only one left he didn't seem to care any more, he merely a sleeping partner now.

Last October, Rose, still a couple of months to go to her eighteenth birthday, had met a twenty-one-year-old lieutenant in the regular army. His name was Bertram Uttley. They had met at a dance, she taken up by his splendid officer's dress uniform and he by her pretty figure and shapely legs, very much revealed by the new, almost scandalously short, skirts girls were wearing. No longer with the guiding hand of a mother to control and advise her, she was pregnant two months later. Married quietly and hurriedly, she'd gone to live with his quite well off parents in Chester, but hoped to move into married quarters once the baby was born some time late September.

Nora hadn't seen her since, had received just one letter full of how happy she was, how wonderful Bertram was, how pleasant her life was and her excitement of the coming baby – not one reference to Mum or asking how Dad was coping, or even how any of the family were.

Nora wrote back wishing her well, her feelings split between missing her baby sister and anger at her lack of concern, in a way feeling foolishly unwanted, not only by Rose but George as well, and even Dad now that he had his son and daughter-in-law to care for him. In her low mood on this dull, cold February day, she even imagined Maggie to have forgotten her. Now, this afternoon, here was Maggie falling into her arms in tears as she opened the door to her knock.

At her side stood two of her children, she supporting seventeen-month-old Donald on one arm, as she threw the other about Nora's neck. Almost suffocated between them, the child immediately began protesting loudly.

Nora pulled away from her. 'Whatever's the matter?'

'I've left him! I can't take any more!'

She looked so pathetic standing there with six-year-old Jack and five-year-old Dora, their small faces puckered with confusion, and little Donald still bawling lustily despite his mother jigging him violently up and down, that Nora moved even further back for her.

'You'd best come on in and close the door! You go into the living room. I'll go and tell Harriet to put the kettle on and make us some tea.'

She'd already told her the last time she'd visited that Harriet Clark, a young woman of around twenty, had been recently employed as a maid-of-all-work, and also worked in the kitchen.

'When I come back you can tell me all about it,' she said as she hurried out of the room.

She was back in no time at all, dropping into the armchair to face her sister who was beginning to compose herself a little, still dabbing her eyes dry while the children now sat on the floor a little more settled.

'Now what's he done?' she began and as Maggie started to weep again, sharpened her tone. 'Whatever it is don't start crying again or I won't be able to make out what you're saying. Now what's happened between you?'

'I've left him.'

'You've said that. Why have you left him?'

Maggie gulped back tears. 'Well . . . I – I think he's left me!'

'He's what?'

'He's been seeing someone else.'

Quickly she told of Donny being out most nights, not coming home until early morning, saying he'd been with his mates and she daring not to ask too many questions in case he flew into a temper.

He no longer worked – their brother George had got rid of him the moment he had taken over from Dad – yet he always seemed to have money.

'At least we live pretty comfortably now-a-days,' Maggie went on. 'He gives me enough to get by on, so I don't ask him where he gets it because it'd start a row, but he knows a lot of people.'

'What's this about him seeing someone else?' Nora prompted, aware her sister was moving off the point.

Maggie gathered herself together quickly to return to her main tale that a week or two ago she'd been out shopping and had caught sight of him talking to a pretty young woman at a nearby stall. Her interest pricked, she'd watched them and saw him put an arm about the girl's waist, then draw her to him and kiss her on the lips.

'It wasn't like a friendly kiss,' Maggie sniffed, tears that had already filled her eyes beginning to run down her cheeks. 'It was a long one like two people in love would do. And when she moved away she held his hand for quite a while before leaving.'

Maggie started to weep again, but seeing her sister's lips tighten impatiently rather than sympathetically, hurried on. 'She looked a bit of a floozie, common, thick lipstick, eyebrow pencil, hair all Marcel-waved, her skirt right past her knees. Then I knew – he was being unfaithful to me. When I tackled him about it, he flew into a temper, said I was a suspicious cow, then he went for me and admitted he was seeing someone else and I could stay there or sod off! He even said that now I knew, he might even bring her home to live with us, or I . . . I could . . .'

Her voice faltered and fell away into tears as the words choked in her throat, making Nora leap up from her chair to go and cuddle her.

Seeing their mother so upset the children had started wailing again, necessitating Nora to try to calm them too, helped finally by Harriet coming in with a trolley of tea and pretty cakes.

Handed her cup of tea, Maggie took a deep breath to control her own misery and sipped gratefully. After a while she looked up.

'What am I going to do, Nora? I can't go back. How could I if he brings that woman to live there?'

'Perhaps he won't,' Nora said futilely, knowing full well that he would but Maggie was already looking up pleadingly into her eyes.

'I've nowhere to go, Nora. I've no money for rent. Where am I going to live? If I could . . . perhaps I could stay with you for a while – until I get myself sorted out.'

Nora was in a dilemma. How could she see her in such a pickle and refuse to take her in, her own sister? As big as this house was, it would bulge fit to bursting: Maggie here and her three children, her own three plus young Robert, now nineteen and courting. And there was also herself and Robert, as well as their maid Harriet and the children's nanny Miss Riley, both of whom lived in at the top of the house. And she herself was now pregnant again, the birth expected around August – if Maggie was still here by then . . .

'Perhaps it will all resolve itself,' she said hopefully, knowing how ineffectual that sounded. 'It might all blow over—'

Maggie almost leapt from her seat.

'Resolve itself! Blow over! You mean me forgive him, go back to him, see him bringing home some young tart to live with us? You must be stark staring crazy! And how long before he turns me out? What then?'

'He might go and live with her.'

'And how do I pay the rent with no money coming in? Knowing him, he can be vindictive enough to give me nothing!'

Nora knew that compared to her own marriage, the money Maggie's husband gave her was paltry anyway and probably irregular. It came from gambling, shady deals and probably a bit of stealing. All his mates were crooks of some sort, though Maggie had never put it into words, no doubt too embarrassed. He was nowhere near being a big time crook, just a small time one, but it was money all the same.

She was at a loss to know what else to say when Maggie said it for her, blurting it out. 'If he don't throw me out for that tart of his, I wouldn't be able to live there. Where can I go?'

There was a short, awkward pause. Then Maggie spoke again. 'If I could come here, just for a while, just until I can get myself together ... where else can I go? No one will rent me anywhere with three kids. I can't walk the streets and it—'

'You'll have to come here!' Nora broke in, without even intending to make that suggestion, as it seemed Maggie was going to rattle on forever. She felt almost dismayed as her sister's eyes brightened with new hope.

'Oh, Nora! Thank you! I'm so relieved. I was at my wits end. I can't thank you enough!'

'There is a spare room,' Nora admitted lamely. It was the only spare room, kept as a sort of guest room.

She'd often spend time in there on her own, away from the children and even Robert, who'd invariably be at home fiddling about with interesting bits he'd picked up from among the scrap metal – old coins he'd scrupulously clean, military cap badges to be shone bright, a few metal gadgets to be oiled and made to work again, and sold for more than scrap would bring in. Her home was never clear of bits of junk, even in the living room.

That quiet little room upstairs was hers to retreat into and do a bit of needlework, or read, or just dream of the holidays they took once a year; a week in August usually, Eastbourne, Dorset or Devon, even Cornwall. No matter how heavily pregnant she was, she never said no to going away, the car packed to bursting with children and three suitcases. This year it looked as if there might be no holiday, for there would be no room for Maggie and her kids, and to leave her behind would probably upset her.

'That'll be good enough for us,' Maggie was saying to her offer of the spare room. 'We'll be spending most of our time down here anyway.'

To which Nora nodded, with a deep sense of dismay.

Thirteen

For months she'd hoped Maggie and Donny would resolve their differences, but it didn't happen. It seemed he had brought his woman back to live in the home she'd vacated. Within a few months, Maggie was suing for a divorce but that could take ages and even then where would she go? Nora was stuck with her, and her sister's tendency towards a bitter nature, which after nigh on a year was beginning to drive her mad.

Now with her new baby, Francis or Frankie as he began to be called, born in September, she was having trouble with her children's nanny, Edith Riley. After almost a year of being moderately obliging about the extra work put on her, she had now begun complaining that she had only been hired to look after her employer's children, not someone else's as well, and was threatening to give notice.

It was left to Nora to explain to Maggie that she must give eye to her own offspring and not expect Edith Riley to take care of them. True, most of the older children were now at school, but they still needed looking after when they came home, and there were the weekends and school holidays.

It was proving hell upon earth with Frankie still a babe in arms, and Maggie's little Donald only just toddling, all of them to be fed and got to bed in the evenings, the whole house disrupted with wails of protest. Nora prayed constantly for some luck to seek out her sister, whereby she would up and find a life of her own, she rid of not only these children but Maggie's constant whining, even after nearly a year, over her broken marriage.

She could fill a whole house with her rancour. And rather than show gratitude for this roof over her head would often remark begrudgingly on Nora's apparent good fortune in her marriage.

Nora bit her tongue as she always seemed to be doing these days. Before her stretched years of her house full of people, nowhere to sit quietly alone. She even found herself looking forward to the children being all grown up and away. At least Richard, now nineteen, was seriously courting a girl called Valerie. It would be one out of the way eventually.

Working for his dad, half the evening when he wasn't with Valerie, the two would sit amid their clutter talking work. Of course Robert loved all his children, but she often felt that Richard, son of his first marriage, was his favourite deep down. At times she'd experience a prick of resentment that young Charlie, the first son of their own marriage and of whom Robert had always been so proud, at nearly six years old and becoming very aware of things, would often look as if he felt pushed out.

Summer 1921 had been a fine one. In fact there'd been an official drought for a hundred days, breaking with a fierce storm around June that cleared the air to her relief, being pregnant again. As winter came along with baby George, she keenly felt the lack of her August holiday. But she said nothing of it to Maggie, who would only have got all uppity.

She hadn't changed, still her carping self and Nora even wondered if that was why she'd picked up with Donny, just to feel ill-used when she'd been unable to have Robert. Typical of her, Nora thought sometimes, knowing the thought unkind. She wanted to love her sister or at least to like her.

Dismayed she told Robert that this baby had to be the last; that she couldn't cope with any more children.

'One after another, it can't go on,' she said.

'But you've got Edith Riley to help you,' he said easily. 'I can't help it if I love you so much. And you do love children too, don't you?'

Of course she did. And looking back she didn't consider that she'd ever had all that much trouble bearing them. And now that Edith. Riley had been persuaded to give eye to Maggie's lot – for a tidy rise in wage – another child shouldn't make all that much difference.

Even so, she couldn't go on bearing children forever. She was thirty-three, surely it was time to stop. Perhaps she was over fertile and as much at fault as Robert when it came to their bed, loving his attentions, enjoying every climax. And if children came from it, what right had she to complain afterwards?

★   ★   ★

George was born in November, named after her brother, popping into the world like an eel out of a bottle.

'I'll never have any more children,' Maggie said on looking at him the day he was born. 'Not now I'm going through my divorce.'

Lying in her bed, weary after her labour, short though it had been, Nora sighed impatiently. 'You might get married again.'

Maggie tightened her lips at the terse reply. 'I never want to marry ever again. I never want to go through what I've been through – ever again! And who'd want a thirty-year-old woman who's been through a divorce?'

But six months later she was like a happy schoolgirl, having met a man the same age as her, in fact younger by one month.

He'd never been married, having sustained shrapnel wounds to his left hip, which had given him a slight limp of which he'd been very conscious causing him to be shy about girls. He was quite a serious type of person. His name was Harry Gresham, an only child living with his widowed mother. They came from Yorkshire and he'd been down to London on business for the engineering firm he worked for and that was how he'd met her – on a bus and they'd got talking, and it had gone on from there.

All this Maggie told Nora in a welter of happiness. 'To think he's still in such a good job, with over a million people out of work today, so they say!' she ended eventually. 'I feel so lucky.'

Nora had never seen such a change in her sister. From being exasperated by Maggie's never-ending moaning, she now found herself being plagued with ongoing accounts of Harry Gresham and how wonderful he was, and how he simply adored her slight Cockney accent.

'Not a bit stuck up. I do feel so lucky!' she would say time after time, displaying yet another present he'd bought her.

'He never ceases to tell me how much he loves me,' she gushed some months later, flashing a diamond engagement ring, her speech amazingly improved. 'I'm the luckiest girl!' Her dismal years with Donny Lea forgotten.

The following year they were married and went to live in Harrogate in Yorkshire. That same year Nora gave birth to a girl she named Eva. Around the same time Richard and Valerie married, continuing to live with her and Robert for the time being while they found a house of their own. It was grand having the whole place to herself again with only her own brood around her.

She wrote to Maggie after their honeymoon in Brittany. Maggie replied after some time saying she was well and happy – no word about her honeymoon. She wrote back asking how she was enjoying her new life. It was four months before she got a reply, and although she answered by return of post it was again months before Maggie bothered to write back. Her letters grew less and less frequent, and they slowly began to lose touch altogether.

Anyway she was expecting again, this baby due early next year. Also Dad, who'd not been the same since losing Mum, wasn't well and that too took up her time.

Once again there was an addition to her family, two in fact. One was her new baby girl called Rose, after her youngest sister, but very soon coming to be called Rosie. The other was Dad.

A stroke claimed the whole of his right side a few months ago, and he now had to be trundled about in a bath chair, having to be washed and dressed, fed and toileted. She'd spoken to George about it, quite expecting him to care for their father, they now partners in the business and he living in the same house as Dad. But George maintained quite ruthlessly that it was unfair to expect his wife, who was only a daughter-in-law after all, to look after the old man, as he'd called him.

Nora had been indignant, but all he said was, 'After all, you're the eldest daughter of the old man.'

'Don't keep calling him *the old man*!' she'd raged at him. But George stayed annoyingly calm.

'Well, so he is.'

'But you don't have to keep saying it!'

It was ignored as George went on, 'Rene is still only a daughter-in-law. I can't ask her to be left all on her own to cope with him when I'm at the yard working for him.'

'Working for him!' she'd echoed. 'What d'you mean? You and him are partners! You take the same profits he does. And you've enough funds to get someone in to look after him. You already pay domestic staff.'

But she too had domestic staff, so she shut up and allowed George the final say. But she was not happy.

Not that she didn't love Dad but it always seemed she was the one they all turned to when in trouble, and she was growing just a little sick of it.

Although she had hired a nurse to help her, it still caused a lot of disruption because Dad had become difficult, his brain also having been affected. There were times when he was fine, but other times impossible, and he could fly into sudden unreasonable temper, he who'd been always been so placid. How she would have coped without the nurse, Miss Webster, she dreaded to think.

Dad died the following June, contracting pneumonia just as his wife had. He was buried beside her on a glorious summer day, the scent of roses on other graves filling the air; his name engraved beside hers, 'A loving husband,' despite her acid tongue having sometimes driven him round the bend.

A generation gone! The thought hit Nora so suddenly as she stood gazing down at the coffin that her heart seemed to stifle her. A whole generation! Mum's two sisters had died some time ago and Dad's family had gone well before that.

She came away from the cemetery, her mind returning to the present. It was now 1926, so much changed since she and Robert were married. Elsie her first child now thirteen, saw herself almost a young woman, where at the same age Nora had been still a mere child. She was already looking forward to hem lines that showed more leg than was good for them – God knows how much shorter they were going to get – stockings rolled down to below the knees, those knees often rouged to be more noticed. Already she was going on about her tiny breasts becoming too noticeable, the fashion being to have almost none at all, clamouring for a bra to help flatten them, and begging to have her hair cut in that ridiculous shingle like some medieval pageboy, though so far she hadn't got her way.

At least arguing with Elsie made the house seem less silent with Dad gone and Miss Webster having moved on.

Elsie wasn't that much of a bother to a mother of seven children. She could control a thirteen-year-old daughter easily enough. What she couldn't control, and should have known better than to try, was the rest of the family getting on their high horses again.

With Dad's death, her brother George automatically assumed he could take over his father's business as a matter of course. After all he'd been a partner and now the only surviving one. What he hadn't anticipated was that the family thought differently.

Maggie and Rose, and even Elsie, came rushing down to London to *sort things out*.

'Everything Dad left should be divided between all of us, equally,' Maggie said hardly had she got through Nora's doorway, the first to arrive. 'Surely Dad must have left a will. George can't go riding rough shod over that and think he can get away with it just because he set himself up as Dad's business partner.'

'Apparently Dad never ever made a will,' Nora told her. 'And George didn't *set himself up*. Dad made him a business partner, him being the only son he had left.'

'That makes no difference, we're entitled,' raged Maggie, lips grown tight, eyes blazing, no moment's thought for the lost son. 'But I suppose you've enough money not to care what happens.'

Nora fought the temptation to rise to an argument. 'Before we get into a shouting match,' she said as evenly as she could, 'let's wait for the others to arrive. Then we can sort things out. Meantime, I need a cup of tea. Do you want one?'

Appeased to some extent, Maggie took a deep breath to control her anger and, composing herself, nodded.

'I needed this after the journey I've had,' she said over her cup, and began to relate some of the more appalling moments she'd had getting here from Harrogate.

It wasn't long before the other two arrived. Amazing, thought Nora, how quick people can get to a destination when there's the possible promise of a bit of money to be got, as each bustled through the door.

'So do you know anything about what's going to happen to Dad's stuff? I mean the house, his business, his things?' asked Rose over her own tea and cake. 'Thanks for the tea – I really needed it, me coming all this way from Chester. I'm famished!'

'So am I,' echoed Elsie, keeping her own council about her father's legacy. Not having had to travel so far, she was the most calm and collected one, and the most reasonable. 'I don't want to bother you, Nora, but I didn't stop for lunch. Will we be having lunch do you think?'

'I've already sorted that out,' Nora told her, but Elsie had more to say, calmly and gravely turning to the matter in hand.

'If Dad hasn't left a will, it'll take some time to settle every-thing fairly. It'll have to go to probate and that takes time, so we shouldn't get too excited, and Dad's house was rented you know. So there's nothing there to concern ourselves about. It really comes down to Dad's business.'

'And George has got no right to claim it all for himself now,' Maggie butted in. 'He really thinks he has every right to it. Well, he hasn't!'

Until the legal wheels settled it the arguments would continue, getting nastier by the day. Even now, as Nora tried to calm things down, Maggie turned on her, saying, 'I suppose, if the truth was known, you're really thinking you being his eldest it should all go to you,' even the other two nodding in agreement, making Nora prickle with anger.

'Apart from his business,' she snapped, 'I don't think there's much to go to anyone! And why should I want it, or any of it? As you said just a while ago I'm quite comfortably off enough, thank you!'

'And you made sure of that, didn't you, marrying the bloke I should have had,' came the reminder, Maggie's voice rising.

'Don't start bringing that up again!' Nora returned sharply. 'You can't say you're not doing all right yourself now.'

'Yes, but look what I had to go through before I was – how much I had to suffer.'

'It was your own fault, rushing off and marrying someone like that Donald Lea.'

'Well!'

In an indignant huff, Maggie was about to say much more but Rose broke in pleading for them all to calm down, which they did, but from her sister's hostile glance Nora guessed that once all the legal stuff was settled it would be a few more years before she and Maggie spoke to each other again.

In the end there was no point to any of it. Dad had left only a few bits and pieces no one really wanted. What was realized from the sale of his business was divided between them equally, George moving out of his father's rented house, finding a nice little house for him and Rene. With his share, once all legal matters were settled, he invested in a small shop and seemed to be doing well the last time Nora heard from him.

With both parents no longer here, they had gone their separate ways. Sometimes Nora lamented the old days but usually she soon got over it. She had her own family, her own large family to think about. They did too, with their own spouses, their growing broods, and their in-laws.

Anyway, time nearly always saw brothers and sisters dispersing as life went on.

PART TWO

Fourteen

For the last three years, Charlie had been doing a course on metallurgy at night school and his father was showing some impatience with it.

'Time you packed up that lark,' he said as the last term before the August break finished. 'You must know enough about this business by now.'

Yes, he did. He'd learned a lot. He'd been working full-time with Dad in the scrap metal yard since he left school three years ago at the age of fourteen. From his father he'd learned how to haggle, clinch deals, what to look out for and what to reject, but he did enjoy studying. It was fascinating. Then so was his work, more interesting work than people imagined, never knowing what you might find among some bit of old rubbish.

Silver coins were his main goal, some Edwardian heads or Victorian, quite early ones at times, young heads as well as turn of the century ones, even Georgian, and sometimes Roman coins, all collectable. He'd learned that even with modern coins there were some quite rare ones and he had learned what years were rarer than others.

Dad was an avid collector too and had books on it. In the evening he'd quietly borrow one and secretly study it, keeping his hobby to himself in case Dad might claim anything he found as part of the profits. If he got a moment to himself in his bedroom which wasn't often, being shared with Frank and young George, he'd get out the cardboard box from under the bed where he stashed his coins and pour over the various dates. If Dad did know he had never said anything.

Lots of interesting stuff came to light among the piles of metal sold on by unsuspecting house-clearance agents, dealers, traders and hawkers. In fact half the house was filled with good quality and sometimes expensive bits and pieces, even nice bits of antiques on occasion, innocently thrown away. But coins were what Charlie quietly competed with his father for.

Now his father dropped his bombshell. 'I can't see much point you going back next term. You're more needed here. A grown man attending classes, it don't seem right. Anyway I need you here what with your mother taking the kids on holiday next week.'

It took him by surprise. 'They're not classes, Dad, they're courses,' he said resentfully. 'And Mum always goes August bank holiday and I usually go with her being there's not much doing here bank holiday – to help her with the kids.'

Mum would take the younger children, Rosie, now seven, Eva, nine and George, ten, down to Eastbourne or Worthing for a few days in August. Dad didn't go with them, not wanting to close down even for August week.

But Charlie looked forward to that break from work. Yet despite nice weather, a chance of swimming in the sea, a rest from ever-lasting hauling heavy stuff about the scrap yard, he would find his mind yearning to get back to his courses when the next term started.

Last year he'd taken up a geology course as well. It made sense that to understand metals and other minerals and ores, learning where it all comes from, was an essential extra, and on the way he had developed a strong liking for the subject. The last thing he wanted was his father going on about his leaving until he felt forced to give in. He needed to dig his heels in.

'I've got the certificate I was after,' he said quickly as his father cast a baleful glare about the cluttered scrap yard where they were standing. 'But I am on another course. It's just a couple more terms then I'll be free.'

Briefly explaining the geology course he stopped as his father swung back to face him, a deep frown furrowing his brow.

'Geology! For God's sake!' he exploded. 'I didn't attend a bloody night school studying that sort of crap to learn this business. This is where you learn a trade, lad, not skiving off, stuck indoors, *studying!*'

That was damned unfair. What about his precious Richard, getting time off for any old excuse – the wife wasn't well, needed his support, had arranged to go out somewhere, for the evening, for the weekend . . .

The words hovered on the tip of Charlie's tongue but instead he said abruptly. 'Tell me how I'm skiving off when I only go to my course one single evening a week and do any studying after work?'

'You know full well we don't stick to office hours in this job!'

'I know, but I'm always here when I'm wanted.' And he was. It was always, 'Charlie, quick give us a hand!' and it was Charlie who dropped whatever he'd been doing to rush off and help.

'All I know is that you're damned-well wasting your time going off to them useless lessons of yours like some kid!' snapped his father.

This time Charlie didn't reply, turning away, leaving him to fume on his own. He had every intention of carrying on with his geology course. He loved it and Dad couldn't force him to give it up when it didn't interfere with work, and it didn't. Dad had stopped paying the fees a couple of years ago, maybe hoping that would work. He now paid them himself. And Dad could hardly try sacking him, his own son.

Charlie smiled grimly. If he did it would mean employing someone else in his place. His Dad was getting on in years and couldn't do the amount of work he used to, still strong though he was. And he smoked like a trooper, which sometimes got him coughing until he grew quite out of breath.

Of course there were plenty of men just waiting to fill a job, any job. The 1929 Wall Street Crash four years ago was still having repercussions in recession, unemployment, many businesses still struggling; even his Dad's still having a bit of a rough time. At first, Dad had done pretty well out of it – people reduced to poverty, selling whatever they could to keep a head above water. But that had dried up and there were now less and less outlets for scrap.

These days he looked as if he was feeling every bit his fifty-six years. He worried far too much about the business, though it was understandable, Charlie supposed. If that went to the wall then what would he do? This job was his life.

Charlie felt sorry for him, sorry to have upset him. Even though it was a relief when his course started again and nothing more was said about his giving it up, he still regretted the argument. But before long he'd have to pack up his studies because Dad needed him. As the years went on, he would eventually have to move aside for one of his sons to take over. He couldn't see Richard, or Dick as they now often referred to him, being much help here, unless he thought to set himself up as a director while others did the heavy work.

Not as long as I'm around, Charlie thought, as he walked back into the office, Dick nowhere to be seen. If anyone was good at skiving off it was his stepbrother, neither did he have any inkling of how to run a business. He could have run it better than Dick any day with what he'd learned these last few years from Dad and night school. But that would be down to dear Richard who, as the eldest son, would naturally expect to take over.

Charlie had been smiling wryly but now the grin faded as he thought about it.

This year there were two of them now working for their father, himself and Frank. He never counted Richard.

It was good to have Frank here. True he was only fifteen, coming up sixteen, but despite four years difference they were very close and Charlie felt he and his brother were allies against a common enemy.

When Dad wasn't in, Charlie would often come upon Richard lounging in the old scuffed swivel chair in the cluttered little office, reading a newspaper, feet up on the desk, having been doing nothing else for most of the morning by the look of the untouched paperwork.

If Dad came in, the feet would come down, the newspaper would be quickly folded and dropped on to the floor, and he would come upright in the swivel chair to begin scanning bills and receipts and order forms, pencil in hand. Charlie had seen it many a time but his father never said a word.

Charlie wasn't daft. He knew Dad hadn't been fooled, but there was never one word of reprimand.

When things had to be hauled, carried or dragged, it was he usually being asked to do it. To mention that his stepbrother wasn't doing anything, would prompt the inevitable answer: 'He's doing something else for me.'

That something else was usually doing the books, but Dick was not all that bright at figures, though according to Dad he was. Charlie knew he was the brighter of the two, yet office work was always designated to Dick while the heavy work was left to him and Frank. There were times when he almost felt he'd have liked to have floored Dick. Tonight he heartily wished the man was around so he could do just that.

Packing up for the evening, his stepbrother having already sloped off some time ago with his father's blessing, of course, Charlie found himself stopped by Dad as he and Frank grabbed their coats, ready to head for home with their father.

He was looking forward to doing a bit of reading up on geology after supper. He no longer attended the classes, almost nineteen seeming a bit old to continue, but he still enjoyed studying his favourite subject.

Tonight, he was looking forward to reading up on some layered formation discovered in Australia, banded iron deposits thought to have come from some sort of action of ancient seas. It was a new concept, not yet fully understood, and it was fascinating. He was dying to get home and reread about it.

Now Dad was asking him to play night watchman for a few hours, until around midnight. 'Being that there's been a few break-ins round here lately,' he said.

Break-ins? What was so valuable here to pinch? There was a bit of lead but all too weighty for a few drunks to heave out, and professionals would go for much larger and profitable objectives.

It wasn't the only occasion he'd been called upon for this. It was about time Dad employed a proper night watchman instead of making these snap decisions to protect the premises. However, having considered the wages involved he'd scotched the idea a long time ago. 'The place is usually safe enough,' he'd say, and get Charlie to step in whenever the fancy took him.

Charlie felt himself beginning to seethe. 'Why me?' he asked, though he knew the answer already.

'You're tougher looking than Frank. Anyway, you can call it a day around midnight. If anyone tries to break it, they'll probably be only drunks. By midnight that sort of toe-rag will have gone home to be sick.'

'I'll need to get home,' he reminded him. But he knew that answer too.

'Take your taxi fare out of petty cash.'

The fact that he wasn't being expected to use his own money for a taxi was in a way a method of not having him protest. He knew too his father would pay him overtime, but in a strange

way that only made him seem more of a mere employee than
the boss's son.

'It would be nice if Dick could take his turn,' he couldn't help
saying, but this time the grate in his tone brought an angered
look to the man's face as he turned on him sharply.

'What the hell have you got against Richard?' he asked, his
tone low and dangerous. Frank was nibbling his lip, sensing an
argument brewing.

'Dad, let's go home – I'm starving.'

'No!' Robert shot at him. 'I want to have this out with your
brother. What he's got against him.' He turned back to his quarry.
'Sometimes you act like he's your mortal enemy. I want to
know why.'

Charlie took a deep breath. 'It'd be nice if, for once, you got
him to do a bit more of the hard graft. He sits there in the office
lording it over me and Frank, giving orders as if he's some office
manager, doesn't do a hand's turn at the heavy work. He's heftier
and a damned sight older than Frank who's still just a lad, but
he never pulls his weight—'

'Now that's enough!' his Dad broke in, his voice brittle. But
Charlie ignored the signs, now championing his younger brother.

'What is it about Dick that you're always giving him the soft
jobs, taking his side against me and Frank at every turn? Well, I
tell you the truth Dad, me and Frank are getting sick of it.'

'So what d'you want me to do? Sack him?'

Charlie ignored the sarcasm. 'At least get him to pull his weight.'

For a moment there was silence. Then his father began to
speak, his voice alarmingly calm. 'If you don't like the way it is,
Charlie, you know what you can do. You're old enough now to
make your own way. So if you don't like the way things are, you
can always leave. Just let me know, that's all.'

With that, he dropped the gate keys on the office desk and went
out, striding across the yard to his car, Frank, with an anxious back-
ward glance at his brother, following behind like some tame rabbit.

That was Frank all over, Charlie thought staring after the two
as they got into the car and drove off – always looking to him
to say what he'd love to say himself but hadn't the courage.

He knew that if he went, Frank would go too. And Dad knew
it. But that was no consolation.

Fifteen

'Where's Charlie,' were Nora's first words as Robert came in the door with only Frank accompanying him.

'Left him behind, giving eye to the place,' Robert said, walking past her towards the sitting room.

'He'll be home just after twelve I expect.' His voice floated back.

She stared after Frank meekly trailing after his father. 'Supper will be ready soon,' she said quietly as if to herself, then a little louder, letting her voice carry. 'What's Charlie eating?'

'He'll get something from the cafe over the road.' Canning Town was full of cheap cafes often open through the night for shift workers.

Nora slowly followed after her husband. Already seated in his armchair reading the evening paper, he didn't look up as she entered. She might not as well have been here. He hadn't even kissed her as he passed but she was used to that.

Years ago when the older children were little he would never have dreamed of not kissing her. These days they didn't even sleep in the same bedroom, hadn't done so for three years. That was understandable. She was in her change and from the very start had been hardly able to sleep for perspiration.

Some mornings she'd wake up wringing wet as if she'd been immersed in a hot tub half the night. And she was liable to fits of irritability when the sweats broke out during the day, not lasting long, but if Robert was around she'd be terse with him, he being a handy brunt of her outbursts. Always a mild mannered man with her, it wasn't fair on him. Little wonder they were being driven apart. But how much longer would it go on?

Probably more upsetting for him was the fact that she no longer took pleasure from sex, hadn't really done so since little Rosie was born. At first it had stemmed from the fact that she'd had enough of childbearing, which had seemed to have been far too regular and too often, and had begun to wear her out. Perhaps refraining from sex had made her change of life happen sooner. The fact was she couldn't and he'd lost interest; it upset her but what could she say?

At supper there was just herself, Frank and Robert. Her two eldest daughters were out, Elsie with her young man named Vic Fairbank whom they'd not yet met, and Eileen still enjoying herself with friends ogling all the young men. The other three, George, Eva and Rosie were already in bed with school in the morning.

Supper was eaten in silence, Robert chewing steadily on his braised steak, Frank who was usually so talkative seeming loath to say much at all. No doubt Robert had a lot on his mind. He seemed to always have a lot on his mind these days, stalking by her as he entered the house, or it felt like stalking, his mind always appearing to be elsewhere. But somehow she felt it more tonight, something had upset him. But apparently he wasn't prepared to say what and she didn't care to pry. Or perhaps she did.

'Is anything wrong, darling?' she ventured, receiving the terse reply: 'Why should there be anything wrong?'

It was too terse but she aimed at a rash guess. 'Is anything wrong between you and Charlie?'

'Why should anything be wrong?' he repeated but she'd caught the look Frank had thrown at him, wary and awkward.

'You and Charlie haven't had a row or something?' Rows between them were becoming more and more frequent. 'What's—'

She got no further as Robert leapt up, his meal half eaten. 'Can I not even eat in peace? Look, it don't matter, Nora! I'm tired, that's all! I'm going to bed!'

Nora chewed her lip as he hurried from the room. She looked at Frank, now nearly sixteen. It was unfair to involve him, he looked so worried. But she needed to know. 'Something's happened between him and your Dad,' she prompted, 'something that's really upset him – worse than usual?'

It was Frank's turn to get up from the table. 'I expect him or Charlie will probably say about it when they feel like it,' he said and there was such uneasiness on his face that she didn't ask any more, merely sat and watched him leave to go upstairs.

It was a long time before she left the table, their present maid,

Hilda, a sweet-faced young girl of eighteen, came in to ask if she wanted pudding before she cleared away, to which she'd shaken her head and got up to leave the girl to it.

Going into the sitting room she took up her knitting – a pullover for Robert. Shortly afterwards, Eileen came in, flushed and weary, saying she'd had a good time tonight in answer to her mother's question; said she was off to bed after getting herself milk and a sandwich. A little later in came Elsie looking dreamily happy, but Nora didn't feel like hearing about her wonderful Vic. Taking the hint, Elsie followed her sister to bed, saying she didn't really want anything to eat after an absolutely lovely meal with Victor.

Nora was still in her armchair in the sitting room, listening to music being played over the wireless, turned down very soft, when she heard Hilda go up the stairs to her room at the top of the house.

She glanced at the clock on the mantelpiece. Eleven fifteen. Charlie wouldn't be home until gone twelve. She'd intended to wait up for him but having dozed on and off she felt she needed her bed. Finally going up after another quarter of an hour, unable to keep her eyes open any longer, she paused at Robert's door to listen, her ear close to the wood. There was no sound. He was already asleep. She went on to her own room next door with no thoughts in her head now, quietly closing the door behind her.

The house was dead quiet. Lying alone in the double bed she could hear a dog barking some distance away and the sound of a passing car, but after that nothing more. She awoke, sweating, in time to hear the click of a bedroom door closing very quietly. That would be Charlie.

She hadn't heard him come in, but then she had to admit to becoming just a little deaf as she got older. Not enough to worry her but often she'd find herself missing what someone was saying to her if others were talking at the same time.

Thoughts turned to Charlie, poor darling. She knew his feelings and wished his father could treat all his sons equally and not have favourites. Maybe Charlie didn't help matters, but he had his reasons for feeling as he did. She wished she could help him. Thinking this she went back to sleep.

*   *   *

The house was silent. Robert had heard his wife creep past his door, aware that she paused, probably listening to see if he was asleep. But he wasn't. He was wide awake, ears trained to the sound of her door closing. Then having waited for maybe a quarter of an hour for any other disturbance before getting out of bed, he donned a dressing gown over his pyjamas and, quiet as a mouse, crept from his room and up the stairs to the room above.

The door opened a fraction to his furtive tapping. A face appeared round the edge. 'Oh, it's you,' came the whisper.

'Is it all right?' he hissed. 'Can I come in?'

He drew in a sharp breath to see that she was naked as she opened the door just wide enough for him to slip inside; a small graceful figure, the waist slim, hips and breasts tantalizingly voluptuous despite this fashion for young girls to adopt an almost boyish shape. He felt his needs move at the sight of her as she came forward, her hand reaching to slip off his dressing gown, undoing the buttons of his pyjama top while he stood mesmerized by her, feeling he wasn't quite in control of the situation.

It went through his mind that he shouldn't have come here, should not have let himself be tempted by those enticing looks he'd seen her give him. This evening, those glances had been so full of suggestion he couldn't help but understand and he'd felt driven to come up here. Perhaps he should go. Now! But her arms wrapped about him, the softness of those firm young breasts against his own bared chest, were sweeping every such intention away.

'You're wonderful,' he whispered. He hadn't kissed her. He was too pent up to. Instead he let her pull him quietly towards the narrow bed, she laying back submissively as he lowered his body upon her.

'I shouldn't do this!' he panted as she accepted him, 'I shouldn't be here!' But he was being overwhelmed and soon all other thought became smothered by the wonderful joy of it all; unburdening the loneliness that Nora's frigid attitude had instilled in him all these years.

Yet back in his own room, furiously chain smoking in an effort to calm his thoughts, he was tormented, only his physical need not his mind, fulfilled, and he was angry – not just with Nora who denied him, not just with Hilda who'd tempted him, but with himself for being so weak.

Robert stubbed out his cigarette and immediately lit another, trying to get his mind off what had happened up there in the tiny bedroom. It mustn't ever happen again. He wouldn't let it. Perhaps he could find some excuse to hand the girl her notice. He must be strong with himself. He vowed this to himself as he drew viciously on his cigarette.

Nora, awoken by another hot sweat, heard what sounded like someone out of breath as if they'd been running, then an almost stealthy click of a door being carefully closed. Too near to be any of the children's. The two attic rooms where Mrs Warner their cook and young Hilda slept were too far off for anything there to be heard through her bedroom door. She found herself listening intently. She could swear Robert was pacing about in his room.

Her hearing wasn't all that bad, and in the quiet of night it was as good as anyone's. What had he been doing? Where had he been? Why had he been breathing so rapidly?

She shook her head in mystification and lay back on her pillows. There she drifted off to sleep, the mystery unsolved.

Next morning at breakfast she couldn't resist asking if he had slept well. Something about his reaction, she wasn't sure what, made her alert. Why had he shot her that quick, almost guilty glance?

She tried to dismiss it but as Hilda came into the room with the fresh pot of tea she'd asked for, the girl's glance went straight to Robert, a faint blush suffusing her cheeks. She didn't look his way again, almost making a point of ignoring him, Nora would have said.

Watching him narrowly from under her eyelashes as she drank her tea she was aware of his gaze stealing towards the girl every now and again.

Normally he'd hardly notice her as she went about her duties, but this morning there was a tension in those jaw muscles of his, and it was only when the girl went from the room that he appeared to relax.

She was left the rest of the day trying to convince herself that maybe she'd read too much into the episode. She'd had a disturbed night and this morning was having to deal with yet another hot flush as she came to the breakfast table, feeling really at odds with the world – no wonder she was making something out of nothing.

But that furtive click of Robert's bedroom door last night, that sound of someone out of breath as if from some exertion . . . brought a cold hand to clutch at her heart. A man hurrying down a steep flight of stairs from the attic, a man who smoked so heavily that breathing these days was becoming an effort, what other reason could there be?

Nora's anger grew steadily as the day went on with nothing to feed on but her own thoughts. Sweet faced little slut! So modest so servile, who'd have imagined? Her first impression of the girl had been amiable, demure and anxious to please. Oh yes, very anxious to please!

When she'd first noticed that sideways gaze, the lingering smile if Robert should address her, the way she'd sidle past his chair at meal times, the words that had come to mind were 'Silly girl.'

Now of course she saw it for what it truly was – coquettish, flirting with him, enticing him with those limpid blue-eyed glances, and he, poor fool, had been taken in by them, she knew that now. The thought of him and that sly little cow together . . . the thought of it made her feel sick!

'She goes!' she burst out as she walked into the kitchen, making Mrs Warner, their cook, jump.

'Sorry, Mrs Titchnell, who goes?'

'That . . . that girl Hilda. I want her out of this house!'

The woman looked taken aback. 'She's a good worker and very clean in 'er ways and respectable.'

Nora paused. What excuse could she give? The description rebounded inside her head, *oh, very clean, very respectable, the evil little bitch*!

'Yes,' she lied, 'maybe she is. But she's becoming just a little bit too cocksure of herself when she's serving at the table. To be honest it makes me feel very uncomfortable and I'm not happy at the way she looks at me when I give her orders.'

'She's very respectful to me.'

'Well she's not to me! You don't see her, Mrs Warner.'

'Well if you're not comfortable with 'er. Shall I warn her as to 'ow you feel, tell 'er that she could be risking getting the sack?'

'Yes . . . no! No, I'll do that. I just want her to leave straight away.'

'You mean this minute? Today? Not even being given proper notice? You pay her wages by the week. If you dismiss her at a moment's notice she could take you to court for wrongful dismissal. Different if she'd been caught stealing or—'

'Of course,' Nora broke in. 'I'll have to let her finish the week.'

'Is she that bad, Madam? Can't you speak to her?'

'I . . .' Nora faltered, chewing her lip.

'I could talk to her, get her to change her ways,' Mrs Warner offered, seeing the anxiety and doubt in her employer's expression.

Nora pulled herself together. 'No! I'll explain to her. We'll see what happens. She might even get uppity and leave anyway.'

She would speak to the girl – tell her exactly what she suspected. No, not suspected, what she knew! That would frighten her off. She'd give her a sum of money and tell her to go; say she could rely on a good reference, but if she decided to cause trouble, then she'd get trouble if that was what she wanted. And who would employ her then? The little hussy wouldn't dare call her bluff.

To her intense relief the small hand snatched the three five pound notes without argument. By the time Robert got home the girl was gone.

For Robert it was more relief than regret. Part of him had wanted it to go on, wanted to experience that wonderful climax again and again, yet fully aware that it could be asking for trouble, could even end with the girl getting pregnant. Then what would he have done?

At supper when told, he gave his wife a bright smile, agreeing that the girl wasn't up to all that had been expected of her and hoping they'd soon find someone to replace her.

'After all we can't expect Mrs Warner to take over all the cleaning of the house and serving meals, as well as cooking them!' he joked and going to her, planted a light, tender kiss on her lips, heartened to have her accept it without her turning her cheek to his lips instead. Yes, he would try to make it up to her. She was a good person. She didn't deserve her marriage to be torn apart. Even if she had grown a little cold and distant, he still loved her.

She might have thought her suspicions unfounded had not Robert suddenly become so suddenly attentive to her. To her raw senses it wasn't natural after years of slowly becoming just two well married people, almost to the point of taking each other for granted.

She had expected him to grow angry, demanding indignantly why she'd dismissed the girl. Instead he hadn't even asked why, and that to her mind declared his guilt for a start. Thinking only of his peace of mind, not hers, the thought screamed at her but she let none of it show on her face. Let him think what he wanted.

Instead she hired the plainest girl she could find. Let him have it off with that one, she thought cruelly. Her name was Molly Shaw whose parents it was told were respectable people, she turning out to be a good and dedicated worker whom she found to be a delightful person.

If one thing did come out of the episode it was that Robert was paying her more attention these days, pausing to kiss her cheek when he came home of an evening. When saying good-night he now kissed her, not on the cheek but the lips, though there was no mention of returning to sharing one bedroom, they having become set in their ways. It was nice having him kiss her. She still loved him. She could forgive him. She could.

Slowly the hurt began to fade but she'd never forget what she'd seen, or imagined she had seen. Even so the idea was there embedded in her mind, which she knew would leap up again the moment she caught him even glancing at a young girl. It sat there constantly like some old wound and she hated herself for the feeling it gave her.

Sixteen

This summer, Charlie was having a great time, despite all the doom and gloom on the horizon: the Spanish civil war with many a young Briton lured by glory; trouble with Fascists in London; Crystal Palace burning down; the death of King George V; Edward VIII threatening to renounce the crown should he be forbidden to make that awful American divorcee Mrs Simpson his queen.

He'd learned to drive. Dad had bought him his first car, a Swallow, second hand but in beautiful condition, its bodywork cream and brown with a curvaceous, chrome-plated speed nymph mascot gracing the radiator cap.

As if pointing the way, her body arched towards the direction in which the car was travelling, arms outstretched behind her with such grace, like a dancer. He would polish her until she gleamed and sparkled, delighting in all the attention she drew.

Dick also had a car but Dick didn't matter – Charlie felt as good as him any day. As yet Frank was without a car, not quite eighteen, his dad deeming him not yet competent enough to drive.

So every Sunday it was off to the seaside with Frank as passenger. At Southend, Ramsgate, Margate, Brighton or Eastbourne, they'd meet up with friends who'd also driven down, chaps and girls, all of them dressed alike in light-coloured linen slacks and striped polo-neck tops. In bathing costumes they'd play cricket on the sands or kick a beach ball about, splash each other in the sea, take snapshots of each other or the whole lot of them sitting on the sand in one long crocodile, one behind the other, legs outstretched on each side, each lying back in the lap of the one behind, or posing with arms about each other's necks, laughing like idiots.

Later they'd guzzle tea from a flask, devour sandwiches and cake they'd brought with them, and cornets and wafers bought from ice cream stands along the promenade,

As the sun went down they'd pack up, bid each other cheerio until next week and drive home to a hefty Sunday evening meal.

This gloriously hot August bank holiday Sunday, Charlie arrived late at their favourite spot on one of Margate's many beaches having had trouble getting out of London. Seeing his friends, he noticed one girl was standing up from the lounging bodies. Gazing seaward, one slim hand shielding her eyes from the strong sun, the other held delicately out behind her, she looked like the nymph on his car.

Breaking into a run, he tore across the sand towards them all, Frank following up in the rear. Christopher Wilson glanced up as he reached them.

'About time too! Thought you two weren't coming.'

At the sound of his voice, the girl lowered her hand to glance round, offering him the sweetest smile he'd ever seen. But Chris was still talking.

'We've already had our ice cream but I can get you both one if you want. The kiosk's only up there.'

'Yes, thanks,' Frank returned instantly, but Charlie wasn't having the man pay for him just because he had arrived later than the others.

'We'll get ourselves one in a minute but thanks anyway, Chris,' he said quickly, tearing his gaze away from the girl to speak to the man.

Glancing up seconds later he found she had already sat down again among the others. He couldn't see her at all now but he was left with a lasting impression of an extremely slim figure, short wavy fair hair, bright blue eyes set in a pretty face and that wide smile she had given him.

It set his heart racing but he couldn't just step over everyone to seek her out. He, like the rest of them, enjoyed a bit of girl company but always in a group, apart from one or two who looked like pairing off for life. He had never been out on his own with a girl, never thought about it. Why? He enjoyed his mates. He was just twenty-one, the reason for being given the car, but in time he would no doubt one day find himself a partner in life.

It now crossed his mind as he thought about it, the girl he had seen standing up amid the lounging group – he'd never seen her here before. Who was she? What was her name? But – and his spirits sank a little – there was not much point finding out. She was probably with another bloke anyway.

'Who's for a swim?' The voice broke into his thoughts, bringing his mind back to reality.

Charlie had thought to put his costume on under his clothes and, standing up, as the suitably attired made off to the water's edge, he saw the girl also on her feet, struggling with a large towel about her body, another girl, no doubt her friend, holding the towel firmly about her. Perhaps after all she hadn't come here with a chap.

He waited as those few also trying to change without revealing too much, one by one departed seaward. Frank had already gone, taking his brother's cue in having come prepared.

The girl looked up as her towel fell to the sand, she now wearing a fetching green and black swimsuit and looking slimmer than ever. Donning a white swimming cap over her curls she looked across at Charlie.

'You were peeking!' she called across, and he realized that the spot where everyone had been a few moments ago was now empty but for himself.

His face grew suddenly hot as he blustered. 'No, honest, I wasn't! Honest to God!'

He expected her to stamp, tell him to keep his prying eyes to himself. Instead she laughed a tinkling, infectious laugh.

'No harm done then.' Her gaze followed her friend now picking her way cautiously towards the gently lapping wavelets.

'You coming then?' The girl asked pleasantly. 'The way my friend is treading I think there may be lots of shingle down there before you get into the water – painful on the soles of bare feet. I might need your help.'

Charlie leapt at the offer, accompanying her down to the smooth wet sand, foolishly hoping there would be stones and maybe he lifting her bodily over them. What would she feel like in his arms, light as a feather no doubt.

There were no stones, or if there were, very few, nothing to hurt her feet. Soon they were splashing in the gentle surf, the two of them laughing and spluttering among the others. When she broke off to swim out slightly deeper he quickly followed to swim beside her, gratified to see her turn her head to encompass him with a bright smile. 'You're a good swimmer.'

And so he was. Often after work he'd go to the local baths, do several lengths in quick succession. He was a strong swimmer, his broad chest powerful. Now with this girl trying to keep up he moderated his pace.

'Not too far out,' she spluttered. 'I'm not as good as you. I don't want you having to save me.'

Give me the chance, the words went through his head, but together they turned and headed back to the shore, he boldly taking her arm to help her out.

As she lowered herself on to the damp sand to recover, he sat down next to her, asking, 'You don't mind, do you?'

'Not at all,' she said pleasantly. 'I'd never dare to go out that far if you hadn't been with me. It was great. I really enjoyed it.'

'Perhaps next week we can do it again,' he ventured. 'That's if the weather's fine and you come here again.'

'I'd like that,' she said and got up, puffing with satisfaction at her swim. 'I think I'll lie in the sun for a while to get dry.'

'So will I,' he said, and instead of leaving her among the returning group, lowered himself on to the sand next to her. 'Maybe we can go and have a cup of tea later?' he suggested.

'I've brought a flask and some sandwiches,' she said, lowering his hopes. 'But sitting over a nice cup of tea would be lovely.'

Charlie's hopes rose again. 'I don't know your name,' he queried.

'Ethel,' she obliged in a soft tone. 'Ethel Allington.'

For almost eight months he and Ethel had been going out together. He'd often hark back in his mind to that first time he saw her on that Margate beach, the only thought then to have a good day with friends, no thought of girls at all. And then there she was. And wonder of wonders she lived at West Ham, hardly a stone's throw away. He could walk there!

They no longer went to the seaside to meet crowds of others and had slowly lost touch with most of their old friends. This year, only a few weeks ago, they'd holidayed in Cornwall, just seven days because Dad wouldn't spare him for any longer than that. They'd gone by train, it being a long way to drive and too tiring, taking hours and hours to get there.

They found Cornwall beautiful and romantic. It was there he proposed to her and she said yes so fervently that they almost made love on the spot – almost, because she had backed away the moment his hand had begun to fondle her breast. She'd pushed him away like this before, seemed almost terrified of making love – a totally different girl to the one he'd imagined on that beach that Sunday afternoon, a girl who had seemed so sure of herself. And she was in certain things, but not in this it seemed.

It wasn't the first time she'd refused to let him go further. Having not had any dealings with this sort of thing before, apart from a disturbing sense of arousal every now and again, he was almost glad at not being allowed to go any further than one touch of her breasts. For one thing he might have felt so awkward afterwards, for another he was a complete novice and feared making an utter fool of himself. Mates had talked about it but few had dared, for any decent girl would have put a stop to that instantly.

One thing he was discovering was that in some things Ethel had a mind of her own when she wanted, although most of her decisions came not from herself but from others. Coming home on the train it appeared that she had already set the date of their wedding.

'Mum said spring can be so unreliable and chilly or wet, and summer can be too hot,' she maintained as if quoting the woman's words. 'So maybe September next year would be just right. But only if you think so, darling,' she'd added hastily, becoming once more eager to please him.

But he was happy to do whatever she wanted to do. She was such a sweet girl, and if easily alarmed by some things it gave him a fulfilling sense of protectiveness, which some girls might not have appreciated.

The only bugbear was Mrs Allington, her mother, another who felt the need to protect her, at times too protective, always her daughter against this and that and everything in between. Ethel's sister, Ann, was very much the same, spinning stories of awful goings on or the horrid consequences of such and such a decision. Charlie never enjoyed going there, having to sit and listen to tales and predictions of misery and disaster; pessimists the pair of them.

Thank God she wasn't like them, he thought now, as he kissed her on the lonely park bench shrouded by the September dusk, with hardly anyone about, his arm about her as she shivered a little.

Yes she was shy and in some ways nervous, but fine as long as she didn't believe all her mother told her. The trouble was that she did tend to believe all her mother told her. But he could cope with that because he loved her and in time, after they'd married and she was no longer under her mother's influence, he'd help her to change, become a good deal more courageous.

It was amazing how fast time flew – 1938 already, September only two months away, and still so much to be done preparing for their wedding, as well as a new flat to get ready. Where had the year gone?

Since last year a lot had happened. Maybe that was why it was flying so fast. Six months ago, Frank had found himself a girl-friend. Mabel Waters was eighteen years old like him, on the short side and slightly plump like him, even their birthdays falling in the same month. It stood to reason that they were soon talking engagement with an eye to marriage early next year, but Dad had put a stop to that saying it wouldn't happen for another couple of years yet, not until both were twenty-one.

Frank was very put out. His brother getting married in two months would leave him living at home on his own as he saw it.

'You'll have your own place when you're married,' he grumbled, 'and I'll be stuck at home expected to do all the dirtier jobs Dad used to ask you to do. He's not going to lumber Dick with them, being Dick's got his own place too, like you'll have.'

'George is there,' Charlie reminded him. George was coming up to eighteen, now working for his dad too though he was a bit of a lazy bugger according to Frank. Charlie grinned quietly to himself, Frank could talk! Frank wasn't exactly the fastest spark in the box, lackadaisical was more the word. George was even worse. Never particularly put out by his father's sharp reprimands, trouble and responsibility drifted over his head like dandelion fluff. But he himself would still be there working – wouldn't dream of going anywhere else. To his way of thinking this was his business as much as it was Dad's.

Meantime the wedding was keeping him and Ethel occupied. The only break they'd had this year was going to Trafalgar Square to see the exciting procession at the coronation of King George VI and Queen Elizabeth. Even that had been cut short when

Ethel had panicked in the crush of several thousand sightseers and he'd had to get her out as fast as he could before she fainted and got hurt. It had been a frightening experience and realizing that crowds did actually scare her, he knew he couldn't take her to any more such gatherings. Still, it was a small point, easily avoided.

There had been two more weddings this year – in February, his sister Elsie now twenty-five and Victor Goodman her fiancé of only six months, and in April, his sister Eileen and Fred Bennett to whom she'd been engaged for nearly a year, a man several years older than her. Dad's business bringing in enough to pay for both his daughters' weddings, they'd made sure they had been splendid affairs, making Charlie feel his own had been rather overshadowed, with smaller presents from guests having had to pay out twice already and several unable to attend. Still, Ethel wasn't partial to having lots of people milling around her so it had probably been a good thing.

They'd gone back to Cornwall for their honeymoon, having loved it there the first time, walking, enjoying the scenery and each other. Coming home they'd gone ballroom dancing, she quite a good dancer, been to shows and the cinema, still lots of people but seated, so long as she wasn't being jostled. They even bought a couple of bikes to cycle off away from London.

Their new home right by West Ham Park had kept her busy. She seemed quite happy to settle into her little house as a young wife, cooking, tidying, rearranging furniture until he came home in the evenings. It was wonderful waking up beside her each morning, instead of Frank and George snoring away.

When he'd first met Ethel he'd got the impression of her being scared of nothing. But as their first year of married life went on, little things began to come to light and he was sure her mother was behind it, maybe innocently, and he wished he could have a talk to her, make her see that Ethel was now a married woman and didn't need a mother's interference. But it wasn't an easy thing to do.

He'd not noticed it at first but he was coming to realize that Ethel was showing an increasing reluctance to be made love to. From the very start of their marriage she'd been exceptionally shy of his entering her, cold and stiff beneath his embrace as if fearing any climax to moments of fondling.

'I don't want to start a family too soon,' she had told him time after time. 'Let's wait a bit.' He, being understanding, had gone along with her wishes although frustrated at times. But now, almost a year later, she was still repeating, 'I'm not ready to start having babies yet, darling.'

It was so beseeching that he felt he had to respect her feelings and hold off, for in so many other ways she was a loving wife.

But sometimes it was so difficult to consider her vulnerability. Until finally this August his patience suddenly snapped, startling even him. He'd always considered he had unlimited patience; saw himself as a person who could state his case but never let a show of anger get the better of him, even if it did tend to simmer for ages under the surface. And now he was fighting with his own wife, reducing her to a flood of tears, and all of it his fault.

Instantly he had gathered her in his arms trying to soothe her as they sat up in bed. 'I didn't mean to get so angry, darling, but you must see how I feel. Ethel, I'm your husband. I love you. And naturally I need you.'

It slaughtered him hearing how pitifully she was weeping while she clung to him, her face buried in his bare chest, her words trembling. 'Please, darling, don't blame me for being frightened. I really am frightened, terrified of being made to give birth!'

He held her to him, his grip tightening. 'I don't expect you not to be a bit frightened,' he soothed the quivering body as best he could. 'If I could have it for you, I would, but women have been having babies ever since people began. My mother had lots of children and look at her. She's fine.'

It seemed to do no good as she continued to weep and tremble, her words tumbling out in a flood. 'My mum often said how excruciating and dangerous it is. She said she suffered terribly having me. And she has never forgotten it. And she said that before that she nearly died having my sister. That's why my sister's never got married or had a bloke.'

He had slowly come to realize that she had been sheltered all her life. Despite that first impression he'd had of her on that beach she had known nothing about sex. Come to think of it, nor did he. But people learned.

All he knew was that following his natural instincts was all that was required. But doing it, proved to be a bit more disappointing than he'd imagined, her body rigid beneath his, her legs held tightly together, not half as fulfilling as he'd heard said. Sometimes he was left wondering what all this talk of fulfilment was about. But they'd at least done what all married couples did as far as he could tell.

'We really should wait a year or so,' she had stalled.

'We don't want to wait too long,' he'd said quite innocently.

'But children cost such a lot to keep.' It was as if she'd been referring to a dog or a cat. In fact she had bought a kitten, a ginger one, which she still crooned over and cuddled almost as if it were a baby. 'And you don't earn all that much working for your dad.'

He shook his head at her reasoning. His mother had had children from the word go and she hadn't needed to spend all that much on them. Still there was plenty of time yet. They could wait a couple more years. Now he knew the truth behind all that fabrication of needing money to have children he could force her to face what was really terrifying her.

Perhaps a talk with her mother might help. But he knew it wouldn't. The harm had been done years ago. But who could tell, one day there might be a small accident and she would learn that perhaps it wasn't so bad having a baby as she had thought.

He'd always had a soft spot for children and naturally had imagined himself a father one day, surrounded by his own offspring, just as Mum and Dad had been. But at this moment it looked as if he might never be a father and his heart sank as he comforted his weeping wife.

Seventeen

Within a month there was more to concern him than this unreasonable fear of hers; the whole nation with more to be concerned about than their own domestic problems.

Sunday morning, he and Ethel sat in their front room, faces stiff as they listened to Prime Minister Neville Chamberlain's dread words informing them that his efforts for peace had failed and consequently they were 'at war with Germany'.

Last year there had been a similar fright, followed by deep relief as he alighted from his plane at Heston aerodrome waving a piece of paper to the huge crowd who'd gathered to cheer him. 'Peace in our time,' had been on everyone's lips then. Now peace in our time had dissolved into thin air.

'What are we going to do?' came Ethel's small voice as stirring, uplifting music followed the end of the solemn announcement.

'Just have to get on with it,' Charlie said in a flat tone.

He felt devoid of emotion, other than a need to keep Ethel from harm as they sat each side of the wireless, she slumped in her armchair, twisting a small handkerchief between her fingers and chewing at her lower lip.

For a while longer they sat in silence, each with their own thoughts. Then Charlie got up to make some tea. The kettle had already boiled for a mid-morning cuppa but he'd turned off the gas beneath when they went into the front room to hear what the Prime Minister had to say. Now they knew.

Outside in the street all was still, but he was just about to relight the gas when that quietness was split by the banshee wails of air raid sirens.

He heard Ethel scream. Blowing out the lit match he dashed back into the front room to find her on her knees before her armchair, her head buried in the seat, arms over her head.

Quickly he lifted her and sat her back in the chair. As he did so he saw through the window the street come alive, people moving in one direction, being shepherded by steel-helmeted policemen towards the ready-built public concrete shelter at the end of the road.

'We have to go!' he cried, trying to lift her up but she fought him.

'I want to die here! I want to die with you!'

'We're not going to die! We just have to go to the shelter.'

'I'm not going! I want to stay here!'

The panic in her voice gripped him, so that all he could do was to crouch down beside her and clasp her to him. How long they remained like this he wasn't sure, as all he could find to say was to repeat again and again, 'We're not going to die. We'll be all right.'

Then came another wail, but a strangely comforting one, even though it had never been heard before, the steady 'all clear' sound, and he stood up and said:

'There. I told you so.' Like some simpleton.

He truly hadn't expected Ethel to cope, but the rest of the day she amazed him as steadily she cut and sewed the blackout material they'd bought on Friday in case war was declared, turning it all into curtains, he fitting them up at the windows. She also helped him paste strips of tape crosswise to every window pane to guard against splintered glass should bombs be dropped.

By Sunday night the little house felt safe, every curtain drawn, the living room light on, the wireless playing soft music while they enjoyed a bedtime cup of cocoa.

He even dared think she might relax her body under him as he made love to her, but those hopes quickly fell as she said she felt too pent up to think of being made love to.

'What if there's an air raid?' she said. 'We have to be ready.'

Sighing, he relented, merely allowed his arm to linger beneath her head while she cuddled up to him, saying, 'I don't think I'll ever be able to sleep again,' her voice shaky, 'in case we get an air raid warning and not hear it. The house could fall down on top of us and if we're asleep we could both be killed.'

'We'll hear it all right,' he soothed, gazing up at the inky black ceiling, totally invisible with no light filtering through the drawn thick curtains, even if the street lamps had been on. Outside was just as inky black, but she had still wanted all the curtains kept closed so that not even starlight filtered in to relieve the absolute blackness.

'We'll be up and dressed before any enemy plane gets here,' he said.

'But we don't have a proper shelter yet.'

The sheets of corrugated iron for the Anderson shelter, delivered a few weeks ago, had still to be assembled, the hole dug to accommodate the finished thing hardly started. He'd been working flat out at the scrap yard, getting together all the suitable metal he could, the War Office needing all it could get to turn into weapons. But after work he'd have to knuckle down and get on with it.

'We'll just dress quick as we can and run to the public shelter,' he soothed her fears. 'Now try and get some sleep, darling.'

He felt her move away from the comfort of his arm to obediently turn over. Soon her breathing slowed to a regular sigh but it was ages before he could fall asleep, his ears alert for the faintest wail of an air-raid warning.

The call of the little alarm clock by their bed awoke him with a start. Clambering out of bed, he yanked back the black curtain, instantly blinded by brilliant sunshine in a clear blue early morning sky.

Another day, like any other ordinary Monday morning! A good night's sleep surprisingly enough, refreshed ready to get dressed, have breakfast and go to work.

Already people in the street below were moving easily along the road all to their place of work, walking or riding bicycles; no hurry, no anxiety, another ordinary day, life going on as usual except that they were at war.

Turning from the window he went and gently shook Ethel awake. 'Time to get up,' he said as her sleepy eyes peered up at him.

Christmas had come and gone, not too bad a Christmas, much the same as any other with all the family gathered around the table at the parents' home in Stratford to eat as heartily as ever, lounging back in armchairs and settee to digest the meal and later enjoy a pleasant evening together with a few neighbours that had been invited in. Come Boxing Day each little family would separate to spend it with the other spouse's family. Next year it would naturally be turn about, of course.

Frank was now in uniform, called up last month but had been given Christmas leave. He and Mabel had spent Boxing Day with her family but came back to Stratford the next day for him to say cheerio to Mum and Dad prior to returning to his unit.

Charlie missed him – no one to grumble with any more about Dick's full-of-himself attitude. It wasn't the same with George, who could shrug off anything Dick said and get on happily in his slapdash way with whatever he was asked to do. Dad, being aware of his easy-going nature, tolerated him as he tolerated his eldest son's self-centred idleness, leaving Charlie to take the brunt of the heavier work, still on the same pay as when he'd first started.

'You know I can rely on you, Charlie,' was his answer if ever he had a gripe about certain jobs, which he supposed might be seen as a backhanded compliment of sorts. But it would have been nicer had that compliment, if that's what it was, been backed with a bit of extra money.

In the end he faced him with it. He was a family man now and as such should be getting a bit more. His father had looked somewhat taken aback but faced with Charlie's determined expression, relented.

Charlie came away with an extra one pound ten shillings to his wages, a warning not to say anything to Dick or George, or even Frank when he came home on his next leave, also an unsettling remark echoing in his head:

'There'll come a time, son, when I'll no longer be here, the business handed over to you and Richard. None of us live forever.'

The words, though upsetting, were overshadowed by another thought: Him and Richard. What about Frank? But he said nothing and pocketed his wage rise, knowing how delighted Ethel would be.

That thirty shillings brought his wages up to over four pounds a week. He was grateful. Would even a bank manager earn much more? With food rationing now in place – Ethel said it was just four ounces of butter, bacon, ham, for each of them, twelve ounces of sugar, meat too on ration – she was saving more than they spent. With her reluctant to go out in the blackout to places of entertainment, he could now put money away for rainy days.

He could understand her not wanting to go out of the house

much this winter. It had been the hardest winter for a long time. In mid January even the Thames had frozen over for the first time in fifty-two years, with a cold wave striking the whole of Europe, and at the end of the month the worst storm of the century sweeping the whole of the country had terrified the life out of her.

As spring got well under way, with daylight saving allowing evenings to stay light for longer, he hoped she would be happy to venture out more. He even got hold of two tickets for the new film *Gone With The Wind*, and to his relief she consented to go, thoroughly enjoying herself and even began to go out to the occasional restaurant, expensive but handy for helping rations to go further. All he hoped now was that it would be some time before he was called up, as he inevitably would be if the war went on for much longer.

He said nothing about it to Ethel but his fear was how she would cope without him. Maybe she'd shut up the place and go back to her mother for the time being. Or maybe she'd surprise him and begin to stand on her own two feet.

Early summer was warm and would have been pleasant but for France and Belgium slowly crumbling before the advancing enemy. Then came Dunkirk.

'Those poor men,' Ethel sighed, while Charlie found himself thanking God Frank was still in England as news came through of what those trapped in France were having to endure, strafed as they stood there on the beaches waiting to be rescued, then the pride he like everyone else felt in those who began taking their small privately owned boats across the Channel to rescue thousands of troops, forgetful of their own safety. They deserved a medal.

At the local pictures that week, he and Ethel watched the newsreel with humbling reactions; war-worn, grubby uniformed, narrow-faced, unshaven soldiers grinned like apes at the camera and offered the thumbs-up, trying not to show what they'd been through, although the endless stream of casualties and stretchers coming off the boats told all, as well as telling of the thousands that didn't make it. Again Charlie thought of his own fate if he was called up, which now seemed even more likely.

There was also the fear that if the Germans now pursued the defeated British across the Channel to invade this unprepared island, surely London would be their first target once they'd overrun the south-eastern coastal towns. And he knew he wasn't the only one to fear it.

In the darkness of the cinema he glanced sideways at Ethel. How on earth was he going to protect her from invaders. With all sorts of wild thoughts running through his head he hardly saw what was showing on the screen, until brought back by Winston Churchill's voice droning across the dark auditorium, saying that they would defend their island, fight them on the beaches, on the landing grounds, in the fields and in the streets and in the hills and would never surrender.

Rather than instilling a sense of pride, all Charlie could feel with his nervous wife beside him was a sense of doom, already seeing himself battling a horde of enemy soldiers in a fruitless effort to shield her.

It didn't happen of course. Unaccountably, Germany went south to strike at the heart of France. Everyone breathed an almost selfish sigh of relief. But everyone now knew that they were alone as Paris fell and France surrendered. An uneasy calm reigned throughout July while elderly men joined a poorly equipped Home Guard in a brave hope to defend their shores should Britain be the next to be targeted, and people dug for Victory in allotments to help fill their larders as rationing tightened.

He got himself one, digging like fury throughout August so as to plant potatoes and brussels sprouts, carrots and onions, as the Battle of Britain began in earnest. The RAF fought soaring dog fights with the Luftwaffe in a clear blue summer sky high above the hop fields of Kent and the allotment holders of Essex. Apart from that and rationing, concern at shipping being sunk around Britain's shores and the dire news from Europe, life went on as usual. This Sunday had been quiet and peaceful. He and Ethel had been to the park, coming home to a nice tea, then settling down for the evening with a few sweets while listening to the wireless, finally retiring early to bed, he having to get up for work next morning.

They awoke with a start to the sound of the air raid sirens going off. It seemed to shiver the very room, practically shaking them out of bed. They'd not experienced that sound since the day war had been declared and it put their hearts into their mouths as they leapt to their feet.

'Quick! Get dressed!' Charlie heard himself yell over the din. 'We've got to get down the shelter.'

Ethel gave a shriek as a terrific barrage started up. 'They're going to bomb us! We'll be killed!'

'No we won't!' he shouted back. 'Come on – just put a cardigan on over your nightie.' Already he was wrestling to get pullover and trousers over his pyjamas.

Still partly dressed, he grabbed their gasmasks and hurried her from the room, down the stairs, into the warm night air, as several huge crashes made her scream again. 'They're our own guns!' he yelled as they tore down the garden path to the shelter sitting in its hole at the end of the short garden, its stark corrugated iron softened by earth and summer flowers. 'They're the guns from the park.'

Inside he lit the oil lamp he kept there, its glow shielded from the night by a thick curtain across the entrance. There they sat on one of the narrow beds, he with his arm about Ethel, feeling her shake each time the guns went off. He eyed the tiny table with its already filled kettle on a tiny primus stove, teapot, cups, saucers and a can of condensed milk.

'We'll hang on for a while until the noise dies down, then I'll make us a cuppa. We need it.'

'It might not die down,' she whimpered. 'It could go on forever until we're all dead!'

'Now, don't be silly!' he snapped sharply. He couldn't ever remember being sharp with her before and she shut up immediately.

Whether he would rue it later he didn't care as he heard the first whine of a falling bomb, making them both instinctively cower. Wherever it had landed, it was some way off. The rest of the night saw them ducking involuntarily if one came anywhere near, but most seemed to be aimed at the city itself. How many there are being killed, he thought dismally.

Towards dawn the racket ceased. The sun rose, beautiful, bright and indifferent to the cares of those it shone down upon. The sky was clearest blue and a warm and gentle morning breeze greeted them as people crept from shelters to resume their lives. But war on their doorstep had begun.

★　　★　　★

Ripping open the official looking envelope at the breakfast table, George pulled out its contents, biting his lips as he read before holding the demand out to his parents.

'I've got to go and register for military service,' he said in a bleak, half bewildered voice, as if he'd never for a moment ever expected anything like this. 'They've jumped on me quick enough, ain't they? Before November's even out, hardly given me time to turn eighteen.'

Gazing at him as she paused in buttering toast, Nora felt her heart sink. Frank and now George! How long before Charlie would be told to go? Already visions assailed her of one or other of her sons lying dead in some foreign field, her mind flying back to the day they heard of the death of her brother Neil. She glanced quickly at Robert but could find nothing to say.

'When do you have to go?' he said, echoing the question that had flashed through her mind.

'Tomorrow morning.'

'Do you want me to come with you, son.'

Surprising them both, George got up, pulling back his shoulders as if already a soldier.

'I'm not a baby, Dad. I can go on my own. Maybe I can get into the Air Force. I wouldn't mind that.'

He sat down again, lifting his breakfast cup to his lips to gulp down the last few drops.

'Well, we'd better cut along to work, Dad. Probably got some clearing up to do. We'll tell Charlie when he gets there. Come on!'

And he led the way, his father following, leaving Nora to gaze after them thinking that already he looked like a soldier, to her mind the easy-going youth gone forever.

Eighteen

As Charlie came into the scruffy little office he found he had walked in on an awkward exchange between Dick and their father. They were standing facing each other, Dick's eyes filled with a staring fear, he noticeably in a panic.

'I know, Dad, but my Valerie can't take it any longer,' he was saying. 'The kids are still evacuated and what if something happened to us and they came home to find they'd no longer got parents? I'm sorry Dad but I have to think of my own family. I'm taking Valerie down to Gloucestershire. We want to rent a place there not far from where the kids are staying. They can come to live with us there. They're not happy anyway where they are. They hate it and they miss us and we can't have them back in London. It's not fair on them. It's not fair on Valerie.'

All through the one-sided outburst, his father hadn't spoken. Now as Dick paused for breath, he said quietly. 'I expect you know your own mind, son. I can't make you stay. I know what it's been like for you and Valerie. It's the same for all of us.'

But Dick was hardly listening. 'We've had bombs drop in the next street, two houses completely gone and people killed. It could have been us. It could be us next and Valerie's scared out of her wits. We've even lost a bit off our own roof and had some windows blown in and plaster come down.'

'I understand,' was the level answer, his father about to say more when both became aware of Charlie standing in the doorway.

At that, he came further into the office, his eyes trained on his stepbrother and by the way the man moved back from him ever so slightly he knew those eyes showed anger. It wasn't often he let his anger show but this time he couldn't help himself.

'Don't you think we've all had some of it? My Ethel's terrified but I can't just go off into the blue and leave Dad on his own with his business.'

'All right for you,' retorted Dick. 'You've got no kids to worry about.'

'Nothing to do with kids – it's leaving Dad on his own.'

'Trouble with you,' Dick shot back furiously, 'You don't want kids.'

'That's none of your business!' Charlie's voice began to rise, not far off from thumping him, and he had to work hard to calm himself. 'If we did have kids they'd be evacuated like yours but I wouldn't start trying to follow them just because I'm as scared stiff as you.'

Dick to his credit for once, began to square up to him. 'Who says I'm scared?'

'I do. Shit-scared! Running away like a frightened rabbit and using your Valerie as an excuse.'

Dick was blustering, stammering, hands clenched. 'N–now you – you – you look here—'

'Pack it up, both of you!' their father bellowed, silencing the pair of them. As clenched hands reluctantly relaxed, his voice dropped to an oddly weary note, almost like someone who'd already given up on his world.

'If you want to take your family away out of it, Dick, then do that. Me and Charlie will manage. Who knows, tomorrow we could get a direct hit and we'll all be out of business. You can build another if you lose it but you can't get another life. I wouldn't want to be the cause of any of my children coming to grief because I said stay. So if you feel you've got to go, Dick, then go.'

'I'm sorry, Dad,' said Dick awkwardly. 'It's just that—'

'So am I, son, very sorry,' Robert interrupted cutting the excuse dead.

To Charlie, listening, there was a bitter ring to those words.

It had become hard going, just him and Dad alone to work the business and lately Dad seemed to tire easily, from time to time complaining of a vague pain in his chest.

'Bloody indigestion! It's what we're expected to eat these days. Bloody rationing! Four ounces of meat each week, how can a man exist on that? Hardly enough sugar and tea to put in your ear, stupid bit of butter, and now even tinned stuff on coupons so your mother tells me.'

'You ought to go and see a doctor about that pain,' he told his father, but he'd have none of it.

'Half of them don't know what they're talking about. They'd only tell me to pack up working. I'm not doing that! I'm all right. It's just indigestion.'

More likely they'd tell you to stop smoking so much, Charlie thought, as his father broke off to cough like some asthmatic coal-miner, but it was best not to put the thought into words. He'd only have got annoyed. He had chain-smoked for years. With an acute tobacco shortage that wasn't easy but being well in with the local tobacconist, he'd slip him a half-crown, a sizeable sum even for cigarettes now up to eightpence-halfpenny a packet, and from under the counter a packet of twenty would be craftily handed over.

'Anyway,' his father said, his gaze roaming about the scrap yard. 'How are you going to manage if I take time off? You can't go lugging stuff around on your own.'

Charlie smiled. His father was sixty-four, looking far older these days and certainly not robust any more. There was really only himself to do the heavy work now. Though he was strong, his chest broad, his arms well muscled and he managed well enough, he missed George and Frank for their help, as well as for themselves. He had little love for Dick but even he'd have made things easier. It was hard not to feel contempt for him, running away, which was all it could be called, and resented the fact that he'd been allowed to leave without an argument, still the favourite if truth was known. What would Dad have said if he'd wanted to do the same?

As it was, he worried about the business if ever he was called up. If Dad, having to manage on his own, were to fall ill, the whole thing going downhill until nothing was left, what would Mum do? She was fifty-two. She'd been a teacher before she was married but too old now to start over. And if he was in the forces how could he ever hope to support her and Ethel? Would his sisters ask their husbands to support her? He doubted it.

But it didn't look like he'd be called up now. When the order had gone out for all married men up to a certain age, not in reserved occupations and without children to enlist, their wives seen as being capable of going out to work to keep the home going, he'd presented himself as ordered. It had been with a heavy heart knowing his wife would be left to cope alone, although she'd have probably gone back to live with her mother and sister.

Instead he was told he could apply for postponement of call-up as the sole supporter of his father's business, the man elderly and not well enough to keep it going alone, in which case his family could well suffer hardship.

That was a year ago. He was still here working for his Dad, no sign of any calling-up papers. Their business was now seen as essential to the war effort, all suitable metal sold on to the Ministry, so with luck it looked as if he'd see this war out as a civilian.

'Do you have to go fire-watching tonight, love?' Ethel implored as he kissed her goodbye at the back door this morning. Her voice was trembling. 'I'm so frightened, left here all on my own.'

'You won't be,' he reminded as he turned his bicycle round to leave. Petrol rationing necessitated him laying aside his car to go off to Canning Town by bike. 'You've got next door's shelter to go into now for company before things liven up.' The Merriwells had been very kind to her.

'But what if you get hurt . . . or killed? What am I going to do?'

He didn't answer straight away. What if it was she who got killed, what would *he* do? It wasn't only the city getting it, the suburbs too. Where they lived in West Ham had been badly hit, sometimes half a street found to be gone when he got back the next day after fire-watching all night. And the thought terrified him of either of them losing the other.

'It's me and Dad together tonight,' he said, evading her question.

'But why do the pair of you have to do it together? Why can't your dad do a turn on his own? You have to.'

He was getting a little impatient with her. 'He does, darling. But he's in his sixties. I can't ask him to stay there on his own nearly every night.'

'But you're hardly ever here with me any night.'

It was true. If he and Dad were there together they'd take turns, each kipping down for a while in the basement while the other stood watch. But sometimes Dad would insist he stay home, as he himself sometimes did.

'I've got old Bennett next door to call on if I need help. Him and his brother are there, they taking turns as well.'

Horace Bennett and his brother Arthur were both a little

younger than Dad but he was still loath to leave him on his own too often.

'Look I've got to go, love,' he said to Ethel trying not to sound abrupt. 'I'll see if I can get home tonight. See how it goes.'

Since Christmas, air raids had got steadily worse. May was enjoying clear starlit nights, if it could be called enjoying. Moonlight showed up the whole of London to the Luftwaffe, the Thames becoming a glittering ribbon to mark the way. For months the city had been fighting to survive beneath that relentless onslaught. He and his father were kept constantly on alert for incendiaries that would burn the place down in no time if unattended. But at least today was Saturday. Tomorrow he'd have all day at home, his father having arranged to be there on his own Sunday night. Hurriedly he kissed Ethel once more and peddled off before she could plead with him again.

Throughout the morning they got on with the job of shifting a heap of heavy metal they'd got hold of yesterday on to a truck to go to a government factory, in the afternoon taking it easy, conserving themselves for another tense night ahead.

It was just as well. Although darkness wouldn't fall until abnormally late this time of year, British time set to hold on to all the daylight it could to keep the Luftwaffe away for as long as possible, it could still be a long night. And a long night it was; one of the worst.

By one o'clock Sunday morning the raid was in its full vicious swing. With incendiary bombs adding to the chaos, soon they were dealing with several at once, throwing bucketfuls of sand over the buggers, water only serving to spread the flames or even explode the wicked little devices.

All the time tons of high explosives were literally blasting office blocks to rubble amid the unending racket of clanging fire engines and ambulance bells and continuous ear-splitting whine and crash of bombs, the night turned orange by hundreds of blazing buildings.

As the sun rose – the Luftwaffe departing just before dawn – Charlie and his father stood on the roof aware as always of that strange silence that seemed to descend after such a night, despite dozens of police wardens, ambulance men and firemen still working flat out, the road still running with water from hundreds of hoses.

The air was filled with the acrid tang of high explosives, the raw stink of burnt wood, scorched brick and a disconcerting odour of chemicals. They themselves were filthy black, dishevelled and exhausted, covered in gritty dust as they gazed across the shattered city. But through the dust and the smoke of acre upon acre of shattered remains of what was once a thriving, busy capital, they could see the dome of St Paul's soaring high above it all, stark, untouched and defiant.

'I can't believe it!' Charlie whispered as he stared. 'Doesn't it make you proud?'

With autumn came blessed reprieve, the Luftwaffe switching its attentions to other cities, breathing space for Londoners – a godsend. A selfish emotion maybe, but like everyone else Charlie put his hands together.

News also came that Hitler had decided to set his sights on Russia, apparently seeing easier game. But it was heaven to go to bed for nights on end. Even more satisfying was that German cities were now getting a pasting from British bombers, though it was becoming a tit-for-tat affair with London getting another dose in December, forcing spotters and fire watchers back on to roofs and busy nights. But at least America had come into the war, which buoyed most people up while others remarked sarcastically, 'About time,' without pausing to give any deep thought to the comment.

Working during the day after an exhausting night Charlie could see it was telling on Dad. He'd find him sitting at the desk, eyelids drooping, head beginning to nod, unaware he was drifting off. Charlie would let him, and as he came awake with a start, would pretend not to have noticed.

God knows what his father would have done if he'd not been here. The business would probably have collapsed by now, as simple as that. Still, there was much more to think about, with no end in sight to this war.

They'd lost their home. Fortunately Ethel had been out, now doing part time war work as expected by the government for married women with no other ties. It had been a devastating shock coming back to find no home, or not one that was liveable any more.

All through the Blitz they'd been so lucky. A year since that ceased, planes were now targeting outer London and other towns. West Ham had been virtually obliterated. Now their house was gone, little left, condemned.

As soon as Charlie got the telephone call he rushed home to find her clinging to a neighbour, almost in a state of collapse, as wardens picked through the rubble of a house two doors down for bodies.

They stood outside, gazing blankly at what remained of two houses next to the one that had received a direct hit; cracked walls, windows and doors blown out, tiles gone, rafters like a set of ribs, outside a few items of furniture and private possessions that someone had kindly rescued.

Ethel clung to him as she stared at what had been her pride and joy. 'What are we going to do?'

'Hopefully they'll rehouse us somewhere,' he said lamely.

'Where? I don't want to go miles away. I don't!'

'We might have to.'

'But I want to be near my mother and my sister.'

He glanced down at her as she began to dissolve into tears again and tightened his grip comfortingly about her shoulders.

'I don't think we get much of an option, love. There are thousands needing to be rehomed. We can't dictate, that's if we're even given another place. There's no room at your mother's. My parents' house is bigger. With Frank and George in the forces and my sisters Elsie and Eileen married, they've rooms to spare.'

Both now lived in Essex. Both had an only child. Elsie's Victor, named after his father, was now seven and Eileen and Fred's Raymond was five. There was only Rosie and Eva left at home now.

'Eva will be getting married to her Harold this June,' Charlie went on to explain. Harold was reserved occupation, something important at London docks. 'And Rosie's courting. I expect she'll be married by next year, that's if her Arthur can get leave.' Rosie's fiancé was in the Royal Air Force.

'I don't want to live with other people if I can't go to my mother's,' she wailed pitifully.

'I'll see what I can do,' he promised, holding her even closer, trying to ignore her reference to his family as *other people*.

There were means of getting a decent place to live and the

idea of a bribe went through his head. But a good deal of money could be expected to change hands. Did he have that kind of money? He could go to his father but already knew his answer. 'Be better if you come and live here, son. It'll be so much easier. You can get to work better from here.'

Anyway, bribery seemed to go against the grain with so many others suffering and destitute. So it was, what furniture they saved from their home being stored in a large shed on his father's property, they went to live there.

It was a miserable winter, bitter and drawn out. The Stratford house was warm and cosy but it wasn't home any more. Even Charlie felt odd, and this was his own family! So he knew Ethel was obviously not comfortable. It was a good job she could escape at least three days a week, working behind a counter, but now having to go by bus instead of walking round the corner to it. He did his best to get her out some evenings, to the pictures mostly.

Searching half of London to find somewhere for them was like looking for gold dust, with so many houses destroyed and so many wanting a place to live. There was no question of them going out of London while his father needed his help. It wasn't until early 1944 that he was able to find a two-roomed flat in East Ham, not too far away from both their work.

The place was tiny, cramped, but Ethel couldn't have been happier. It might have been a mansion she was so happy. And seeing her, so was he.

Nineteen

Charlie stood watching the huge bonfire in East Ham's Central Park. It lit up the sky. In almost every street across the country, people were dancing and singing to pianos dragged out of doors, letting off fireworks, drinking beer or whatever they had, light pouring from every door and window, blackout curtains, which had so long shielded the smallest chink of light from the dangerous sky, thrown out on to the cheery fires.

Beside him, Ethel had her arm linked through his. He'd have liked to have gone to join in the celebrations in the heart of London but of course she hated crowds so they'd stayed in. But tonight he'd persuaded her to go out to watch the bonfire and the fireworks in Central Park before going home to bed. The celebrations continuing well into the small hours kept them awake for ages, Charlie mesmerized by the unaccustomed lights flickering on the ceiling.

It had been a strange day. All morning with nothing officially said, people had gone outside to begin putting up Union Jacks and red, white and blue bunting that they'd probably kept for years from the Coronation, all in a somewhat subdued and uncertain way, but slowly enthusiasm began to pick up. At three o'clock the Prime Minister was to give his announcement that the war in Europe was over and at five minutes to three the streets emptied as if by magic, everyone to his wireless to hear the long awaited message for themselves.

Sitting forward on their chairs, Charlie and Ethel listened. Outside all had been quiet. But hardly had Churchill uttered the words, 'Long live the cause of freedom, God save the King!' the world seemed to suddenly burst into a frenzy of utter joy and Ethel had burst into tears.

Later that week, going off to the local cinema seeing a newsreel of the celebrations in London, crowds singing, kissing, cuddling, dancing even in Trafalgar Square's fountains, girls linking arms with service men of all nationalities to prance in long lines, the girls jauntily wearing the men's caps, he again wished he'd been in the midst of it all, he and Ethel together.

It was a wonderful summer. Rationing was still pretty tight but they could now look forward to better times. The whole family had survived the war, air raids, doodle bugs, V2s. Frank was home, having gone through the North Africa campaign and after that in Europe. So too was George, and so were their sisters' husbands, all of them unscathed. Sometimes it seemed like a miracle knowing what others had lost.

Dick too was home again in London. Ironically having run away with his family to escape the bombing, two years later he'd found himself being yanked into the forces. Charlie admitted to getting some satisfaction from that. Now they were all home again and it was marvellous.

It was becoming a year of weddings, hardly a week going by without seeing two or three gatherings on the same day at each church, the groom often still in uniform. Rosie too got married, somewhat hurriedly to Arthur in December – registry office and few guests – and went to live with his parents.

Frank had introduced his fiancée some time back on one of his leaves as the war was coming to an end and already had the wedding day planned. Her name was Mavis, something of an unsmiling girl about the same age as Frank, who to Charlie's mind seemed to take the lead in all things. It was she, not Frank, who'd declared the date of their wedding – March next year.

'Frank and me thought it ought to be soon because we want to get a place as soon as possible. If we wait too long with everyone coming out the forces and accommodation so scarce we could miss out.'

She was right of course. But it was the way she took charge, leaving Frank to merely nod in agreement to whatever she said, that made Charlie dislike her.

George, too, was getting married. Jolly, chubby, friendly Betty had everyone warming to her. She would look to him to make decisions, he one of the most easy going, unambitious persons ever, who'd hardly ever made a firm decision in his whole life. How the pair would ever make their way in life, Charlie dared not imagine, or perhaps that would be their secret for happiness.

For Frank's wedding in March, with clothes rationing still

operating, Ethel made Mavis's wedding dress for her from parachute silk she'd got hold of. She did the same for Betty for her wedding three months later, saving a good deal of expense. Both dresses turned out so beautiful, the brides over the moon with them, that Charlie took a huge pride in her efforts, though she seemed to take their gratitude in her stride. She was a good dressmaker. She could also knit and crochet. Her hands were hardly ever still, always working away on something or other while he would help with most of the household chores, so she wouldn't have to stop and do them.

She made several things for Mavis, who seemed unable to put two stitches together without getting wool or cotton in a tangle. Ethel and Mavis soon became firm friends. They'd meet and chat for hours, which was good for her, and for him a great relief to see her happy.

But there was a catch to it when in September Ethel came bursting into the flat.

'Frank and Mavis have found themselves a house,' she gabbled hardly had she got her jacket off. 'In Upton Park. Just by chance Frank heard of it. He's been scouring the whole of London for a place. It's near the shops and the railway station and he'll be able to get to work on the train in only twenty minutes or so.'

Until then they'd been living with her parents in a cramped little two-up-two-down, his parents having George and Betty, the housing situation even harder, men still being demobbed and no new homes yet being built.

Hardly had the two moved, he and Ethel invited over to see the place, than she began asking, 'Surely we can find somewhere better to live? After seeing where they're living I feel so ashamed of this place.'

'They are only renting it,' Charlie reminded. 'They don't own it.'

'But Mavis said when we were in the main bedroom, if her Frank can do it, surely you can. I think she thinks you're not really trying.'

He could have throttled dear Mavis! He had been trying for months, knowing how discontented Ethel had become with this tiny two-roomed flat.

'Your dad gives you good money and maybe he'd lend you

the down payment to buy a house. We could pay it back bit by bit. If he ever makes you a partner we could repay it in no time and have a really nice house somewhere, all bright and airy like the one Mavis has got.'

Mavis had no doubt been boasting, making her feel inadequate and he being blamed for it when he'd been trying so hard but so far with no success.

'Surely we can afford something better on what you get,' she insisted as the months went by until he felt he was being slowly ground down. 'After all you can afford to run your old car again. So surely, darling—'

'It's not a case of affording a better place,' he interrupted, trying not to sound sharp. 'It's *finding* it. You just have to be patient, love.' To which she huffed and walked out of the room leaving him seething.

The word 'partner' was even plaguing his dreams lately. He could think of nothing else. But there seemed little chance of that happening, he was still seen as the worker, the mere son, the untried one and it wasn't fair. He had a diploma in metallurgy behind him, all that night schooling, he was good at figures, mental arithmetic, but what had Dick got. Nothing! Yet was being regarded these days as the king pin of the business. It *wasn't* fair!

The boys were all working here now, post war providing plenty of scrap metal, governmental bodies still buying it to help with rebuilding homes and business premises. They were all needed here now, allowing their father to sit back a little after years of just the two of them, him and Dad, slaving to keep things going. After all he was getting on to sixty-seven but he seemed indifferent to the fact.

'I'm still as fit as anyone half my age and I'm not ready for the scrap heap yet, and don't any of you think I am!'

To prove it he smoked as heavily as ever and though no longer lugged weighty stuff about, was always there supervising, never one day off. He'd be in the tiny, messy office, Dick usually with him, dealing with the paperwork, leaving the rest to do the hard work.

'Charlie! Frank! George! Come here quick!'

Hearing Dick's alarmed voice bellow across the yard, all three dropped what they'd been doing and raced through the November downpour towards the office. Bursting through the doorway they saw the old man on the floor, chair over-turned, Dick crouching beside him, shaking him as if he were a piece of rag.

Pushing him aside, Charlie knelt down, lifting the limp head on to his lap. The face held a strange, bluish pallor, but the eyelids seemed to flutter and he was sure there was faint, rapid breathing. He heaved a sigh of relief, glancing up at the three standing above him helpless.

'Could be a heart attack – someone phone the hospital for an ambulance!'

As Dick leapt for the phone on the desk, shouting into the mouthpiece to the operator the need for urgency and where to come, he began pumping his father's chest, stopping to listen for a heartbeat, then pumping again. It was all he could think of doing but carried on until there came the clanging of an ambu-lance bell. Relieved, he stood aside as ambulance men hurried into the office.

Feeling totally helpless, he watched his father lifted on to a stretcher and borne off. 'Can I come along?' he asked and receiving a nod, following them to the ambulance.

'I'm coming with you,' Frank said, hurrying out after him. 'Dick, lock up. You and George go and tell Mum. She'll need to know. Dick you can drive her.'

Charlie had never seen him so efficient but was too pent up to make much of it, except to be only too glad of his company.

Robert had recovered but it was months before he was well enough to return to work, all the while champing at the bit, driving Nora mad with a constant stream of choleric assurances that he was as fit as he'd ever been.

Ever would be, was Nora's opinion as she watched how he had slowed up, the anxiety of seeing him light up a cigarette, imper-vious to her and the hospital's warnings, telling her to mind her own business.

'I've smoked all my life. I know what I'm doing,' he'd argue irascibly.

'Yes and the doctors said you should stop.'

'A lot of bloody idiots – what do they know, sitting there telling me what I can and can't do like they're some bloody God! They smoke all right!'

'But they've said it could kill you, Robert.'

'Kill me? Not being allowed to have even an odd cigarette now and again will see me off anyway!'

But it wasn't the odd cigarette. It was almost as many as before, her warnings falling on deaf ears. These last few years he'd grown obstinate and demanding, refusing to listen to advice even from his sons, getting on their nerves. He got on hers too, now at home under her feet, fretting to get back to work despite being told he couldn't. And in this weather too.

The winter of 1947 was turning out to be the cruellest they'd known for ages: since Christmas people were unable to get to work due to snow and freezing conditions. How did he ever expect to go to work? Even when things finally improved, he still wouldn't be well enough, maybe never well enough again to manage the business in which he'd been so successful.

What he should be doing was allowing his sons to take the reins. But he was loath to see the business go out of his control, though it could very well do so if he didn't hand over some responsibility to them, all four now dependable, married men who knew the business inside out.

This February morning she awoke to find Robert not here beside her. She was usually the first up. Now her first thought was had he got up and perhaps gone downstairs and there had had another turn?

Running to George and Betty's room, she tapped on their door. George would have gone to work earlier probably by bus, his father no longer able to drive him there.

'Have you seen George's father?' Nora demanded the moment the door opened to reveal her sleepy-eyed daughter-in-law. Half awake Betty shook her head.

'Never mind,' Nora snapped, leaving the girl gazing after her as she hurried back to her own bedroom to hastily dress and go downstairs.

'Minnie, have you seen my husband about?' she asked their middle-aged, part-time domestic help busily vacuuming the carpet in the hallway.

Minnie frowned. 'I saw him go out in his outdoor clothes about half an hour ago. He went to his car.'

Fear clutched at Nora's breast. Going to the front door, braving the bitter frost, she peered out, her cardigan clutched to her throat. The garage door was wide open and she knew the car had gone.

Twenty

Charlie was surprised and dismayed to see his father's pre-war Citroen being slowly manoeuvred through the gate and into the yard, its wheels ploughing through the thick layer of snow that had fallen during the night.

It was around ten thirty. Even he, as well as Frank and George, had found it almost hopeless getting here through the awful weather. Still no sign of Dick, but Dick seldom needed much of an excuse not to be here.

Hastening to help his father from the vehicle in case he slipped on an icy patch, he found his hand pushed roughly aside.

'I can do it! I'm not bloody helpless.'

'Sorry,' he apologized, as Frank emerged from one of the sheds, also having seen their father drive in.

Of George there was no sign, as he and Frank followed close behind the old man to the office, expecting any minute to be told to get on with whatever they'd been doing. But as they reached the door he turned and asked, 'Where's Dick?'

Frank didn't reply, Charlie answering for them. 'I expect he's held up by the weather.'

Charlie grinned. Found out at last. Not that the old man would have much to say about that. And nor did he.

'Well, when he comes in,' he said unruffled, 'I want a word with all four of you. And where's George?'

'He was here before us but I don't think he heard you arrive.'

'Then go and get him wherever he is. I can't wait for Dick.'

He'd hardly spoken when his oldest son's little Ford moved cautiously into the yard, its front wheels slipping and sliding gently to a halt in the snow. 'There's Dick now.'

So stern was his father's face that Charlie felt uncertain as to what was on his mind. Or was that tight expression coming from the strain of driving here after so long at home? But it was still good to see the look on Dick's face as he noticed his father's car sitting there.

He came over to them at a cautious run. 'Sorry, I'm a bit late this morning. The weather . . . Had a hell of a time . . .'

'Just come into the office,' ordered his father, ignoring the excuses and at the same time acknowledging George entering behind his stepbrother. 'Ah, there you are! There's something I need to say to you all.'

Charlie's heart sank. The old man looked just about all in. Already he could hear the voice, weary, flat-toned, defeated, saying that he was closing down the business as it was beyond his abilities.

'I've decided,' the words cut through his thoughts. 'I've decided I'm getting a bit beyond running this business. So I've come to a decision.'

Charlie held his breath – in fact they were all holding their breath as his father paused to take a deep sigh.

'I've decided I need help now. So I've decided there must be a change.' Again he paused before continuing, taking in each of them in turn.

'I've been talking to your mother and she agrees with me that in the present situation it might be right to make you, Dick, and you, Charlie, and you too, Frank, partners in the business. The firm will be Titchnell and Sons. How do you feel?'

He gave each a broad smile but while Frank returned the smile, the faintest scowl touched Dick's expression, no doubt feeling he alone ought to have been made a partner. Charlie too remained straight-faced.

'What about George?' he said quietly. 'Why've you left him out?'

He saw his father nibble at the corner of his upper lip, a sure sign of annoyance before turning towards his bewildered youngest son. 'It might be better, George, to wait a year or two for that, don't you think?'

'George like the rest of us is a responsible married man with a family on the way,' Charlie cut in before he could reply. 'A little'n expected around October. He works hard as any of us and I think deserves the same credit.'

He knew this wasn't quite correct. Though his brother worked well enough, his nature was such that he'd never ever be that dedicated to be anything more than a worker. But how could one tell him that?

'I think it's only right to include George along with the rest of us,' he added.

'I disagree,' Dick broke in. Charlie turned on him.

'No one asked you!'

'That's enough!' His Dad's deep voice silenced the pair. 'I'll sort George out at some later date.'

'I still think he shouldn't be left out,' Charlie replied adamantly.

His father glared. 'I'll be the judge of that. And if there's going to be a load of squabbling over what I see as a generous gesture to you all, it can easily be changed back.'

The dire words brought everyone up sharp. Robert gave a satisfied humph and continued.

'Right then, if we're all in agreement, I'll have the necessary papers drawn up in accordance with the Registration of Business Names. We'll then be a firm in every sense. I trust you all agree.'

He regarded the gathering steadily and they nodded, even George, if somewhat glumly. Deep inside, Charlie seethed for him. He could see him never being elevated to any position of trust and caught himself thinking that when the old man eventually expired, he'd make sure George was made a partner. It felt only right.

Seconds later he was hating himself for even daring to dwell on his own father's death, one who'd been such a vibrant part of his life, the two of them carrying the business together while others were away fighting, working side by side through Blitz, fire, buzz bombs and V2s.

Dad was right. George was too irresponsible to be relied upon in this business for all his good nature. He knew what he was doing.

Little had changed. They still worked as hard as ever, shifting scrap metal, loading it on lorries, while Dick and his father took charge of buying in and negotiating deals. Trouble was, Charlie felt entirely on his own here – George with his couldn't-care-less attitude, Frank seemingly with no mind of his own looking to him to make every decision, and Dick trying to lord it over everyone.

With them all pulling different ways he could see the firm collapsing if they weren't careful. Not a way to run a business, one that was started by his father's father way back around the

1880s, and had been going for nearly sixty years through two wars and a bad recession.

If it went to the wall, it would break Dad's heart. It would break his too, wondering how his Mum would cope if it did go under. All due to this underlying hostility since Dick had been made a partner and George hadn't.

As if in compensation, Dad had found him and Betty a small house in Canning Town not far from the firm, having slipped the local postman a few quid to keep an ear to the ground for any opportunity that might come. And it had. George and Betty were over the moon about it, he seeming to have forgotten the earlier slight.

'I can't thank the old man enough,' he said to Charlie, as together they manhandled a heavy load of scrap metal picked up at a nearby factory from their lorry. 'He's been really good to me and Betty.'

'I'm glad you're glad,' Charlie told him unenthusiastically, but George hardly noticed the bite to his brother's reply as he ploughed on.

'Apparently this woman's husband died and she wants to sell it and move back up north to her family. The place is going for a song and Dad has forked out the down payment for us. He says he don't want it back. Betty couldn't be happier. She's getting near her time so it's come at just the right moment. If all goes well, we'll be moving in around July or August.'

Charlie just nodded. Dad could be generous at times.

George and Betty's baby, a boy they called Simon, was born three months later.

With a heavy heart which he kept to himself, Charlie accepted their invitation to be a godfather. Everyone in his family now had children except him. He'd hoped that when Mavis had had a baby, she and Ethel being such good friends, Ethel would have changed her mind about pregnancy. Best friends or not, she was envious of her; Mavis had this, Mavis had that, Mavis had a nice place of her own and we're stuck in this rotten little flat, and so on. So he'd hoped envy would extend to wanting a family but it seemed it wasn't to be. Her main goal in life was apparently merely to have a nice house of her own.

It was still almost impossible finding a place to live – nearly all men now demobbed and young couples looking to marry and settle down and though new houses were being built and new towns were springing up, a place to live was still hard to find, unless one had the money to buy – which most hadn't. Working in one of the new towns could ensure a council house, but he wasn't prepared to leave the firm to go and work elsewhere.

When next visiting his Mum, he took Dad aside to ask that as he'd helped George whom he'd not made a partner, could he help him who'd been at his side all through the war. He wasn't prepared for his answer.

'You've already got a place of your own.'

'I know, but we can hardly move in it and if Ethel decided to have a baby . . .'

'I can't see that happening after all this time. Maybe she can't have kids,' came the reply, his father's lips quirking into a one-sided smile.

It was hard to conceal the hurt and anger the remark brought. 'I just thought,' he said as evenly as he could, 'as you helped George, maybe . . .'

'Because they had nowhere else to live, except with me and your mother. Not a satisfactory arrangement for a young married couple with a baby on the way. But I consider you quite capable, lad, of standing on your own two feet to find a better place than you've already got without my help.'

The answer was like a blow between the eyes. All he could think to say was. 'If that's how it stands, Dad, I don't need your help. But thanks, I'll sort myself out.'

The bitterness in his tone seemed to stagger his father as he turned and strode out of the room, knowing that nothing would ever induce him to ask for help from his parents ever again.

Last winter had been dubbed The Big Freeze with non-stop blizzards and huge snowdrifts, hardly any transport movement by rail or road, power cuts, people living by candlelight, some factories staying closed, and all the while rationing grew worse than it had been in the war. In March, melting snow brought flooding everywhere making life even more miserable. It had often been impossible to get into work yet Charlie had always managed to make it somehow, even if it meant cycling the whole way to Stepney, staying overnight and going home by the same means the next evening, it being too much to do in one day.

Ethel had done a lot of moaning about it but it was the only way to protect the premises from break-ins; scrap metal, especially lead, was an easy way for a thief to make money. He and Frank took turns.

It was a relief to see the weather finally relax its grip, if not rationing, with even the humble potato in short supply. Despite it all, it had been a nice summer, with autumn highlighted by the engagement and marriage of Princess Elizabeth to Lt Philip Mountbatten.

All through the year, Charlie had saved every penny he could. He wasn't short of cash by any means, the rent on this tiny flat taking little to find, and it being just him and Ethel.

They spent Christmas at Stratford but he and Dad said little to each other. There was now a distance between them and Charlie wasn't ready to narrow it.

'Is something going on between you and your father?' his Mum asked as she came into the small sitting room after she and Rosie had washed up the Christmas dinner things.

He was sitting in the room alone, those of the family spending the day ensconced in the larger dining room and lounge, chatting, drinking or merely dozing, the radio full on.

He looked up at her. 'Why, should there be?' he evaded.

She came and sat next to him. 'You and your dad used to talk like mad to each other. Now this silence between you . . .' She leaned forward from the armchair where she'd seated herself opposite him and took his hand. 'What's wrong, love?'

Charlie looked down at the hand. It was veined and faintly wrinkled and he remembered the vibrant young woman of his childhood. A sudden pang caught in his throat. They were getting old, his parents. One day . . .

He looked up sharply. 'It's just work,' he said offhandedly, 'nothing for you to worry about.'

'But I do worry. Is it the partnership?'

Somehow he knew she suspected things were not right. She'd always been intuitive. Suddenly he found himself blurting out all the things that were indeed wrong, including Ethel's refusal to have a family and his father's seeming indifference to the conditions in which he and Ethel still lived.

She listened without expression but all the while her hand tightened on his. Finally when he'd finished, she spoke quietly.

'I know your dad can be difficult. But he wasn't always that way. I know he did help George to get them their own place to live. I know he knows George's failings and sees you as the stronger brother. He needs to see you stand on your own two feet. And secretly he admires you.'

'Pity he doesn't show it,' he responded, unconvinced.

'But it's you he looks to. Dick is self-centred and in a way a bit of a disappointment to him, I think. Frank will always be a follower. He lets his wife make all the decisions. George . . . well, we know George. But you, he knows you could go far. And look at you, love, you've studied this metallurgy thing and one day it'll stand you in good stead. I know it will. I don't know how, but I feel it will and he feels it too.'

'Then why doesn't he help me?'

'He doesn't like to show favouritism.'

'Wonderful!' Charlie observed bitterly.

'And he's not well,' she went on. 'He hasn't been well for quite a while though he refuses to bow to it. He's like you, love, refuses to allow things to get him down. He's a battler, always has been, and so are you. Stick with him, Charlie, please. He needs you.'

He didn't answer and silence fell between them. In the other rooms they could hear laughter, conversation, music. Someone came out to the kitchen, passing the closed door of the little sitting room.

At last she spoke. 'Darling, I want to give you a start in getting a better place to live. I've savings—'

Charlie jumped. 'No, Mum! I'm not taking your money!'

'It's a loan – just for a down payment on a house when you find it.'

'No, Mum!'

'Darling, please, to please me. I *want* to do this. No need to tell your dad. Just let him think you've saved it up. Please, Charlie.'

He said nothing, and after a while Nora let go the hand she

had been holding all this time and went out of the room leaving him sitting in silence with his thoughts.

So far he hadn't taken advantage of his mother's offer. She had not pressed the offer but he knew she was only waiting for him to ask and would not insult him by referring to it again. They knew each other implicitly in a sort of personal common bond and always had done. Though neither ever spoke of it to the other, it was there deep down under the surface unlike the relationship he'd had with his father.

Not wanting to abuse her offer, he let nearly a year go by without it being referred to again, instead secreting away money as a miser might, not even telling Ethel in case she got too carried away.

His mother was right, Dad was not as well as he made out to be, obviously keeping it to himself and dare anyone ask how he was; he'd fly off the handle so that they refrained from asking again.

This way, work jolted from one setback to another, all of them getting at each other and every day a hint of seeing the end to the firm.

Breaking point came six months later in the April of 1948. George had come in late and Dick, who had for once come in early, went after him, calling him a lazy sod, a fit-for-nothing idiot, too dim to pull his weight. Charlie immediate went in defence of his brother at the very moment their father drew up, getting out of the car to hurry over to the squabble, his face flushed, his breathing harsh.

'What the bloody hell's going on!'

As they stood away from each other, he glared at both men. George moving even further back than the others, Charlie found himself the object of his father's glare. 'What the bloody hell do you think you're all doing?'

'Dick had no need to come the high hand with George just for being a bit late.'

'Well, George *should* have been here same time as you lot.'

'Maybe, but he's never as late as often as this one is,' Charlie returned sharply, indicating his stepbrother with his thumb.

'I don't bloody care who's late and who isn't! Just get on with the work, all of you.'

'Dad, you're not including me in—' The rest of Dick's protest was silenced by his father's glare.

'If this sort of bickering is what comes of making you partners, I'm sorry that I ever . . . ever—'

He broke off, taking a sharp breath, one hand going up to his chest. Charlie took a step towards him, taking his arm. 'You all right, Dad?'

His hand was pushed roughly away. 'Of course I'm all right. But I'm not hanging about here listening to you all quarrelling. I'm going home.'

Turning, he stomped to his car seeming suddenly older than his years. They watched silently as he got in, started up the engine and turned the vehicle, driving out of the gate.

After a moment, Dick said, 'Now see what you've done.'

About to make a retort, Frank looked to Charlie for support but he'd already walked off, too weary of the whole stupid affair to bother to argue.

'He needs taking down a peg,' Frank said, aggrieved, as he hurried after him, catching him up. 'He needs to be told to stop bossing us about.'

'Then you do it,' Charlie said heavily over his shoulder.

'Me?'

'If you feel that strongly.'

'Well . . .' Frank began but said no more as he resumed the task they'd been doing, manhandling a pile of rusty iron rods into a neater stack by the back wall of the yard as Dick returned to the office.

They worked steadily through the morning in the open. It had begun to rain and George made for one of the sheds, Frank too, saying they would be better doing something in the dry. Charlie stood looking after them, then turned and went over to the office instead, guessing Dick might probably do with some help, there on his own, especially today no doubt with a few long lists of figures to tote up and work out without Dad's help, Dad quick at figures and he not.

He didn't look up as Charlie entered, still surly at being included in his father's bad books along with the rest. When the telephone began to ring he snatched it up as if it were the sole cause of his chagrin.

'Yes!'

It was no way to answer a business call but seconds later he was staring up at his stepbrother, his face drained of colour, his expression one of bewilderment, as if he couldn't believe what he'd heard.

'It's Mum,' he whispered hoarsely. 'She's in a terrible state. Dad got out of the car at home and collapsed. He's dead! Just collapsed and died. Just like that.'

Twenty-One

He hadn't realized how many friends Dad had had, the church full to overflowing: many of his Masonic brethren into whose lodge Dad had introduced him three years before; friends and neighbours, business acquaintances and of course family – so many there who thought highly of him. Only later in life had he become crusty and impatient, but Charlie now understood that this had sprung purely from deteriorating health. How could he have not seen it, blaming the man himself for those shortcomings? How could he have been so insensitive?

Mum was clutching his hand so tightly that even through her black gloves the nails were pressed into the flesh. She'd not wept. It would have been better had she done so, maybe made his own heart less heavy, filled with guilt knowing that the last words he and Dad had shared had been full of discord.

He went over and over them and wanted to weep. But how could he when his mother remained dry eyed, carrying her loss so silently? He'd seen the looks the rest of their family had given her, stupidly assuming her hard and callous. It seemed that out of all of them only he knew how much she was grieving.

The day of the funeral he'd sat beside her at the front of the mourners in the crowded Stratford church, later at the graveside in the cruelness of bright spring sunshine he was still there beside her, holding her hand as she'd grieved silently.

Today he was beside her again, again holding her hand but in the quietness of her lounge as he had done so many times these past months, he nursing his own quiet anger even as he comforted her in her grief – a different sort of grief this time, one that came from the discovery of just how hurtful people with greed in their hearts can be.

A few weeks earlier Elsie had been beside herself when the contents of the will had been made known.

'I can't believe he done it!' she'd railed at her husband the morning after it had been read. 'Everything left to Mum – I mean *everything*! The house – yes, I can understand that. She has to have somewhere to live but that big rambling place with only her in it – she should be somewhere much smaller, more convenient. But Dad's business, his entire business – I mean what does she think she's going to do with it?'

From the breakfast table Vic had regarded her with some concern. He agreed with her, but he knew what she was like once she got her teeth into something and she'd been going on about this affair half the night, keeping him awake.

'It's not entirely hers, love. Your brothers are partners in it, they've got forty-nine per cent between them and she has fifty-one.'

'Which means she owns a majority share, and what have we got out of my father's will? A paltry few quid!'

In fact it was a couple of thousand, but to her it was peanuts. 'An entire business left to a woman of sixty-one. How can a woman her age manage a scrap metal yard, I ask you?'

'I've told you, love, they'll be running it for her.'

'They'll run it all right! They know where their bread's buttered – all that money and us with a few paltry quid!' The fact that Victor held down a well paid job didn't come into it in her estimation. 'A few lousy quid!'

In fact Rosie, Eileen and Eva had received likewise, but so far there'd been no reaction from them, though it was early days.

'I think we should get together and have a little talk about contesting the will,' she said flatly. 'I'm going to get in touch with them, see how they feel after they've had a chance to think about it.' Her mind made up, she took a great gulp of scalding hot breakfast tea, almost choking on it.

A few days later she wrote to her sisters saying what was needed was a family meeting – just they and their husbands. Having stirred up a hornet's nest of discontent, everyone was now gathered at her home looking quite concerned.

'I don't feel it right to go contesting Dad's will,' Eileen murmured, aware that her words could instantly isolate her from the others. 'After all she is his wife and our mum. Personally, I don't feel it's right.'

'*Personally,* I think it is!' Eva shot back at her while Eileen's Fred put a hand on his wife's arm to stop such silly ideas.

He himself did not earn a great deal as a motor mechanic working for someone else. They lived in a bungalow in the country, practically falling to pieces, threadbare carpets and much of the furniture made by him, and a huge garden to upkeep. A bit more money would come in very handy.

'The decent thing to do,' Eva went on, glaring at her sister, 'would have been for her to have shared at least a bit of it between us. After all we are her daughters and probably need it more than she does at her age, or at least some of it – certainly a bit more than a couple of thousand!'

Her husband nodded in agreement but Rosie turned on her, hands waving about in that batty way of hers whenever she talked.

'I can't see as you need it. Your Harold don't do too badly.'

Eva's husband was in publishing, a popular motoring magazine or something.

'That's none of your business!' Eva shot at her and Rosie subsided back into her chair, while her husband Arthur sat looking daggers at her for even daring to suggest her sister be content with what they had.

He ran a smallholding and just about made a living. With two young daughters to keep, it took a lot of work to make enough to live in the comfort that Eva and Elsie did. A larger share of his mother-in-law's inheritance would come in very handy. He didn't want Rosie spoiling it for him with her silly observations.

'We could all do with a bit more,' he said quietly, the others nodding in full agreement.

It was a profitable afternoon, all of them enjoying a nice tea together and later on a nice drop of wine, the conclusion turning out very satisfactory indeed: to procure a good solicitor and set the ball rolling.

'I don't know why they're behaving like this towards me.'

Sitting with his mother, Charlie knew why only too well. Seeing money to be had, money they thought themselves entitled to and had been done out of, they had got together, his family, and damn how much they were hurting Mum.

Oh, they'd look after her all right, as they were promising.

That meant putting her in a smaller *more manageable* house as they termed it, selling up the Stratford house and reaping the difference for themselves. After all, why would Mum at her age need all that cash the Stratford house would bring, so long as she had a nice little place to live?

Schemers, the lot of them! Seeing money to be had, had even hired legal help. Well, he would see they couldn't get away with it. What Dad had left was Mum's and hers alone.

'I never thought everything would be left to me,' she was saying, her lined face pallid and taut. 'I thought he'd leave the business to be shared between you all, his family.'

'I know you did,' he soothed but she did not seem to be listening.

'I was his wife. Natural he wanted to see me comfortable. And as his sons you four are partners. But he should have given the rest of his family a little say in the firm – a few shares each, so they could have had a say in the business.'

Charlie didn't agree. It could have split the business up, each of them pulling this way and that, ready to quarrel at any slight, not one with any knowledge of the way this business worked, none of them ready to soil their hands. But he said nothing.

'Maybe that's what's upset them,' she went on. 'But they're acting as if it's my fault. That I got round him to cut them out of his will. I didn't.'

Charlie gripped her hand to show that he knew she hadn't.

'How can they be like this towards me, my own children,' she said, pulling her hand away to cover her brow and eyes, such a gesture of despair that he got up from his chair and hugged her to him.

'I'm not going to let them hound you, Mum,' he soothed. 'You've got me. I'll fight them. They can spend all they've got on solicitors but I shall see they won't get a penny of what Dad left to you.' And he meant it.

On the face of it he remained friendly. From what was being said he deduced Elsie to have been the instigator of their unrest, with Eva a close second; Elsie a naturally envious woman and Eva who saw herself a lady.

He found out that Rosie and Eileen, especially Eileen, had both been reluctant to resort to legal help but were being pushed by their husbands whose eyes only saw profit coming their way with very little effort.

Eileen was a sweet-natured, fair-minded person who would let herself be ruled by her somewhat forceful husband. Rose had more go in her but was vivacious and giddy, flitting from one idea to another, the life and soul of a party though sometimes got on the nerves with all that chatter and giggle. But she was not greedy. Life passed by her at an easy rate. It was her Arthur who was the bugbear, his eyes too, seeing money to be had.

But try as he might to show friendship, they obviously saw him as the enemy even as they accepted him into their homes. He and Ethel would pop in to one or the other as frequently as he dared. But he knew each smelled a rat no matter how sociable he tried to be, especially Elsie who had always been open with her feelings.

'You've always been the blue-eyed boy,' she had said waspishly one afternoon, Vic being at work, when he'd turned up. 'I wouldn't be surprised if Mum didn't wheedle Dad into giving you the biggest share after herself.'

'I wish,' he quipped as evenly as he could, accompanied by a laugh. 'He treated us four boys all the same. That was way before we lost him.'

'And cut us girls out altogether!'

'But you weren't working there. If your husbands had been—'

'That's beside the point!' She cut in, sipping furiously at the tea she'd brewed for them on their arrival. 'I still think we should be entitled.'

He wanted to add, 'To the point of hiring legal help to get at it.' But he didn't and let the conversation drift on to more convivial things.

He could see this affair dragging on for years, they unable to see that to fight Dad's will was a waste of time, his wife being lawfully deemed, as he saw it, Dad's main beneficiary. But Dad had appointed him executor of his will and he meant to carry out his father's terms and fight any legal battle that ensued over it. And he knew how unpopular he was with the others.

It was some time last year, before their falling out, that his father had taken him aside, saying, 'I'm not a well man, Charlie. The old ticker isn't quite what it used to be and I've decided to

appoint you to take care of things for me when I finally pop off.
That's if you agree.'

'You're not going to die!' he'd burst out but his Dad had lifted
a hand to stop him, giving him a broad grin.

'I'm not going to die this minute, son. But things do need to
be sorted out. I made a will years ago leaving the business to
your mother so that's OK. The thing is, I don't want to leave a
muddle behind me and now's as good a time as any to talk to
you about it while the other three aren't here.'

He had got up from his desk to close the office door to the
yard before coming back to draw his chair closer, his voice
lowered.

'You boys have worked for me all your lives and deserve your
shares in the firm. But you're the only one I feel is sensible and
level-headed enough to be made executor of my will. So will
you do it?'

'Of course,' he'd said readily, 'but what about the girls?'

'What about them?' his father had countered. 'Their men have
got jobs. And none of them come very often to see your mum
except maybe at Christmas or sometimes on her birthday. Oh,
I'll leave them all something, obviously, but you four boys keep
your shares in the firm as well as a decent bit of money – I can
tell you that now. Your mother will of course be the major share-
holder. She'll have the house and money enough for herself. I
think that's good and fair, don't you agree, son?'

Yes, he had. But now he had to bear the brunt of his sisters'
ill will. Couldn't they see that if he didn't protect her, their
grasping greed could bring about the death of their mother if
they weren't careful.

The year dragged itself out towards a miserable winter. The only
guests at his mother's Christmas dinner were him and Ethel, George
and Betty and their two boys, nice looking youngsters but for the
most part bored and wanting only to go home to their Christmas
presents.

He and Ethel were spending New Year's Eve with her mother
and sister, but he'd make a point of popping in on his own
during the afternoon to see her, staying only a short while,
for since losing Dad she no longer bothered with New Year,

preferring to go to bed early as she did much of the time now.

But he was becoming worried about her health. For a couple of months she'd not been all that well. As the weather had grown colder she'd developed a rather persistent cough which was affecting her breathing quite a bit. The doctor whom Charlie insisted she visit, had diagnosed chronic bronchitis. 'Understandable in one your mother's age,' he had said as he prescribed a bottle of cough mixture and some pills before dismissing her.

It hadn't done much good or she wasn't taking it as she should, but New Year well behind them, this winter hadn't helped the cough one bit.

'I don't want any doctors!' she told him when Charlie insisted she see her doctor again. 'And don't go creeping behind my back to call one in,' she warned. 'As soon as the weather starts to warm up it'll go on its own.'

But it was now April and it wasn't going, in fact was becoming ever more chronic, but still she insisted he keep away from doctors.

'But you can get me some more cough syrup from the chemists. That seems to ease it more than anything the doctor has given me. I'll be fine well wrapped up nice and warm in my own home. They'll only start wanting me to go to hospital and I don't want to leave my nice home just to be messed about with in hospital. It'll clear up of its own accord given time.'

Despite her assurances it wasn't clearing up, sometimes draining her of all energy. At times it seemed as if she didn't care if it cleared up or not. He knew what she was frightened of – not so much hospitals but her home left unoccupied, fair game for her daughters and sons-in-law to lay claim to it and arranging for her to go into a home.

The truth was that she was being worn down not only by what was obviously a bronchial illness but by them and the many solicitors' letters she was receiving. He would read them when he came to see her then throw them straight into the fire. When she panicked and said he couldn't do that, he'd say that he could and would, and the less she responded to their blackmailing the better.

'Never give those people the benefit of a reply!' he said. 'Then you can't be accused of being antagonistic. Do nothing. Let them fork out money if they want. The only ones who'll end up benefiting from all that bother will be solicitors. They always will. So don't you worry, Mum. You've got me.'

It did his heart good to see her smile. She smiled so little these days.

As spring melted into summer she had improved a little but it was obvious bronchitis would be with her to stay, to lay her low at the first hint of change in the weather.

It was obvious, too, that she shouldn't continue living on her own. Her daughters were not slow to point that out, all agreeing that rather than hire a private nurse to care for her in that rambling house of hers that took such a lot to heat, it would be better if they arranged for her to be cared for more expertly in a comfortable home for the elderly, there to get all the attention she needed.

'Oh, no they don't!' Charlie said knowingly to his Ethel when he got wind of their scheme. 'And get their hands on the house? Not if I have any say in it!'

Ethel merely shrugged. It wasn't up to her to say one way or the other but Charlie already had the solution. 'What do you think of us giving up this flat, love, and going to live there? You wouldn't have to look after her. I could afford to pay that private nurse, with no need to fork out for the rent of this place.'

He had expected an argument but Ethel thought of all the room she would have after this small flat. So many times had she nagged him to get somewhere larger but he always seemed too preoccupied with other worries to listen. She could do things with a house like the one in Stratford, have it modernized, painted nice and bright, with nice light curtains, maybe a few bits of new furniture. They'd get someone in to clean and do the washing and cook their meals, leaving her to sit back to knit and do embroidering. She loved knitting, hated housework, in fact in this tiny flat Charlie often did many of those jobs for her. But now they could have proper help.

He could hardly believe how quickly she'd answered and to see the relief on his mother's face was a tonic. Within a couple of weeks they'd given up the flat and moved in.

'What cheek!' Eva burst out when Elsie phoned her. 'He knows full well what he's up to. Out to inherit that house when Mum goes. But what can we do about it? My Harold can't afford another legal battle.' The other proceedings had broken down with nothing achieved but ill will. 'And what happens to the business if Mum goes?'

'I hope she'll go on for ages yet,' Elsie answered sharply, a sudden stab of guilty conscience and superstition that Eva was almost inviting their mother's death. That was wrong. She was their mother.

Picking up on her tone, Eva blurted out a hasty, 'Of course!' and with a brief goodbye put the phone down.

Nothing more was said about it, certainly not to their husbands or their other two sisters who would have been appalled. Yet as autumn's damp weather began to affect their mother's health again, it felt as if she and Elsie had been willing it. They made a point of going to see her more often, sitting with her in an effort to compensate, but it felt to both that she saw through their cheerfulness. It made the visits uncomfortable and tedious and slowly as autumn came, the visits dropped away.

To Charlie it seemed as if she couldn't have cared less, that spark that had kept her going all through the summer months, beginning to dwindle.

'She should be in hospital,' her doctor said again and again, 'But if she won't go, I can't make her. At least she has her nurse.'

'I need to have a little talk with you, Charlie,' she said one evening after the doctor had left and her nurse, Joyce Bell, was in her own room.

She was sunk into the armchair in her bedroom where she preferred to be these days, Ethel downstairs watching the little television he'd bought them. He'd come up to see if she wanted to go down and watch it with them but she'd waved away the offer with a weary hand.

'I couldn't concentrate,' she said. 'What I want . . .' A fit of coughing caught her making her lean forward, her handkerchief to her mouth until breathless and weak she let her head fall back on the headrest.

'I'm sorry, dear,' she said feebly.

He took her hand. 'Mum, you've got to let the doctor send you to the hospital. You can't go on like this.'

'I'm not going to hospital!' she said with a little strength returning. 'I'm not having my home taken away from me.'

'It won't be. I'm here now,' he said, knowing fully what she meant. 'No one's going to take it away from you, Mum, while I'm here.'

She sat up slowly, putting her other hand over his, looking deeply into his eyes. 'I don't know what I'd do or where I'd be without you, love.'

She suddenly seemed to gain some strength. 'To tell the truth, I don't think I'll be going on much longer in this world.'

She stopped him with the raised palm of her hand as he made to protest. 'I don't think I want to. I'm tired. I need your father. Let me say what I want to say,' she added as again he made to interrupt with a protest.

'I need to see your dad's solicitor. Tomorrow will you call him, love? I've decided that when the time comes I want to make over my shares in your dad's business to you. You know what you're doing. None of the others seem to know and I – I . . .' She broke off, exhausted.

'I just need to sleep,' she said, closing her eyes and after a while he got up and left her, bidding her nurse to get her to bed.

Twenty-Two

It was the last serious talk they ever had together. Today, a cold November day, Charlie sat in the front pew of Stratford Church remembering the last time he had sat here gazing at his Dad's coffin, holding his mother's hand. Now it was his mother's coffin he gazed at and there was no longer anyone's hand to be held, Ethel sitting beside him with hers in her lap, no real need of solace.

The day after Mum had given her wishes to her solicitor, making him her executor, 'to save the bother,' she'd said when Charlie said that he and Frank would take on the responsibility, she hadn't seemed inclined to talk to anyone and as the week went on she had sunk into a decline, her breath laboured, her face taut with a new pain in her chest.

The doctor had diagnosed pleurisy but it was too late for hospitals, and that night she passed away, almost it seemed as if having done what she'd done, she wanted no more from life.

Watching her coffin being reverently born on the shoulders of the ushers out of the dim interior into the bright October sunshine, he was convinced that it wasn't the illness that had taken her but that she had just given up, her heart broken by the thoughtlessness and greed of the girls she had brought up with love and self-sacrifice. Maybe the thought was being a little dramatic but he felt he would never forgive them for that.

The contents of his mother's will sometime later did his heart good when he saw the expressions on Eva and Elsie's faces, and their husbands'. He'd taken what seemed to him fitting satisfaction having them come to the house for it to be read by his mother's solicitor in the old way of doing things.

He'd watched Elsie's lips working with fury, she ever the bitter one ever ready to stir up trouble, while Eva ever the cold fish, presented a face like stone, only her grey eyes revealing how she felt.

But he couldn't help feeling for Rosie and Eileen both of

whom had found it hard to hide an honest grief at the loss of their mother. In fact the tears just rolling unchecked down Rosie's face, she who had always worn her heart on her sleeve, made his heart melt towards her. She had been led into that legal business and probably so had Eileen. He'd always had a soft spot for those two and it had hurt when he'd discovered all four had had a hand in trying to contest his Dad's will. Well, no one was going to have a go at contesting his mother's wishes, he'd see to that.

He now held the majority share in the business. But it wasn't what he'd wanted, to his mind not only alienating him from his sisters but from his brothers as well.

George hadn't batted an eyelid at his brother's good luck, if it could be called that, he still the easy-going soul he'd always been. Dick chafed, but he wasn't concerned about what Dick thought. Dick could think what he liked. What he hadn't reckoned on was the slow animosity that had begun to smoulder, a couple of months going by before it really began to reveal itself – the strained atmosphere, Dick's odd resentment of him coming into the office more often, leaving Frank and George short-handed as he put it, although they had never complained.

'If that's how you feel about them being short-handed,' Charlie finally told him, 'why don't you go out and give them a hand yourself?'

'I've always been here in the office,' was the sulky reply. 'Dad wanted me here. And I don't see why I should leave it now and go out there.'

'And I need someone else outside!' retorted Charlie before thinking.

'Then you go!'

It was all that had been required to start a nasty situation but he was no longer prepared to be spoken down to by Dick. With a certain amount of control of the firm, he had every right to ask him to help out in the yard. It was then that he suddenly realized he was behaving exactly as Dick would, quite unlike his usual self. What was it that someone had once said? Power corrupts – or something like that. He pulled himself up sharply, but his stepbrother wasn't finished.

'Just because Mum favoured you over the rest of us, you think you run the bloody place now. But I bet you did a bit of wheedling on the quiet, getting round her, going to live with her and all that, cunning bugger!'

He ignored the swearing. 'It would've been nice if you'd spent a bit more time with her yourself.' He refrained from adding the lot of you.

'Getting on the right side of her, like you, you mean!' Dick finished angrily. 'She always did have a soft spot for you – too blind to see what you were up to, too blind to see through you, the silly old fool!'

Charlie moved towards him. 'Don't ever talk of my mother like that!'

Dick had leapt up from his chair to face him. 'I'll talk as I please. Nor am I going to have you ordering me about—'

The next thing he knew was a hard slap across the face, jarring his head back on his neck as Charlie leapt at him. Collapsing into his chair, hand to his face he stared up at his assailant, his cheek stinging.

Charlie had stepped back, wondering at himself. He'd never been of a vicious nature but this time had in fact gone to aim a punch, at the very last moment using the flat of his hand instead. But he was fuming, having his mother insulted in her grave.

'I tell you what,' he said, glaring down at his stepbrother. 'If you want to try running this business, then I'll leave you to it. That means you buying and dealing on your own. I won't be here. Just remember, I hold the majority shares and I can sell off this business any time I want.'

'You wouldn't—'

'What do you care? You hardly bother to come in sometimes. With Mum and Dad gone, and the rest of the family wanting to be a part of the business but not prepared to contribute anything, you can have the worry.'

Leaving him gaping, he grabbed his coat from the hook on the back of the office door and stalked out, going to the shed where the other two were busying themselves.

Frank looked up and saw his brother's angry face and the coat he was carrying. 'Where're you off to? What's going on?'

Quickly he told them what had transpired, George standing looking quite blank and bewildered, while Frank's face slowly adopted a deep frown of concern.

'How we going to manage without you here?' he asked.

'I don't know, and I don't much care. This place is slowly going to pot anyway without Dad's hand and I can't deal with the bickering that goes on.'

'What are you going to do?'

Charlie thought for a while. 'I'd like to set up on my own. Not scrap metal. I've had enough of that. I might get a shop of some sort. I don't know what yet.'

It was something that had been on his mind for a while now – a little business of his own, started by him with no one else to interfere.

'What are *we* going to do?' It sounded so pitiful the way Frank said it, that Charlie felt for him.

'Do whatever you want.' He could find no other way to say it, seeing Frank's features crease up with anxiety. But George merely gave a shrug.

He could see George leaving too, in time, maybe to find himself a less harrowing job, working for others probably.

Dick had come out of the office and was standing looking at them. He didn't move even as Charlie went to his car, got in and drove off, leaving behind him a bewildered trio. Maybe none of them believed he really meant it, he thought as he drove towards Stratford. Now that he was away from the place, he hardly believed it himself. Perhaps he had been a bit stupid but pride would not allow him to go back, at least, not yet.

He needed to get away, start a new life. Since losing Mum, Ethel had begun to complain that the house was too big, made so much work, cleaning and dusting, forgetting that she had paid help for that sort of thing.

'I don't feel comfortable with domestics around all the time. I feel I'm always being watched whatever I do. I'm beginning to hate the place.'

'How can you hate it?' he'd asked. 'The way things are with anywhere to live still hard to come by, thousands would love something like this.'

Almost five years since the war finished and still finding somewhere to live was at a premium. New towns springing up outside London, council houses going up at a tremendous rate, yet waiting lists were still long and seemed to be getting ever longer. Ethel didn't know how fortunate she was. Any one of his sisters would kill to get their hands on this house to show off in; large, rambling, just a stone's throw from the city. What it would be worth if sold beggared the imagination. But Ethel wasn't happy.

A thought was taking shape. The rates on this place were exorbitant and if he found somewhere else to live, the money saved could go on paying the rates on a shop. He had no intention of letting his sisters get their hands on this place, not after all they'd said and done. He would simply close the house, forbid any of them taking possession.

A certain satisfaction had stolen over him at the thought. Anyway, should he allow any of them to take over the house it would start another family war, the rest deeming they should have been the ones entitled. No, it was his, had been left to him by Mum. The last thing she would have wanted was for one of her scheming daughters taking possession. He would close it up and buy a house, not too small, with a shop close by. Ethel could work in it with him, just the two of them. She'd like that.

Today he was telling her that he'd had enough of the bickering and ill feeling between him and Dick and had walked out on them all. He was about to reveal his plans but she was staring at him in horror.

'You don't mean you've given up the business? What will happen to us? It's not going broke, is it? We've not lost everything, have we?'

She would have raced on had he not stopped her with a chuckle, reaching out to take hold of her shoulders.

'Of course we're not going broke, darling. Just that I no longer intend working there. I just need a change. What I'd like to do is go it alone, buy a little shop somewhere, say a grocery shop maybe somewhere out of London.'

The words 'somewhere out of London' made Ethel's eyes brighten. 'You mean we'd move away from here?'

'Yes, darling. I'll close up the place and buy us a nice little house. We should find somewhere away from London but not too far. Across the river would be nice.'

'Will you sell this place?' she asked rather too eagerly.

'No.'

He almost shot the word at her. This was where his parents

had been happy. He could never bring himself to betray that which he felt lingered still or insult their memory by selling it. This had been their home and still was.

'I shall just close it up,' he said firmly, quickly adding as he saw her face change, 'but we'll never live in it again if you don't want to. I promise.'

He'd not been near the yard since walking out a few weeks back and at times wondered how they were all getting on. Oddly he missed the place, in a way wishing he'd not been so quick off the mark. Then he'd think of Dick and all his resolve would come flooding back, strong as ever.

He'd seen none of the family over Christmas, not even Frank and Mavis. He and Ethel had spent Christmas Day with her mother and sister and Boxing Day here, just the two of them, quiet and cosy.

This evening, he sat lounging in the sitting room reading the stack of brochures he'd picked up from various estate agents giving details of shop premises and homes around the Plumstead and Erith areas. They wouldn't be too far from the Blackwall Tunnel, making it easy to pop over to keep an eye on this house whenever he could.

It was late. Ethel had already gone to bed. She would be asleep by the time he went up. She'd done this for a long time now, for years in fact. He often wondered if it wasn't a way of escaping the possibility of his getting amorous, he hating to wake her up and no danger of something happening to get her pregnant. That he would never do against her will. Her well-being had always come first, but sometimes he wished . . . but no good wishing.

The brochures idle on his lap he let his mind wander on how it would have been to have a couple of little ones running around his feet. He could almost imagine them. Too late now though. Ethel was thirty-four and though still able to bear children, he couldn't see her coping with a kiddie now.

A weight began to fill his heart as he sat thinking how it could have been. Elsie and Eileen both had a son, Eva and Rosie each had two girls, George had two boys – at least they would carry on the family name. He didn't even bother to consider Dick's kids, but even Frank had a daughter. Quite a crowd! He was the only one without children and that heavy feeling was beginning to flood over him, as it often did when he was alone with his thoughts.

The doorbell startled him. He glanced up at the clock on the mantle-shelf. Half past eleven. Going to the door he opened it a fraction, one foot against it in case whoever it was thought to barge in. But it was Frank. He'd not seen Frank since walking out of the yard that day and had naturally assumed that, offended, he hadn't wanted to see him.

'I walked out today,' Frank said, hardly had he got through the door.

Charlie gazed at him as he paused in the hallway. 'What d'you mean, you walked out?'

'Like you did – I just walked off the job.'

'Why?'

'I had a brush with Richard,' he said, hoarse with emotion, pushing past his brother to make towards the sitting room from which bright light was filtering into the hall. 'Another one!'

'Another one?' Charlie said, following close behind. 'How many of these brushes have you had with him, then?'

It sounded almost sarcastic. Frank personally having a set to with Dick was news, Frank who before would have left him to cope with their arrogant stepbrother, now forced to fight his own battles. Still amazing to hear but he couldn't help feeling that Frank was following his lead, even in this.

Moments later he was confirming it. 'I heard you're planning to start up on your own – buying a grocers shop or something.'

'Where did you hear that?' he asked, surprised.

'Mavis told me. Ethel told her when she was at our place on Monday.'

Ethel had told him she'd popped in to see her sister-in-law though no reason why she shouldn't. The two were still as thick as thieves.

'Are you still thinking of doing it?' Frank furthered.

Charlie nodded reluctantly, already reading his brother's mind with a sense of the inevitable creeping over him. How would Frank fare, facing the working world on his own? None of them had ever had to do that. It was even a bit daunting to him. Taking a deep breath he bowed to the inevitable.

Twenty-Three

Ethel clung to his arm, her face lit up with excitement. 'What do you think, darling? I think it's just right. It's just what we've been looking for.'

They stood gazing at the empty shop centred in a parade of shops. Already having been a grocers it would need little alteration.

'What do you think?' Ethel urged again. 'We've looked at so many places I don't think I could go on looking for much longer.'

He had to agree. They'd been searching for weeks but nothing had come up to what they'd been hoping for. This one at least looked promising, though Erith was a little further from London than he'd have wanted. He'd have preferred to be a little nearer the Blackwall Tunnel, Woolwich maybe but nothing in that area had inspired him and Ethel had been lured by the thoughts of somewhere more open than Woolwich.

Now they stood gazing at this attractive place with the Thames only just down the road. 'We can take walks along the river on a Sunday and half day closing,' she begged.

His reply was non-committal. 'That's if we can find a house nearby.'

A flat, quite roomy, went with the shop but as soon as she heard this her reaction was instant. 'I don't want to live in another flat, love, ever! Perhaps we could rent it out to someone – make a bit more money.'

It was an idea. Having looked the place over he knew this was what he wanted. He'd have been happy enough living upstairs but not Ethel. As luck would have it, having allowed her to drag him off to the estate agents at the end of the parade, they were shown a reasonably priced place two streets away and with her begging, 'Please, darling! Please!' the deal on both premises was settled a few weeks later.

When Charlie and Ethel went there to tea the Sunday previous to tell him, Frank immediately saw himself being left in the lurch. 'You do still want me to come in with you, don't you?' he asked anxiously.

In truth, it wasn't he who wanted Frank to go in with him but Frank who'd asked to go in. So far it had only been word of mouth, nothing signed and sealed, Frank merely taking it for granted.

'I assumed it was all cut and dried,' he could only reply.

'But I'm in Upton Park,' added Frank. 'It'll be a job going over to Erith. I thought you'd be looking for a shop here.' It was like an accusation.

'Ethel wanted to get out of London,' Charlie said quickly.

'But wouldn't she want to be near her mum? Mavis, you wouldn't want to move that far away. Especially since your mum became a widow.'

Mavis nodded in agreement. Her father had died ten months ago leaving her mother rattling around in a three bedroom, bow-windowed terrace house in West Ham. Neither did she get on all that well with her neighbours. Mavis was always there listening to her complaints about them.

'She couldn't possibly leave her behind on her own,' Frank went on, in his anxiety forgetting to eat the piece of cake Mavis had put in front of him. 'And I'm sure your Ethel wouldn't want to leave her mum either. Maybe if we could find somewhere around here, we could—'

'I can drive Ethel over to see her mum any time she wants,' Charlie broke in, hoping his brother might be backing out, 'probably on a Sunday. It's not that far by car. Straight through the Blackwall Tunnel.'

What he really wanted was to work alone for once, not to have to make decisions for others, as he knew he would for Frank. As for Ethel, she was so excited about seeing herself behind the counter of her very own shop that suddenly her mother wasn't an issue any more.

But Frank was thinking rapidly. 'Ethel said there was a flat above the shop. She said you were going to let it out and I was wondering . . .'

He let his words fall away but his eyes were trained on his brother like a dog pleading to be taken for a walk. Now he turned to Mavis. 'I know your mother hates that place of hers since she lost your dad.'

His round face grew bright with anticipation as he looked

back at his brother. 'If Mavis and her mum agree, maybe her mum could rent it.'

Filled now with enthusiasm he turned to Mavis again. 'What do you think, love? She's got no ties here and if we went to live over the other side she'd be all on her own.'

'I could speak to her,' Mavis said, her own expression brightening while Charlie watched in growing dismay as Frank went on.

'We'd soon give up renting this place. I've got enough for a mortgage. Houses must be cheaper that side of the river and easier to get. I know you still can't get a council house for love or money but we'd be buying!'

'So long as it don't take *all* our savings,' answered Mavis, the pair of them seeming to have forgotten the other two. 'But I think Mum would be over the moon to get out of her place, have a little flat of her own – she'd love it, I'm sure. I'll go round first thing tomorrow and talk to her.'

She seemed suddenly to realize that they still had guests. 'So that's what we'll do. Just give me a day or two, Charlie, to sort things out.'

Frank said no more, merely sitting back in a haze of relief. Charlie too sat in silence with his own thoughts, as Ethel and Mavis could hardly conceal the excitement of their future.

Things were going well despite his misgivings at having his brother go in with him. The cash he'd put in, though not as much as he'd have liked, was helpful and if they should one day sell the shop Frank would only get as much as he put in. It also gave Charlie a bigger say in what they'd do.

He was pleased too with the place he and Ethel had settled upon; quite roomy but not too spacious like the Stratford house, which pleased her, and it did him good to see her happily planning the redecoration of the entire house with new carpets and curtains, even new furniture.

'I don't want anything from that place,' she said flatly. It hurt a little, the way she called it *that place* but he said nothing, only too glad to see her content.

The outlay on new furniture was an expense he hadn't counted on, of course, but the shop began to do better than he had dared hope from the word go. There was also the income from the flat – not as much as he might have got from an outsider but helpful.

Soon they were also starting up a small delivery round to the local elderly who were unable to get out easily, for a little extra charge and no need for the expense of a van.

It was Frank's job to do the rounds using a pushbike with a large basket on the front to carry things like eggs, sugar, butter, milk and the like. Frank had sold his car to help towards the house he'd bought. He could have rented but Mavis insisted on buying. Charlie still had his car so as to go over to Stratford to keep an eye on the house and attend his Friday Masonic lodge. Often of a Sunday he and Ethel would see her mother or sometimes visit the mates he'd kept up with from his earlier years, especially his oldest friend, Tom and Win Wilmott, now living at West Malling, not all that far away.

The shop was doing well. He was working hard, money was rolling in, both he and Frank benefiting well from it. Ethel and Mavis would go up to London to window shop and come back excited with the clothes they had bought. He didn't mind. It was good to see Ethel so happy.

Summer had seen him and Frank run off their feet, especially when a small greengrocer not far away closed down, the man retiring, and they began selling root vegetables in the shop. Potatoes washed clean of mud, bagged up in five pound bags, the same with carrots and parsnips, and delivered to customers should they want that service, had proved a success. Frank was still using the pushbike, not wanting to muck up the new car he'd bought with enough money to do so. It was good to see them both doing so well.

Now in late autumn, the till wasn't looking as full as it had been yet trade hadn't diminished. It was a puzzle but he had little time to dwell on it, his mind more taken with how things were going with the old firm with only Dick and George there to manage it.

Occasionally he'd hear from George complaining that Dick was hardly ever there, how he would come in a bit late because of the winter weather to find the gates still locked.

'To tell the truth,' he wrote as the year began to turn, 'I'm just about fed up with the whole thing and Dick is talking about moving out into the country, going back to that place where he evacuated his family during the war. Says he's fed up with London. If he leaves, what's going to happen to the firm? I said to him I can't carry on, not on my own. He said he wants to sell his shares. If he does that where do I stand?'

It was worrying. It meant him constantly having to run over there to sort things out, often allowing little time in the shop, forcing him to let Frank take charge. To his surprise Frank turned out to be running it quite well, even if the money coming in seemed a little less these days.

But reading George's letters, brought thoughts stirring in Charlie's mind. The firm had had its day. He himself had very little interest in it. Frank certainly hadn't and nor had the other two by the sound of it. There was only one solution – the business would have to go, it was sad, but one couldn't continue hanging on to sentimental memories. What he'd do would be to buy his brothers out. He'd always been thrifty. There was enough funds in the bank to buy their shares from them and they'd probably be well relieved to have the money in their pockets, rather than tied up in a failing business.

It hadn't taken long. It was now all his to do what he wanted with. What he wanted was to sell it. But he reckoned without the rest of the family.

'Sell it! You mean you want to sell it? You mean Dad's business – you want to sell it?' Elsie blared at him, idiotically repeating herself over and over in her anger when she heard.

Her and Vic having driven all the way over to Erith, hardly had she entered the house, refusing even the offer of a cup of tea, she now stood in the centre of his living room, Vic hovering behind her nodding vigorously in agreement to every syllable she uttered, while on the settee, her small son Victor sat quiet and subdued by her raised voice.

'It would have been decent to have given the family some idea of what you intended to do. Sell Dad's business? How you can disregard his memory beats me! No, it's money, money, money! All you've ever been interested in. Greed, that's what it is!'

So far he had said little except to voice surprise at seeing her turn up. It was two years since he came here to live and in all that time she'd not once come to see him.

Rosie had been the only one to visit, a cordial Sunday afternoon, she and Arthur and their two little daughters. She'd kissed his cheek as she left, Arthur shaking his hand, a little reluctantly he'd felt, she thanking him as he gave the two little girls two half-a-crowns each, she protesting that he shouldn't have given them all that much, but pleased anyway. Five shillings each would keep them in knickers as well as sweets for a couple of weeks.

Eileen hadn't come over. She and Fred weren't all that well off on their smallholding, but she wrote quite often; friendly letters, all about how they were getting on and how her son Raymond was doing. Charlie loved hearing about his nieces and nephews, even though it always raised a lump in his throat that he alone was still without children.

Eva, of course, had never visited. He expected she never would. A cold fish, something of a snob like her husband, and Charlie didn't have to guess that she looked down on him as having come down in the world, a mere shopkeeper, forgetting that he could actually afford to buy his brothers out. Now here stood Elsie, ranting and raving about disloyalty and greed.

'So what do you expect me to do?' he asked curtly.

She hardly noticed the sarcasm. 'What I thought you would do was to have given us a chance to air our views on what happens to Dad's business.'

'Such as?'

'Giving us fair warning about what you'd intended doing with the firm, not even allowing us to have a say in it.'

'But it's not yours. It belongs to us four. We've worked there, put money into it, kept it going, you didn't want to have any hand in it at all.'

'Nor were we given a chance to.'

'But you've never wanted anything to do with it as I recall,' he went on. 'And now you do?'

'I should think we deserve to be included,' Elsie said through tight lips, 'so as to keep the firm going in memory of Mum and Dad.'

He made a play of thinking for a minute while she and Vic watched in anticipation. When he spoke his words were steady and friendly. 'If that's how you feel, then if Vic puts in some time coming to the yard and getting stuck in, perhaps we can keep it going.'

He looked directly at Vic. 'Maybe you and the other three can all come and each put some time in. That would help.' He was calling Elsie's bluff and glowed inwardly and wickedly to hear her and Vic draw in their breath.

'I – I can't do that,' Vic stuttered.

'No, he can't! He's got his own six-day-a-week job. So have the others. They're all working,' echoed Elsie.

There was a long pause while Charlie once again made himself look thoughtful. Then, as if he'd had a brilliant idea, he looked at his sister.

'I tell you what – if you really want to have a say in the firm, what I could do is from time to time bring a lorry load of scrap metal, that factory stuff that comes in regularly, and dump it on your front lawn so Vic can sort it out and dispose of it without having to come all that way to Canning Town. That might be more convenient for you, Vic.'

The appalled look on their faces was a tonic, the pair of them stunned rigid. Elsie was the first to break the silence.

'You can't do that! No, I can't have that!'

He could see her mind working, the thoughts of her beautifully tended front garden ruined by piles of metal and mounds of junk, what would the neighbours say?

'No, I won't have that!' she almost squealed, stepping back from him.

He'd never had visitors vacate his home so quick. Not even the offer of a cup of tea taken up, young Victor hauled off the sofa almost by the scruff of his little neck and trundled out of the door, Elsie huffing and puffing, 'I've never heard the like!' Vic leading the way to his car fast as he could go, she depositing her son on the back seat to scramble in beside her husband, the car speeding off without a wave from either of them. Following that visit no more interest in the business was ever advanced by any of the sisters.

George was over the moon with the money from his brother and later wrote him a long, badly worded letter of gratitude saying he'd got a job as a bus driver for the London Transport.

It suited him, regular hours, regular pay, extra for overtime, just to drive from one bus stop to another until breaking off time; making friends in the depot – George made friends easily – and just letting life drift by, right up George's alley.

Dick hadn't even said thank you to him for having bought him out, leaving him with money in his pocket. There hadn't even been a letter of acknowledgement, apart from the legal ones.

The last Charlie heard was a letter from Eileen saying he'd moved out of London and bought a house somewhere near where he had evacuated himself and his family during the war, but that she didn't have his new address. It was the last Charlie ever heard of him.

Twenty-Four

More unrest from Elsie, what else did he expect? It was what he'd been anticipating for quite a while, she maintaining that as he had vacated their parents' house, leaving it empty and uncared for, it should be handed over to one of them rather than being allowed go to rack and ruin.

But it seemed that this time she was alone in her cussedness. Rosie and Eileen were not interested. Living in the country they wanted nothing to do with London – the old sores were in the past and they'd had enough of paying out for some solicitor to chase yet another pie-in-the-sky idea.

Charlie didn't even bother to reply to her. It was his house. He'd keep it or sell it as he felt fit and he had no intention of selling, ever. Besides he had enough to think about running his grocer shop.

Something else that had come to the fore was an idea of putting to good use what he'd learnt from night school all those years ago. Lately he'd become intrigued by accounts in the *Financial Times* of Australian mining for minerals and metals. Soon he was taking careful note of what was coming out of the ground. What he read delighted him. With careful speculation the odds could be good, provided he knew what he was doing, and he was sure he did. He had enough money behind him to take a risk. Dad used to dabble on the stock exchange quite successfully, so why shouldn't he?

Through his bank, he bought his first securities in a mining company that looked promising and every day followed the company's progress. Within a few months they had doubled his investment. Taking a gamble, he told his bank to hang on. A few weeks later the shares had tripled their value and he sold at a profit. It seemed not only was luck on his side, he apparently knew what he was doing.

But he wasn't prepared to rush headlong into any risk taking. But it was enjoyable studying what mining companies were up to and he came to realize, when some time later a simple change of a director of one company sent one of his investments soaring, that it had as much to do with politics as with getting minerals out of the ground.

He said nothing to Frank. His investment affairs were quite separate from what the shop brought in, which just lately began to seem peanuts compared to what he was making from the stock market. Mavis though had become curious about how many nice new outfits Ethel possessed and the new furniture recently bought for their house, and he and Ethel going just a little too often to London to a show or pictures on the odd Saturday night.

Obviously she'd spoken of it with Frank who remarked, 'I don't know how you afford to lay out on them sort of things, Charlie. Wish I could.'

And rather than be pleased when in May Charlie took them all up to the 1951 Festival of Britain, closing the shop all day that Thursday, paying for everything, Frank, frowning at every penny spent, whispered to Mavis when they were on their own for a moment: 'God knows where he's getting all the money from. The shop's not bringing in that much.'

Charlie thought so too when later Mavis told Ethel about what Frank had said, she repeated it to him. In fact, it had set him wondering lately that while custom seemed as good as ever, the equivalent in money wasn't exactly matching it, as he could see from a past few stocktakes.

The discrepancy wasn't that alarming but it was puzzling. There could have been several reasons: a regular pilferer at work, or Frank's lamentable book keeping, or the IOUs Frank's mother-in-law was wont to leave in the till not being honoured until several weeks later.

He disliked IOUs but to say so would cause ill feeling, so he let it go. But that couldn't account for the drop in takings.

The bewildering part was that as the year went by the loss stayed relatively the same and a suspicion began to arise in him which he was unwilling to entertain. Was Frank fiddling? But of course not, why should he? He and Mavis hardly ever went out living it up, much less buy any luxuries. It couldn't be anything to do with Frank. But something wasn't right. Although the shop was paying its way, the monthly stocktakes never seemed to balance with the takings. It wasn't huge and hardly ever changed, but always this worrying regular discrepancy. He told himself he was being paranoid. They were doing well, so why get all riled up about it all? But it was puzzling.

As spring came he felt he needed to share his concern with someone. He could only think of Ethel. He waited until they had closed up for the evening, then in the quietness of their living room he told her how he felt.

She looked at him as if he had gone off his head. 'Frank would never do anything like that. Pilfering, your own brother, he put his own money in the shop.' She gave a little laugh. 'Oh Charlie! It'd be like robbing himself!'

He remained unsmiling. 'Maybe not him, but what about his wife?'

'Mavis? We're friends.'

As if that made it all right! 'Well maybe not her, but her mother could be helping herself to a few things and not paying for them.'

Ethel ceased to laugh. 'Now stop it, Charlie! You can't go accusing your own family just because you and Frank can't balance the books properly. That's just wicked and I'm not having that. If Mavis knew what you were thinking, she'd have fifty fits and never speak to us again! Anyway, the shop belongs to both of us so what's so bad about taking what we need?'

He realized he'd aired his thoughts a bit too openly as Ethel continued to gaze at him.

'And as for Mavis's mother,' she went on, 'we know she puts the occasional note in the till if she's short of money and pays what she owes later when she gets her pension. How can you stop her doing that? She's an old lady.'

Even old ladies could be crafty, came the thought. But he would keep a closer eye on things from now on, even though he felt a cad doing so. But he knew he was trapped. The last thing he wanted was trouble between him and Frank. There was enough bad blood between them and the rest of the family as it was.

Even so, throughout summer and autumn, stocktaking discrepancies became more pronounced, not as to be starkly noticeable but he was now sure he knew what was causing it, though there was no way to prove it. Then around the end of

January, arriving home a little early from a lodge meeting, there came a whim to stop by the shop even though it was closed. Going in by the side door, as usual, he was surprised to find Frank still here. He was behind the counter removing bits of paper from the till into a rubbish bag.

Seeing him standing there in the doorway, Frank shot upright, eyes wide and staring, his mouth dropping open, alarm on his face for a split second before relaxing into a grin of relief, it seemed, as Charlie came forward.

'Oh, it's you! I – I thought we had burglars.'

'No,' said Charlie. 'It's me. I thought you'd have gone home by now.'

'Oh, yes . . . er . . . we've been upstairs just chatting to Mavis's mum. Mavis went home while I made her fire up to keep her nice and warm and got more coal in for her. It's so cold outside. Thought while I'm at it I'd do a bit of clearing up before going home. Save doing it tomorrow morning.'

'I see,' said Charlie. 'Well, don't worry, I'll finish off.'

'No, it's all right, Chas. I can do it while I'm here. Thought I'd just burn this bit of rubbish in the yard before I go home.'

'Not this time of night, Frank. In case the neighbours call out the fire brigade!' he added making a joke of it. 'You pop off.'

He saw his brother nibble his lip. 'OK then, I'll just stick this bit of rubbish outside before I go – might as well keep the place tidy.'

Frank had never been tidy in his life, but Charlie watched him take the bag outside, telling him he'd close up behind him. He saw Frank hesitate but after giving a submissive shrug, he said goodnight and left.

He waited until he was sure Frank had truly left before going out into the yard. A ten minute search of the rubbish bin, all the time feeling like a snoop and hoping not to find what he was seeking, he discovered, screwed into tight balls, five IOUs, three signed in Mavis's mother's childlike hand and two by Mavis herself, but none countersigned as having been paid. Worse was that two of them were for quite substantial sums, one of them Mavis, the other her mother.

It wasn't so much that which hurt but the underhandedness of it. He knew he should let Frank know he was aware of what was going on, but he knew he wouldn't. He would go on nursing the hurt to himself fearing hostility, ill feelings, maybe he and Frank never speaking to each other ever again. There seemed no choice but to be around when Mrs Gardner came down to do her bit of shopping. It wasn't easy. He hated this playing detective on his own family.

Over the next two weeks not one IOU appeared in the till. But rather than ease his mind it only emphasized what was going on when he wasn't there. It would need a good few weeks of trying to look innocuous to prove it.

He said nothing to Ethel. She'd only look horrified and might even tell Mavis. She could be silly enough to do that and it would really finish things. He dreaded to think how she would react when the truth did come out, as it would eventually. It would wound her deeply, he knew.

He loathed the prospect of telling her but by the Wednesday other things had taken over, that morning's newspapers reporting of King George having passed peacefully away in his sleep; the nation plunged into deep mourning, places of entertainment closed, the BBC transmitting the solemnest of music and only a few snippets of news that were deemed necessary. Not a time to go raising Cain over his own paltry concerns.

It lasted over a week until the state funeral that following Friday, newspapers showing the sad pictures of the three queens heavily veiled, in mourning; Elizabeth the widow, Mary the mother and Elizabeth the daughter, now Queen Elizabeth II.

Saturday, the country had returned to normal and Ethel and Mavis went shopping on their full day off together. Both helped in the shop, Ethel three mornings a week and Mavis for two afternoons. The rest of the time, Frank would be behind the counter, Charlie less so, more often attending to the paperwork, seeing goods in or talking to reps, but rather he than Frank doing it.

Frank was honest enough on his own account, if a bit slapdash, but it left him wondering if Frank wasn't being placed in an awkward situation by his wife and her mother. In a way it was the same dilemma he was in. And if it made Frank equally at fault, maybe he too was at fault, turning a blind eye to what was going on, trying hard to avoid a nasty outcome.

Lately a lot of his time was being taken up studying the Australian mining companies and the minerals coming out of the ground. It was going very well for him, occupying his mind maybe too much. Then there was the ongoing business of the sale of his father's old firm still distracting him.

Another distraction was Mavis's little daughter Veronica. She'd bring her with her when she was on the counter leaving her with her grandmother. But Mrs Gardner liked her afternoon nap and the child would wander downstairs to the store room where Charlie would delight in entertaining her.

'I hope she's not being a trouble,' Mavis would say, but he was only too glad to have her there. She took the place of the child he'd never had. Having Veronica around filled that gap; making up stories for her, playing simple little games, drawing pictures, giving her sweets. She adored him as much as he adored her.

It was probable that his absence in the shop at these times gave her mother ample time to help herself to whatever she fancied. He knew she'd delved into the biscuits by the crumbs left behind on the counter, snacked on ice creams, chocolate and the odd cake. She always brought a shopping bag with her, the zip done up when she left and suspiciously bulging. But how could he challenge her to open the bag for him without making what he suspected so obvious?

With no one to confide in it weighed heavily on him, unable even to tell Ethel. The last time, she had defended her sister-in-law to the hilt and saw Frank as a darling. And of course he was – not a spiteful bone in his body, just that he was so easily led. And how could he accuse his wife and her mother to his face and not make an enemy of him? One way out would be to get rid of the shop and not have to declare what had been going on. But what reason could he give? It was doing moderately well, even more so if this other thing wasn't going on.

Though it would never make them rich, he wasn't exactly hard up for cash – Dad's scrap-metal business had eventually sold at a decent profit, which was all his, he having bought out his brothers.

Neither Frank nor George had grumbled, though his sisters had no doubt complained that he'd probably well feathered his own nest with not one penny coming their way. Nothing was said but he hardly heard from them, at least not Eva and Elsie. He'd visited Rosie and Eileen a few times, both of whom were happy to welcome him and had never mentioned Dad's business having been sold, but they had never come over to see him or the shop.

Coming to Erith had in fact cut him and Ethel off from quite a few people they'd known in earlier years. At first they'd kept up with them but it slowly fell away, except for one couple he'd known from their early teens, Tom Wilmott and his wife Winnie living here in Kent. It was Winnie, a lovely lady, in whom he finally confided about the problem of the IOUs.

'If I were you,' she'd said after careful thought, 'If I found I couldn't do anything about it I would try and look on it as part of the overheads. You'll feel easier that way.'

Good advice but one he couldn't take with more screwed up IOUs finding their way into the waste bin outside the back door. Rifling through it after closing – not a pleasant job – he kept asking himself why he should be creating so much unrest for himself, and that he should take Winnie's advice and forget all about it, but he never could.

As she said when he told her and Tom about the moderate success he was having on the stock market: 'Then why make enemies over a few light fingers? You're enjoying yourself playing the market, studying all those essays on the ore you say these Australian mining companies are bringing out of the ground. Why make a burden for yourself for some petty-fogging little shop?'

And he had to agree. It was just that it went against the grain being diddled. It *was* getting worse and he was weary of it, and of the shop. If only he could find a way to close it down, but what excuse could he give?

The excuse came just after the New Year of 1955 – a shop opening up just down the road, more a self-service store, a great deal larger than his and selling not only groceries but vegetables, meat, household goods and almost everything else. Before long customers were drifting away to the new store, first out of curiosity then as regular customers, happy with this mode of helping oneself to goods straight off the shelves, instead of waiting to be served while the shop owner and the customers gossiped.

It was the excuse he'd been looking for, a unique opportunity to say that they were losing far too much trade to keep going. He could get away from the constant frustration of being taken for a fool by Frank's womenfolk.

He spent half the summer mulling it over. He'd had enough worrying about it, the same old routine tied to opening times, his social life sacrificed for it. It was time to go, and whatever Frank thought on it, too bad. Frank would have to make his own life. He wouldn't be caught again. But he would have to find something in which Frank would not instantly assume he could come in with him.

That August he took Ethel on a holiday to Switzerland, leaving Frank in charge. Returning home on the Saturday he found the shop virtually empty of customers and according to Frank it had been like this the whole couple of weeks they'd been away.

'It's that blooming self-service place doing it,' was his answer.

Charlie had to admit to agreeing. Yet, though the takings were not up, the stock appeared mysteriously to be well down.

'I didn't think it worth reordering the way things were going,' Frank said hastily when asked about it.

Sprang the thought, 'No, because your lot have been ransacking the place.' But he kept it to himself because he now had the motive he'd been looking for.

'We're not doing at all well,' he told Frank as summer waned. 'I think at this rate we're going to have to call it a day.'

Frank's face was a picture of alarm. 'We can't! What will we do?'

'We have to face it, the shop's not paying. Go on like this and we'll be broke in no time. It's better to pull out while the going's good, put it up for sale. We should get a decent price. It's in a prime position and it doesn't have to stay a grocer shop. And the two of us would split the money evenly between us,' anything to get Frank out of his hair.

He saw Frank's eyes light up, no doubt a better deal than he had expected, but almost immediately the gleam faded. 'What about Mavis's mother? Where would she go?'

He hadn't thought about her. 'She's a sitting tenant. Maybe she can stay on.'

Dismay showed on Frank's face. 'We couldn't leave her here

on her own. I think Mavis would want to go back to live in
Essex. We couldn't leave her mum behind.'

'Then take her with you.'

He watched Frank gnaw at his lip, faced with a dilemma what
to do with his mother-in-law once back there.

'I'll talk to Mavis,' he said glumly after a while, realizing that
selling up was now inevitable. Yet his glumness wasn't all that
dark. It might even have been a relief to him, no longer bound
to covering up for his womenfolk's days of endless freebies, and
Charlie felt for him.

Twenty-Five

He couldn't wait to be out of it. But Ethel was uneasy, only able to see her world falling apart around her.

She greeted him as he came home to tell her that the estate agents had just told him of someone who might be interested in buying the shop. 'But what are you going to do now?' she asked anxiously.

'Start to take it easy for a bit,' he said, putting the shop keys on the hall table.

'But you're going to have no income unless you start thinking about what you intend to do. And what about this house, will we still be able to afford to keep it?'

'Of course we can afford to!' he laughed. 'I don't *have* to work. I'm doing all right on the stock market and—'

'But that's gambling!' she broke in, panic rising in her eyes.

'Not gambling, darling.' He continued to smile. 'Investing, it's called investing.'

'Whatever it's called, you can't rely on that. What if things go bust? Then what will you do?'

The fear in her tone made him stop and think. She was right. He was doing well in that direction but what if his good fortune was to tumble down around him. It could happen. He'd been so sure of himself – too sure, even to dibbing into money from the sale of the scrap metal business to play the market. What if one of those mining companies should fail? Investments could become worthless almost overnight, an investor could lose everything in one go for all sorts of causes. It had happened back in 1929. Perhaps it was time to give thought to what he was doing and to what he was going to do.

The last thing he wanted was to move back into London. There was still the house in Stratford, he still went back there from time to time to check on it and see it was still in good order. It was beginning to smell musty and needed to be lived in but Ethel wouldn't want to move back there. And what could he do in London – another shop? He didn't much care for that.

He knew about metal – could become a scrap metal merchant again. He didn't much care for that either. Also Ethel had become quite besotted by the open air. The Thames flowing by just down the road, she enjoyed their taking a stroll on a Sunday afternoon or else a car ride into the countryside, virtually a stone's throw away. It was that last thought that gave him a sudden idea.

'What do you say we move to the coast?' he shot at her.

Who cared if they moved further out? These last few years he'd begun to lose touch with their old friends. And his family didn't matter. Tom and Win he still saw, and from here a move to the coast wasn't all that far from them by car, not like crossing the river to get out of London, queuing at the Blackwall Tunnel. Just get in the car and go!

Ethel looked startled at the suddenness of the suggestion but her eyes had lit up. 'The coast?' she cried. 'Where? What coast? When?'

'Whenever you like, darling. Where ever you like. Margate? Ramsgate?'

'No, I'd prefer the south coast. It's warmer. Let's say somewhere near Brighton or Hove. Oh, Charlie! I'd love the south coast.'

As if it was already cut and dried.

The shop successfully sold to become a flower shop, a change of use going through unopposed to the new owner's delight, the house put up for sale and went to the first buyer, luck seeming to follow in their footsteps. But it was late autumn before everything could be finally concluded.

Frank and Mavis went back to Essex, taking out a mortgage on a house in Upminster, her mother finding herself a little flat nearby. Frank got himself a job as a caretaker at a local hospital.

'What are you going to do about the house in Stratford?' he asked Charlie just before they moved off.

'I'm keeping it,' Charlie told him flatly, relieved to see Frank nod in agreement.

Elsie getting to hear about the closure of the shop had written to him saying it wouldn't hurt to sell their parents' house as well. 'If you're not going to live in it,' she wrote, 'what's the good of keeping it? It could do us all some good.' As if she expected a share in the proceeds.

But he couldn't bring himself to dispose of it, though it meant often having to drive to London to air it and make sure it remained in good order.

'I think you're being quite selfish,' Elsie wrote back when he told her he wasn't prepared to sell, 'hanging on to the place like some magpie with a string of shiny beads. It's doing exactly nothing sitting there and Eva agrees with me that it should be sold and the money divided between everyone.'

He ignored the letter.

Eileen wrote too saying that she supposed it was his business what he did with his own property, but her Fred was moaning about how he could have done with a bit of cash to mend the roof of their bungalow.

'The water comes pouring through into the kitchen every time it rains,' she wrote. 'We have to put buckets underneath. Fred says he dreads to think what it'll be like once winter comes. But he needs what money we've got to keep the smallholding going. We have to work on a budget these days.'

He certainly wasn't going to get rid of what had been Mum and Dad's home just to finance Fred, but he sent him and Eileen a cheque for quite a substantial amount from his own bank account for the roof to be mended and a little more beside. It wasn't her fault she'd married a loser.

The trouble was that when Rosie's husband got to hear about it, it came to Charlie's ears that he had been speaking to Elsie's husband and they'd both agreed that it was, 'All right for some!'

He decided never again to fall into the trap of giving to one giving to all, but Eileen had always been special – a sweet girl who deserved a better partner than the one she had and he didn't regret giving to her. There was nothing wrong with Rosie either, but he couldn't go on handing out to this one and that.

While they waited for the sale of their house to be completed, he and Ethel took several trips down to Sussex to look around for something suitable but nothing seemed quite what he wanted.

He was beginning to feel despondent as he and Ethel now sat in the car with a wind-driven November rain hitting the windscreen and the side windows, gazing across the lane at the FOR SALE notice.

For a long time he'd been toying with finding some land and maybe building a nice house on it. The Stratford house was surrounded by quite a bit of ground but being in London it was still hemmed in by other houses. The Erith house had had a decent size garden and with the countryside on their doorstep so to speak, he'd developed a liking for the open air. Ethel felt the same but this place he was looking at felt like too much open air.

Just beyond the notice across the lane there stood a shoddy-looking bungalow and behind it some six acres of now bare fields rising up to a low hill. Was this what he wanted? He wasn't at all sure, but Ethel had squealed in delight as they slowly pulled up to stare at the place.

'It's lovely!' she breathed now. 'Imagine what it would look like on a warm sunny day, and the sea is only just over that hill. If we get building permission we could make a lovely place out of that bungalow.'

The place was going for a relatively small sum, which Charlie tried to ignore as pointing towards something possibly being wrong with the place while he haggled on the purchase, while wondering what on earth he would do with it other than use it as the smallholding he'd planned to have.

He had to admit that by the time he'd concluded the deal his mind was already working on what he intended to do with it. He'd made enquiries into its previous use, being told that for the most part it had been a chicken farm with some arable land on which the previous owner had grown a few vegetables for the local market. That would do him.

Ethel would have her open air and there was a little village hall down the road that catered for a few women's groups which she could join. A dance was held there now and again and there was the pub of course – more social life than he had first thought.

His time would be taken up learning all about rearing of chickens and growing of vegetables. The rest of the time he'd spend going up to London to keep an eye on his Stratford house and attending lodge meetings. He'd also have time to study the stock market more fully. If he remained lucky there'd be no need to worry too much about making a living here.

Within months the place was theirs. By June and July the work of tilling some of the land and sowing seed was reaping benefits. They also had quite a few poultry with the old chicken sheds renovated and weatherproofed. He'd had workmen in to extend the bungalow and smarten it up considerably. Ethel had got herself on the WI committee and had made some friends. He too found himself getting along with locals, finally having lost their wariness of someone down from London.

As the following year warmed up, he and Ethel took long walks to Beachy Head and its lighthouse far below the chalk cliffs. Sometimes they'd drive to Brighton and wander the narrow Lanes or visit the Pavilion, or they'd go into Eastbourne, or take a drive to Ashdown Forest, going through all the pretty little villages. Other times they'd visit old castles – Hurstmonceux, Pevensy or Lewes. He'd never known such freedom. As a youngster working for his father, then after his death managing the business, then the shop claiming almost every hour he had, he'd had little time for himself. Now he had.

Making a living from this smallholding was not all that crucial either, though to his surprise he was doing well; doing well too with stocks and shares, apart from a brief blip, losing around five thousand pounds in one go on a British brick company that looked good at the time, only to go suddenly bust. But what he was realizing from Australian shares more than compensated that rather alarming setback, he vowing never again to invest in anything other than Australian minerals.

He soon settled into an enjoyable life, doing just what he wanted. He was happy enough and so was Ethel, always lively, energetic, a different woman, other than sex.

It came as a shock then when over Christmas dinner which he had helped to cook, she saying she felt tired and a little under the weather, she putting her knife and fork down beside her plate, the meal hardly touched.

'What's the matter?'

She shook her head. 'I don't feel all that hungry.'

She gave him a wan smile as he frowned, then as he continued to look at her, bewildered, tears began to fill her eyes.

'It's nothing. I've not been feeling quite right for days. I don't know why, but . . . well . . . one of my thing-me-bobs feels odd.'

She touched her right breast with the tip of a middle finger, as if the mere action was not a nice thing to be doing in front of him.

'How do you mean?' he asked. She hated anything to do with the body as he had known to his disadvantage since they'd first married.

'Just odd, achy,' she replied. 'A sort of muscular pain when I touch it, as if I've been in a draught.'

'Like a backache?'

'I suppose so. The wind has been cold and I hung up some washing outside a few days ago when it was blowing. I must have caught it then.'

'Which one of your breasts?' he asked, seeing her frown at the word but she answered frankly enough.

'The right one. Either it was the way the wind was blowing when I hung out the washing or else I strained myself using the washing machine.'

He'd bought it when they'd first come to live here – one with a handle going down into the suds needing to be turned by hand. New ones had come out that did it automatically – top loaders. He ought to get her one of those, save all that work. They'd go out next week and buy one.

'It's not much,' she was saying, 'but it's miserable.'

'Well, try and finish your dinner after having cooked it. Afterwards, I'll rub some embrocation into it for you.'

'No, I can do it myself!' He knew that guarded tone of hers. Whenever he went to caress her after whispering goodnight, he would hear that same tone. 'It's late, Charlie,' or 'I need to get up early tomorrow, love,' or just an emphatic, 'Goodnight, darling.'

'If you want,' he said now. 'But it might be a bit awkward trying to do it yourself.'

'I'll manage.' She said, and giving up he let it go at that.

Twenty-Six

February and the strange pain was still there, not all that bad, which was maybe why it had been ignored, still in one spot but sometimes he'd notice her wince if anything touched it. It wasn't right.

'I think we should go and see the doctor,' he'd suggested once or twice but each time Ethel's eyes would take on a look of alarm.

'I hate doctors! It'll go away once the weather gets better,' she told him sharply. 'These muscular pains can take an awful long time to go and I don't need a doctor to tell me that!'

He couldn't remember a time when she'd been to see a doctor. She had always enjoyed good health, apart from the odd cold which she would nurse herself and in a couple of days was fine again. A couple of years ago she'd gone down with that Asian flu which had laid so many low, but again insisted on nursing herself. Within a week she was up and back to normal. But this pain of hers had a different feel to it.

'I still think we ought to pay him a visit,' he insisted. Doctor Harris was in Newhaven, a very good man whom Charlie had signed on with the time a metal fence he'd been trying to shift had fallen on his foot, cutting it quite badly. Doctor Harris had been their practitioner ever since. Quite a way to go for one but it was seldom that they ever had to.

'You ought to be looked at,' he went on, but she refused absolutely.

It was a month later when the pain suddenly worsened, so much that she was left crying with it. And this time he bundled her into the car and against all her protests drove her into Newhaven. After listening to what he had to say, Doctor Harris frowned and said he needed to examine her, that she would have to undress and Charlie should wait outside.

Already on the verge of wanting to run out, Ethel turned to him in panic, her trembling voice pleading, 'Charlie! Please stay here! Don't go!'

'I have to, love,' he told her helplessly.

She had never undressed in front of him in all their married
life and now she was being required to expose her body to a
complete stranger, albeit a doctor. A picture of the young girl he'd
met all those years ago flashed through his head, audaciously standing
up in a bathing suit among a mixed crowd of friends on that beach.
She'd looked so slim, slim and frail but full of life, and with a way
of carrying herself that had set his heart racing, and when she had
turned and smiled at him, it had raced even more.

Letting his eyes fall away from hers, he hurried out, ashamed
for his lack of support, for not putting up an argument, trying
to find comfort in telling himself that she'd have been even more
embarrassed had he stayed.

Called back after having sat outside for nearly half an hour,
he found her seated on the chair by the doctor's desk.

She looked up at him as he entered but didn't return his smile
and looked immediately away, her posture stiff.

He was aware of the doctor speaking and turned his attention
to him.

'I am sending your wife for a hospital examination where they
can go more deeply into your wife's condition,' he was saying. 'I
deem the need to be quite urgent.'

'What's wrong with her?' Charlie asked and found himself
being immediately led from the room.

Outside, the doctor explained, 'I have to tell you I suspect a
breast cancer. I've not told her that, only that there is a lump on
her right breast that needs investigating, no more than that. She
strikes me as the sort of woman who might panic. But I must
tell you that it looks quite serious. She will need to go into
hospital for treatment.'

'Hospitals frighten her,' Charlie said lamely, as if that mattered.

The doctor looked a little cross, his tone sharpening. 'Well,
she'll have to overcome her fear and you will have to help her
to overcome it. When did she first feel the lump?'

'She's never felt a lump.'

'Oh, come!' the voice was impatient. 'When she bathes, washes
her breasts, when you touch her, surely you must have felt that
something wasn't right?'

The question was like a piece of his flesh being ripped

out. 'She doesn't touch herself, well, not in front of me, and she's never let me . . .'

He hesitated and the man put a hand on his forearm. 'I understand. It happens. However, the fact remains I will be sending her to hospital.'

'I can't go to hospital! I can't!'

She'd almost collapsed beside him in the car, still standing idle outside the surgery, her voice as near a cry of distress as he had ever heard. He sat staring through the windscreen at nothing in particular, the engine still not switched on. 'You really should go, Ethel. You'll get proper treatment there.'

How could he tell her what Doctor Harris had told him, terrifying her out of her wits? It was terrifying him. He just didn't know what to say to her. She hadn't answered him and all he could do was switch on the engine and drive home.

Within days a letter arrived from the hospital. Seeing the distinctive logo Ethel refused to open it, so he did. It was an appointment to attend that Friday, to bring nightclothes and toiletries for a short stay while the examination was taking place.

'I'm not going,' she said with some force, quite unlike her.

'You have to, they've set a date.'

'I *don't* have to! And they can't make me.'

Other than dragging her there, there was nothing he could do to make her see that this was for her own good. So against his better judgement he secretly replied with an excuse that she wasn't very well and couldn't keep the appointment.

Almost immediately an alternative appointment arrived as he knew it would. Hardly had he opened it than it was snatched from his hand and torn into four pieces, she crying out, 'No one can force me to go.'

'What if I tell you that you should – for your own sake,' he coaxed but it was no good. He hadn't replied to it and now a third lay on the table, she sitting there staring at it like one drained of energy, wrung out as if she had been forced into doing an endless stint of hard labour.

'Why can't they leave me alone?' The statement was hardly audible, pitiful. It was time for him to take proper charge, mortally afraid for her.

'You have to. Without treatment this thing could—' He stopped in time from uttering the words 'kill you,' but she looked up at him sharply, the truth she saw in his eyes slowly sinking in.

'Thing?' she echoed slowly, shakily. 'This . . . *thing* the doctor found? This *thing*?' Her voice was beseeching him. 'He said what it was, didn't he?'

What could he say? All he could do was nod in reply. But her voice grew strong, startling him.

'I'm staying here, I can nurse myself! I hate hospitals – I really do! They frighten me. People die there.'

He almost laughed but it would have been a bitter, sad laugh. 'There's nothing to be scared about, Ethel. You'll get the best of treatment. It's most probably benign and the only way to find out is to let them take a look at you. They'll be able to operate and get you better again. Why are you so frightened of hospitals? They can only do you good.'

The words breast cancer had not once been mentioned but there was no need to. For a while she didn't answer, then slowly as tears began to glisten in her eyes, she said, 'My father went to hospital. He was well enough when he went in but he died there.'

She was blinding herself to the fact that, as she had told him years ago, her father had died whilst being treated for kidney infection, having ignored his condition for years until it was too late.

Fighting to remind her that her condition, if caught in time, could be cured, he knew there was no guarantee of that. It had been left for so long. If she had recognized the signs earlier, if only she'd told him about it earlier . . . If . . . If . . . Such a little word that carried so much weight. So much agony.

All he could do was crouch down in front of her, take her hands in his and look up into her face, seeing her stare back.

'Ethel, it's just a check up. The doctor said it could be benign,' he lied. 'They won't know until they examine you. But if you refuse to let them you could go on never knowing and be in fear all for nothing. They'll take it out and you'll come straight home and be back to normal.'

'It's an operation. It was an operation my father had. He never came out.'

He was at his wits end to answer that. He stood up. 'Well, what do you want me to do?'

'Let me stay here,' she said her voice strengthening.

So, one appointment after another was ignored and while he waited for each one, he watched her stiffen as pain caught her, her face going tight and grey, as she tried to hide it – all so as not to be dragged off to that place she so feared. And all the while he tried to make light of her illness for her sake, it was destroying him.

It was the worst time of his life, weeks of trying to coax her to go for an examination, weeks that stretched into months, each appointment torn up in a frantic wish to escape that place she so feared. In the end he wrote saying that he could not compel her against her will other than by force and that was out of the question of course.

Pills, painkillers, long nights sitting beside her, washing and dressing her, bandaging her breasts in an effort to ease her, this had become his life. The year crept by, the smallholding untouched and running to weed, he had no interest in dabbling in stocks and shares though he received nothing but good news on that front – ironic to be so fortunate in all things monetary but not in what really mattered to him.

Winnie and Tom came often to support him, more or less every other weekend, arriving on the Saturday and leaving Sunday afternoon – staunch friends in this time of trouble.

He felt deeply indebted to them and often wondered what he would have done without them. Especially having written to the family of Ethel's condition, the only one who came was Frank, he and Mavis turning up almost as soon as they heard. Frank wasn't all that regular a visitor but Charlie appreciated his efforts and it was good for Ethel to have Mavis here to talk to.

Eileen turned up once, deeply sympathetic, for once compelling her Fred to bring her. But it was only the once, Fred most likely dominating her as he had always done. Rosie too came once with Arthur, she and her two girls, filling the house with squeals and giggles and either non-stop chatter or bursts of weeping at Ethel's illness, leaving Ethel exhausted by her sister-in-law's over-exuberance.

George and Betty, of course, carried on their own casual easy way and wrote promising to come and visit but never did.

Slowly the visits stopped except for Tom and Winnie. Even so he was feeling isolated. Ethel was beginning to say she hated the place; that this was where she'd contracted this cancer as though the place itself was to blame.

'I want to go back to live near where we used to. Can't we go back to Erith or maybe Dartford?'

She had no interest in the London or Essex side of the river now. A few months back her mother had passed away, another trauma to hit her between the eyes, she too ill to travel to attend the funeral. Shortly after, her sister who'd met someone some time before, got married quietly and moved off to Derbyshire, Ethel again being unable to go and see her married.

Her desire to go back to Kent, to be in a town, gave him food for thought. Maybe having a doctor only just down the road and a hospital almost within walking distance might make her feel a lot better about going into hospital, though it was getting a little late for any hope of her being cured.

The problem would be trying to sell this place – who'd want a few weed-infested acres and a house out in the sticks? But the house wasn't so much in the sticks as it had once been. Over the years more houses had been built, adding to the few there had been down the road. It was 1960 and those with a bit of money were eager to move out of London and commute instead, looking for larger houses on the coast, not exactly in town, but with room to expand. New estates were springing up, building firms looking for land on which to build them. Charlie found his financial luck paying off yet again – a building contractor, seeing his land as a likely prospect, coming to him with an offer to buy. They already had building permission for a new estate and his property was just what they were looking for. The sum offered was far more than he'd ever expected, one which when he promptly refused, they immediately returned with a better offer, which this time he accepted.

By autumn they'd settled in Dartford, in a house with open views that she could see from her bedroom window and a small garden needing little work, leaving him with time to devote all his attention to her. What was more, there was a doctor within easy reach in the very next street.

As far as her condition allowed, Ethel was happy with the house but he had no love for it. This was where he would lose her eventually. He knew that now. His heart aching, he no longer spoke of hospitals, doing all he could for her, not caring if he wore himself out, sitting up with her for hours on end at night trying to ease her pain, staying on long after she fell asleep under the influence of the painkillers Doctor Denman prescribed. He would wash her, read to her, talk of this and that in a light vein but inwardly he raged at seeing her slowly fading away.

Then, in late November, there had been a terrible two days with her – she wrenched with pain, he at his wits end calling in the doctor to administer yet more painkillers, he saying in a strangely confident tone that she would sleep easier now, but it could be that she might very well not last the night and that he should be prepared for that possibility. Nor did she; leaving the world peacefully in her sleep in the early hours of the morning, as the fog from the river drifted silently over the town to enfold it in a hushed blackness.

He was alone. The loveliest girl he had ever known was gone.

The funeral was a quiet one, few people attending. Had they still been in Newhaven, those friends he had made and those from her WI would have been there in force, but they'd been here too short a while to make friends.

His family came – for the sake of decency he felt. No genuine sorrow.

They came back to the house for a bite to eat but left soon after in an almost irreverent haste, each saying they'd got quite a way to get back home.

Only Winnie and Tom stayed on, despite now being only down the road as it were, and again he wondered what he would have done without their kind and genuine company.

'Now you call on us whenever you need to,' Winnie told him before they left, warmly taking his arm in both her hands and kissing his cheek. 'Remember, any time at all. We're only nearby, don't forget.'

Tom shook his hand as if loath to let go. 'Cheerio, ole man. Winnie's right. Whenever you want us, we're nearby.'

Twenty-Seven

He couldn't keep running to Winnie and Tom, bothering them, but he thought of them constantly as he sat alone in the empty house. Even after six months of losing Ethel the place still haunted him, every room, every piece of furniture, even the cups and saucers, reminded him of her. While she had been alive he'd given no thought to furniture being alive too. Now, everything had a sense of having died with her, a sense of lifelessness which he could never have described to anyone.

At times he still imagined he could hear her calling from the bedroom and he was finding it harder and harder to stay there. He'd drive over to Stratford to check on his parents' house. But that too had a forlorn, forsaken feel, even though a few of the neighbours he'd known were still there and welcomed him. He occupied much of his time in freemasonry. They were supportive and many of them would come to see him when he was there, or phone him in Dartford asking how he was.

He had thoughts of coming back here permanently to live. Like his reluctance to get rid of the house where he had nursed Ethel and where she had died, he was equally reluctant to get rid of the one his parents had lived in all those years back. Well able to keep both places going, paying the rates, gas, electricity and any other expense, he divided his time between each place giving himself something to do with his time, if only going back to Dartford to pick up any mail. But it broke his heart each time he did. There it sat, empty and desolate, a reminder of unhappy days that he clung to in an unreasonable need to relive them.

But as summer waned he found himself more often in Stratford, alone in the larger house, wandering around it trying to lose himself in its upkeep, decorating and repairs, often wondering what he thought he was doing. All he was really doing was torturing himself. Yet still he couldn't bring himself to get rid of either home. Not yet.

★   ★   ★

'You know, Charlie, you need to start getting out more,' Frank said as he and Mavis sat drinking the tea he'd made for them.

'I get out,' Charlie defended, watching little Veronica, now six, as she wandered aimlessly about the room, nothing to play with, obviously bored.

He got up and picked up the sweet dish he kept on the sideboard for when she came and offered her one, seeing her blue eyes light up as she took a boiled sweet.

'You shouldn't be giving her any more,' Mavis said instantly. 'She's had enough. And they ruin her teeth.'

'It's only the one,' he said and, replacing the dish, sat back down.

'She doesn't have sweets at home. You spoil her. You shouldn't be encouraging her every time we come here.'

More's the pity, he thought. It lightened his life whenever he saw her, but at the same time, widened the emptiness in his heart still more that he had no child of his own to give sweets to, to spoil, to worry about.

He looked back at Frank. 'I'm pretty well caught up with the lodge these days. That takes up most of my time.'

He was studying hard in the hope of eventually going through the chair and becoming a past master. In a way it had become his life. He'd made some good friends there, had come to realize that he was popular, willingly doing little jobs that were needed; at the moment he was painting the railings around Stratford Church for the Revd John Fox, with whom he had become good friends.

'You don't call that getting out, do you?' Frank said as he sat down again. 'You've been hanging around this place for a whole eighteen months since Ethel died, doing nothing.'

Eighteen months! Where had those eighteen months gone? A picture of Ethel flashed through his mind, sending a pang of longing through his chest – he and Ethel walking arm in arm across the downs towards Beachy Head, the sun on their faces, the sea breeze playing through her fair hair, ruffling her summer skirt, her voice animated with happiness.

'I mean, you could find someone at least to go with you when the lodge has its ladies night,' Frank was saying, 'You have to have a lady.'

'I'm not interested, Frank,' he said quickly, brought sharply back to the present.

'But you don't even go out to a pub.'

'You can't stand in a pub on your own!' Charlie retorted. 'You look a fool standing at the bar – like you're just on the lookout for a woman or . . . or a man. And sitting at a table you look like some old twerp no one wants.'

'Well, if you call forty-six old, there's no hope for you,' Frank quipped but he had little idea how much that hurt. Forty-six – no, not old, but too old to start thinking of marrying again, even to start thinking of having a family. He let his thoughts run. He'd be well into his sixties by the time a child was off hand. He silently resigned himself to remaining childless, he who had so enjoyed his brothers' and sisters' kids when they were young, loved playing with them when they came. Now he saw none of his family, nothing of their children. He was alone in this world.

'By the way,' Frank said as they made to leave. 'Elsie's been on to me about how she'd like to see you some time.'

'Why,' asked Charlie, kissing Mavis then Veronica goodbye. 'She hasn't bothered herself to see me for years, apart from Ethel's funeral.'

'I know. She says she feels guilty not going to see you when you were in Dartford except, as you say, for Ethel's funeral. Says we all ought to stay in touch. Says she'd love to see you if you wanted to visit any time. Said she tried to ring you there several times but couldn't get any answer.'

'That's because I'm seldom over Dartford way these days,' Charlie said tersely.

'I told her you were here now most of the time. Why don't you get rid of that place in Dartford?'

Charlie said nothing and Frank shrugged. 'Well, you know best. Better get going. Give Elsie a ring. Be nice if you and her got together again.'

Watching the three of them climb into the little green Hillman, he closed the door thoughtfully. Perhaps Frank was right. It wasn't nice for families to be split. Someone ought to break the ice. Maybe it should be him, and yes, he would get in touch. From time to time he'd heard from Rosie and Eileen and he had replied.

Nothing from Eva of course, she'd always been a cold fish, didn't deserve to be contacted but at least Elsie had mentioned him. And he would respond, bury the hatchet – if there was one to bury. But first he had something else playing on his mind.

The house was causing him some concern. He couldn't go on rattling around in this rambling place trying to keep it in order – for what? To cling to the past! Frank's seemingly inane advice on getting himself out and about again was beginning to make him think, but in a way Frank wouldn't have thought of.

Having speculated for years on the stock market and still doing pretty well, he began to put his mind to this house he was living in most of the time. So long as he stayed here he'd be going nowhere. And he *was* only forty-six, still with plenty of life left if he allowed it.

Lately all he had been doing was occupying his mind with Masonic matters, more or less for something to do. Yet even this didn't seem to heal the feeling he got sitting here all alone in his parents' old place. It had come down to knowing that he wouldn't be able to take it much longer. Yet to move away and see it still standing there, forever having to have an eye kept on it, was something he couldn't contemplate. And selling to someone else, other people occupying the house he'd known from a child, a house that his parents had enjoyed all their married life, wasn't something he wanted either. Finally he realized what he needed to do – have it demolished, a block of flats built in its place. It wasn't the money he'd be making from such a project, but knowing that strangers would be living in an entirely new environment to the house he'd known seemed far more acceptable.

The more he thought about it the more he felt excited. But he couldn't just tear the place down. He'd have to let the family know what was in his mind. And how would they react? He could well imagine. There'd either be gasps of horror that he could even think of doing such a thing, or else intakes of breath in eagerness at some of the money from such a scheme that should come their way. Yet he couldn't *not* tell them. They'd know soon enough once it was done and clamour for their share, no matter that the house had belonged to him not them.

The best person to talk to about it would be Frank, closer to him than any of them. He waited until the next time Frank and

Mavis came to tea then after they'd all eaten and he'd played awhile with young Veronica, casually broached the subject.

Frank was left looking shocked and astounded. 'But it's Mum and Dad's home,' he said in a tone of bewilderment.

'*Was* – not is!' Charlie corrected. 'They've been gone thirteen years. The place is falling to bits. It needs care and attention and I've not got the incentive or heart to do it.'

'But to pull it down? Why not sell it or rent it? What about the rest of the family? What do the others say?'

'Yes, it's their mum and dad's home as well,' put in Mavis. 'Have you stopped to take into account their side of things? Or are you going to rush in despite their feelings?'

Charlie smiled at the bombardment of questions. It was really none of Mavis's business what his family thought. She too hardly ever saw any of them, a family that to his mind had never been close knit. But he took Frank's point and briefly explained that the house had nothing to do with any of them any more.

'I inherited that house from Mum, fair and square, and, as far as I see it, none of them have ever been interested in its upkeep. In my opinion, they shouldn't have any interest in what happens to it now.'

He heard the gasp from both of them while little Veronica played on with the doll he had bought for her the last time they were here.

'You can't just go ahead and tear down the place without telling them first. They'll get to know anyway once it's done and be really angry that you didn't even tell them. No matter what you think of them, they've got a right to know even if you don't intend to listen to their side of it. You have to tell them. Two wrongs don't make a right!'

The old cliché would have made him smile again if his brother's words hadn't begun to hit home. Of course he had to tell them. He still meant to do what he'd intended with the house, but Frank was right, he should tell them or ask for an irreversible gulf to open. There'd always been a gulf of sorts but this time it would be of his own making if he wasn't careful.

To his surprise, having expected a cold reception, Elsie gave him an extraordinarily warm one. Seeing him on the doorstep, she gave him a huge kiss, and as he entered the living room he received a hearty handshake from Vic. Though his son Victor, now nineteen, who'd been lolling on the settee as he came in, got up and left, ignoring him, probably having heard his parents talking about his uncle, and had, like most young people, formed a set image of him that he wasn't prepared to alter without a fight.

He wasn't offended. Victor was a good lad according to Frank, only youth, no doubt, armouring him against changing his opinion. With just the other two he set about telling them his decision to demolish the Stratford house and have flats built on the empty site. He knew it was going to be hard but it was far harder than he had imagined, seeing initial shock change to horror then to something like malice.

'Oh, no, Charlie, that's not on!' the cry came from Vic while Elsie's fingers curled themselves into claws, a torrent of words wrenched from her:

'Demolish Mum and Dad's house? No!' she raged. 'How dare you think you could do such a thing? We won't let you! I'll see you dead before I ever let you do that!'

Why he said it he never knew, but suddenly he was saying without giving it any proper thought: 'I thought of dividing some of the money I get from it between all of the family. It *was* Mum and Dad's home as you say and it's only right.'

Fool! But Elsie had calmed like magic, her eyes opening wide, claws retracting. 'You mean that?' she queried, almost in disbelief.

He'd have laughed if he hadn't felt so contemptuous. Yet in that instant he had made a friend of her. The news would go round the family like a wild fire. Now he had to think fast.

'It'll take a good couple of years, maybe more – getting planning permission, paying for an architect and building contractor's fees, legal fees, laying proper drainage and public utilities.'

His tone had become professional. 'It all takes money, a good deal of money, and time. But when it's all up and running, money will start to roll in. But we have to be patient.'

He had never seen such a change in expression, joy on both their faces. And joy would be on the faces of everyone in the family no doubt – nothing to pay out, but the promise of ongoing riches to come in.

But as he talked his brain was working. It would be nice to

see those flats rising, but did he need to make money? He was doing so well with his shares, knew what he was talking about now. Why get caught up worrying about all the possible problems that could arise from delayed contracts, building dates set back, legal matters taking ages to complete and all the other little things that can go wrong in that field?

He left Elsie's with a sense of satisfaction. He had made friends with the family again. Not that it was so important to, but in his heart he felt easier in that respect than he'd felt in years.

Twenty-Eight

Standing here on the empty site where the house had once been, he hadn't expected to feel such a sense of emptiness as now came over him while he watched the site agent approach him.

'That's the lot, sir. All done,' the man said, brushing his hands together as if he had carried out the demolition process all by himself.

The work force had departed, the last truckload of rubble driven away, leaving a silence made more noticeable by the distant rumble of traffic from the main road, emphasizing the forlorn air of the empty site like a mute condemnation by those who had once occupied the now demolished house – his parents. He hadn't expected to feel this way about it.

'Thank you,' he said automatically and watched the man walk away still brushing his hands together.

It was surprising just how much ground there was. It hadn't seemed as much as this when the house had stood on this spot, or even while it was being demolished amid all the dust left suspended in the May sunshine.

While most of the demolition had been going on he'd gone back to Dartford, preferring not to be around should any of the family come to gape at the destruction, not so much to lament as to nurse the prospect of money rolling into their pockets when the promised flats went up in its place. That was if the flats ever did go up.

Planning permission had been granted but it wasn't to say he would be going ahead with the project immediately. He might not get around to it for years. Maybe as the expiry date loomed, he might. It all depended how much it was going to cost to build them.

He smiled reflectively as he let his gaze wander about the area. It would be a wonderful investment, building flats on this site. He'd promised the family a share of the profits when they were sold, singly or in their entirety. In the meantime, most of the family were being more than friendly to him.

'You ought to come and see us more often,' Elsie was writing. 'We'd like to get over to Dartford but it's such a long journey. But do come to us. You'll be more than welcome.'

Old sores seemed to have miraculously healed but he was happy to take up on her invitation. Living back in Dartford had brought a strange sense of loneliness despite the summer weather, worse than he'd felt in the old house. Again and again he thought of putting this place up for sale, move back to London or Essex, but somehow he had no interest lately in being anywhere with Ethel gone – 1960 was now almost three years ago, and the old drive he'd once had when she'd been alive had died with her.

If there had been children he might not feel that way. In a way it seemed to set him apart from everyone else in the family.

It was this that made him take up Elsie's invite and despite her one or two digs on how well off he seemed to be, he was rather glad he went, even felt better returning home with a promise to go again, and often.

On the strength of that he was now taking himself off to Rosie's and to Eileen's, who'd always been his favourite sister. He even visited Eva, though only the once. House proud to a fault – her home more like a show house – it was enough to give any visitor an inferiority complex; it suited her personality, and her husband didn't help.

Harold was the sort who tended to look down on anyone lower than an accountant. Charlie knew he looked down on him, seeing him as little more than a manual worker having worked in a scrap metal yard, no matter that he had actually owned the place at one time, and as a smallholder the lowest of the low, and now someone who apparently had no work at all.

He'd been glad to get away. Not being an entirely tidy man himself, the discomfort of having a cushion plumped up afresh the moment he stood up was too much. And a cup of tea apparently required a small side table, a napkin, a piece of cake on a pretty plate and a fork to eat it with; the little side table was wiped swiftly afterwards with a damp cloth before being slid back into its hiding place.

Living on his own so long, he was more used to wandering around the house, a slab of cake in one hand, a mug of tea in the other. He decided that the less he saw of Eva and Harold the better.

Eileen's place, and Rosie's too, were, to a point, more congenial for being fairly untidy. Both had small bungalows with nowhere to put anything, but the kettle was always on for the inevitable visitors who apparently would call in on them all day long. It was homely and comfortable. He felt at home.

George's place in London wasn't far off being the same, he was still the slapdash, good-tempered, happy-go-lucky brother he'd always been. As for Frank, it was more often that Frank would drive over to see him rather than the other way round, though lately that had fallen away a little.

He'd phone saying, 'Mavis isn't feeling too well today,' apologizing.

He understood. As he could recall, Mavis had never been much of a happy passenger in a car. Though whenever he went to Frank's he could see Frank was telling the truth. These days Mavis was looking quite washed out, pale and listless.

'How long have you felt like this?' he'd said the last time he was there.

It was Frank who answered, she looking to him to do the talking, that in itself unusual, she always the one to be up front.

'It's been, oh, a couple of months, hasn't it, love?' he'd said, regarding her questioningly. 'The doctor said you're a bit anaemic and he's given you iron tablets for it, hasn't he, love?'

Mavis had sighed, puffed and looked aside, disinterested, before going off to the kitchen to pour the tea for her visitor. It wasn't unexpected for her to be offhanded when she fancied to, but very unlike her to say so little.

'She looks thoroughly washed out,' Charlie remarked after she'd gone out, but Frank had shrugged. 'What she needs is a holiday. So we're taking a trip to France next week, taking the car on the ferry and popping along the coast to Brittany for a couple of weeks. That'll put the colour back in her cheeks and she'll be as right as rain.'

Charlie's thoughts were that she needed to eat a bit more heartily. She hardly ate a thing now according to Frank.

But when Charlie next visited she seemed to be just as miserable as ever and he stopped going quite so often. It was a shame because for all Frank's faults, which weren't all that many or serious, he and Frank had always been close.

He still continued to visit the others. Oddly enough it was Elsie he seemed to see more of these days. True her home was a bit like her sister Eva's, almost too tidy, but at least it had a much warmer atmosphere. She would phone him, ask him when he was coming, would give him a dinner or a full tea, always seeming to be worrying about his welfare. And young Victor was a lot friendlier too, intelligent, talkative, making him wish he'd had a lad like him, a thought he'd quickly brush aside as they chatted together.

Elsie though was beginning to plague him with her constant concern over his continuing single state. 'Haven't you met anyone else yet, Charles?' she'd asked outright last Christmas.

When he shook his head, she'd gone on, 'You can't spend the rest of your life, pining for Ethel. It's not natural.'

Now it was Christmas again and she was reminding him, 'Your Ethel has been gone all of four years, Charles. That's a long time. You must get so lonely sometimes. What you need is company. You're not the single type, Charles. It's time you started to get your life together again and to go out socializing. You never know, you might find someone and get married again.'

He didn't want to *get his life together again*. He had no wish to replace Ethel. And anyway, where did a man of forty-seven find himself a wife? Most women his age were married. Anyone younger and unmarried could be a stiff-faced spinster or a bit of a flighty one. Nor did he have any wish to find himself a divorced woman – or anyone for that matter.

He said all this to Elsie in as light-hearted a way as he could and after she and Vic had thought the remark highly comical, Elsie became serious again.

'I mean it, Charles, you can't spend the rest of your life pining.'

'I'm fine,' he tried to assure her but it made no difference.

'If only you and Ethel had had children. Such a pity! I wonder why.'

'That's his business,' Vic cut in but she ignored him.

'It would have been such a comfort to you now if you had. It was so silly. Why didn't you?'

He had no intention of answering that, but if he had she would have given him no chance as she hurried on: 'You know, Charles, you really should start going out, seeing people. You never know who you might meet.'

'Maybe one day,' he said, just to satisfy her. But he had no intention of doing so, not now, not ever. Ethel's memory was sacred to him and always would be.

The phone was ringing as he came in from this Friday evening's Masonic meeting in London; it was a long meeting and a long wet journey home through the dark of October and it was now late. Who'd be phoning him at this hour?

Quickly he dropped his briefcase on the floor to answer the summons before it rang off, at the same time struggling free of his raincoat.

'That you, Charlie?' It was Frank's voice.

'It's me, Frank!' he added unnecessarily. The tone sounded extremely urgent. Charlie was immediately alerted.

'Anything wrong?' he queried.

'It's Mavis – she's been taken into hospital. This afternoon. I've been trying to get hold of you.'

'I was in London, at my—'

He was given no chance to finish the sentence or ask why Mavis was in hospital.

'She's had that anaemia for a long while as you know. But this week she'd been really under the weather. The doctor sent her for blood tests and this morning he asked us to see him. It's turned out she's not just anaemic. It's pernicious anaemia. They took her into hospital straight away.'

'Why didn't you let me—' he began but was again cut short.

'They've done tests on her this afternoon and they've sent her to Kings Cross hospital. She's in there now. Apparently it's very bad. We didn't know. We just thought she was a bit anaemic. I've been trying to get in touch with you but you weren't there. I'm in the hospital now. I told Elsie and she and Vic came here. They're here with me now.'

'Right, I'm coming straight there,' Charlie said, ready to put the phone down, but Frank interrupted him, still rattling on erratically.

'It's late. Nothing you can do now. They've told us to go home and come back tomorrow. They say she's quite comfortable and there's nothing we can do staying here.'

'I'll go straight there first thing in the morning then,' Charlie said as soon as he could get a word in, but again was cut short.

'There's no visiting in the mornings. The hours are from two to four in the afternoons and in the evening.'

'OK, then. Look, I'll be there tomorrow afternoon. Are you all right?'

There was no answer. The phone had gone dead, Frank no doubt in his state of panic having put it down

Mavis had been in hospital a week. While Frank and her mother sat with her, the others waited outside – Elsie and Victor, his father needing to go on to work after dropping them, George's Betty, being the nearest to the hospital and coming by bus, and Frank with young Veronica. When they were let in, Mavis lay inert, seeming to have no energy to talk to them, just a ghost of a smile for her daughter, her face so pale that it didn't seem true.

That first day Charlie had gone back to stay with Frank and Veronica for a couple of days. He seemed grateful of his company but after Mavis's mother said she would stay with them, he'd shrugged and left her to it, Frank seeming not to be caring one way or the other.

This afternoon he was on the point of leaving home for the hospital when the phone rang. It was Elsie.

'Oh, Charles,' she began. 'Frank can't come to the phone so I'm doing it. Mavis died this morning. He's too upset to tell you himself, so I said I'd do it.' The cold way it was said, took his breath away.

His mind winged back to when Ethel had died, then to Frank again. 'Where is he?' was all he could say.

'He's here at the hospital. I'm here too. I didn't know until I got here.'

'I'll be there soon as I can!' he shot at her and put down the phone.

For a moment he stood staring at it, then as if a great darkness had descended, he put a hand to his eyes, fingers pressing tightly again the lids and took a shuddering breath. It was like losing his Ethel all over again.

Twenty-Nine

Eighteen months since Mavis died and Frank was still driving over to him nearly every Sunday, usually on his own, Veronica now eighteen just having started university.

He liked Frank well enough but not every weekend. By now he would have expected his visits to fall away a little. He had his own life to get on with and sometimes Frank coming interfered with his taking up invitations from one or other of the family to Sunday dinner.

At home, not being much of a cook himself, he tended to eat whatever came to hand as and when he fancied. Being asked to Sunday dinner by Elsie or Eileen or George's Betty, a marvellous cook if she did do far more than one could eat, was a treat to look forward to. Not so often to Rosie who, like himself, was quite slapdash, most of her meals usually eaten on the hoof so to speak. And certainly not to Eva if he could help it, who could turn any meal into an uncomfortable ritual.

The trouble with Frank was that he would never stop talking about Mavis and, as much as he felt for him, Charlie was sure he hadn't burdened others with endless references to Ethel. As far as he could, he'd kept his grief to himself. He hated admitting it but Frank had begun to get on his nerves somewhat.

He found himself making excuses to be going somewhere when he'd phone to say he'd be coming over. It was perhaps unkind but there was only so much one could take of another's harping on the one subject all the time. The only excuse he could make to keep Frank from going along with him was to say he was going to see Elsie. Frank couldn't abide her and her incessant digs at this and that.

Oddly enough, he too was beginning to tire of her increasing digs at why nothing yet had been done about the block of flats he was going to have built on the Stratford site.

'It's been going on for such a long time – four years. You've got the planning permission for them. I should think it's about time you started doing something about getting them started before permission expires.'

He had always avoided bringing up the subject of their contributing to the cost of building. Though he'd mentioned the costs when the house had first been demolished, he always knew that the moment he referred to it again, Elsie would incite a small rebellion among the rest of the family.

He didn't want to make enemies of them again. He'd had enough of that. But sooner or later they'd have to be reminded. Maybe if he approached it carefully.

Suddenly, today, he heard himself coming out with it as they sat back full to the brim from Elsie's splendid dinner of roast lamb, followed by a delicious trifle and a few suitable glasses of wine.

It might have been the wine that made him fail to look before he leapt when answering that inevitable enquiry of hers.

'The fact is, Elsie, I don't think I can afford to have them built. I must have mentioned it ages ago, that to get them built and the family to have a share of the profits, we'd all have to chip in with the cost of building them. Surely you remember?'

There was a sudden silence. 'If I'm going to go ahead with it,' he went on, 'I think we'll have to have a few meetings to thrash out how it's to be done, form a company or something.'

The silence continued. He saw Elsie and Vic look at each other. Young Victor had left the table and gone to his room, bored with the conversation.

Charlie had to say something. 'You did expect to shell out at least something towards it, didn't you?' he queried the two stricken faces remaining. 'Even if I hadn't spoken of it.'

'How much?' asked Vic.

'Well, I haven't gone into it yet, but—'

'Coffee?' queried Elsie, jumping up from the table.

Not waiting for anyone to answer she made off towards the kitchen, the subject appearing to have been closed for the time being. Vic too said no more but also got up from the table to stand with his back to his brother-in-law, as he gazed out at the sunny Sunday afternoon, fiddling with a packet of cigarettes he'd taken from his pocket.

★   ★   ★

So far nothing more had been said on the subject but at least there was no return to the old gulf there had once been.

Elsie was still going on about his expectations of meeting someone, something he in his turn evaded. He told himself he was content with his own company, he was self-sufficient, kept himself occupied doing things for the Masons, visiting the family and especially Tom and Winnie, studying the shares market. It was enough.

Then there was Frank, having taken to coming over on Saturdays, though not as frequently as he once did. In fact he hadn't seen him for several weeks. Perhaps he was settling down to his single life at last.

Frank had phoned this Saturday morning saying he needed to pop over to see him, that there was something he had to tell him. When Charlie opened the door to him he was looking as elated as someone who'd just won ten thousand quid on the pools.

'I'm going to have to tell you sooner or later, Charlie,' he said grinning from ear to ear as he barged into the house.

He went on into the living room to throw himself into an armchair, gazing at his brother who sat himself opposite him to hear what wonderful news Frank had to tell him.

Frank leaned towards him. 'I've met someone, Charlie. A young woman.'

Why should he feel shocked? Unable to find anything to say except to echo, 'A *young* woman?' he could only stare at him.

Mavis hadn't been gone two years yet, three weeks off of two years to be precise, and here was Frank going on about some young woman he'd met. It struck him as almost sacrilege and he nearly said so but curbed his tongue and said instead: 'How young a woman?'

'Well . . . she's about twenty-eight, twenty-nine.' He sounded briefly apologetic but brightened almost immediately. 'Her name's Lorna.'

Charlie continued to stare at him. Frank was coming up to forty-eight. It made her eighteen or nineteen years younger than him. Staring at his brother's broad face, showing its age a bit, he wondered what a woman of twenty-eight would find in someone like Frank, short in stature and with a tendency towards fleshiness, not a snappy dresser by any means and a bit tight on the pocket to boot.

'Well, say something,' Frank's voice broke into his thoughts. 'Aren't you pleased for me?'

Now he said it. 'Mavis has hardly been gone two years.'

Frank's grin faded. He frowned. 'I've not forgotten her, what we had together. I'll never forget that. But I'm not like you, Charlie. I need someone to be with, to keep me company. I wasn't looking for someone if that's what you're thinking. It just happened.'

He ignored Frank's half peeved, half beseeching tone.

'How?'

'Well, I met her one day when I popped down to the corner shop near my place. She was with her mother. I didn't take much notice but then she dropped her groceries and I helped her pick them up and we got talking and after I saw her in the shop once or twice on her own, we ended up having a bit of lunch together in the high street and . . . well, it went on from there.'

Charlie remained silent hearing Frank rattle on like some young lad.

'She's never been married. She lives with her mother. She told me she was rather frail as a child – had a lot of illness – and that she still does suffer from a sort of frailness which she says she's always been conscious about and never expected ever to marry. But, well . . . we get on OK together and we have a lot of things in common and—'

'How long have you known her?' Charlie cut in.

'About three months or so.'

That made the time Mavis had been gone even shorter. How could Frank put her aside like that? How could he be in love again so soon after losing her? He had a sudden picture of Frank at her funeral, back at the house sitting apart from the others, slumped in his chair, grief-stricken, his daughter Veronica with one arm about him trying to comfort him.

'Do you love her?' The question bursting from him sounded utterly inane. He couldn't believe that he'd asked it. Frank's face broke into a smile.

'I know we get on well. She's quiet. Mavis never stopped chattering and it's nice having someone who doesn't chatter on all the time. We get on well . . . I said that, didn't I? But we do, and—'

'You intend to get married again?' Charlie cut him short once more. His feelings were beginning to penetrate and Frank frowned at him.

'Would it be so wrong if I did?' The words were a challenge. 'I can't bring Mavis back. She wouldn't have wanted me to go through the rest of my life like some miserable recluse, pining. If I'd been the first to go I'd have wanted her to be happy again and we all need a bit of companionship in our lives . . .'

'Have you talked to her about marriage?'

'Lorna? Yes. And she's agreed. She's looking for companionship too. There's nothing wrong in that, Chas. I don't want to stay single the rest of my life and nor does she. Otherwise where will she be when her mother eventually goes and leaves her all on her own with no one to care? So yes, we're going to get married.'

'When?'

'In about three, maybe four month's time.'

'And you've only just got around to telling me.' He could hardly keep the bitterness out of his tone. 'You've been coming here all this time and said nothing.'

'It was only this week we decided. That's why I'm telling you now.'

For a moment Charlie couldn't bring himself to reply. Gazing at his brother he became aware of a face now tight with anxiety, silently pleading for approval. Frank was the sort who needed company, he realized that now. He had no right to be judgemental. It was Frank's life not his. Relenting, he let his lips widen into a smile.

'I'm glad,' he said briefly, then finding a need to enlarge on it, added 'I'm really glad for you'. And seeing the relief spread across his brother's face, he knew he really was glad for him.

It was a register office wedding, a simple, quiet affair as would have been expected considering Frank's earlier marriage.

Frank had asked him to be chief witness to which he had consented. Behaving churlishly would have done no one any good, but he couldn't avoid being painfully aware that it was taking place in September just short of two weeks from the day Mavis had passed away two years previously.

Bad timing on Frank's part, but that was the man all over, never thought ahead. At least he did feel a little easier in his mind about the union after having met Lorna. He felt a little unkind, but she was no oil painting by any means – plain, thin, taciturn to a point of rudeness that seemed to have little to do with shyness or frailty, but more a couldn't-be-bothered attitude.

To be asked how she was or how her mother fared barely received a response much more than, 'All right,' not even a thank you, much less enlarging on the subject, which made it hard to hold any sort of conversation.

She seemed to have no care for social graces and appeared not to be that bothered by what others might think of her, though he suspected she had a large chip on her shoulder against everyone, but why, he couldn't fathom. It would account for her unsociable attitude but thankfully it was Frank who did the talking for the pair of them, and so long as he appeared happy that was all that should matter.

Elsie and Eva had been appalled by the unfortunate timing of the marriage and had downright refused to attend the wedding, which struck Charlie as strange when all Elsie ever did was try to persuade himself to find some female companionship.

Rosie, George and Eileen had all been happy for their brother, they and their spouses attending the wedding, each armed with a wedding gift, heartily congratulating the groom and complimenting the bride.

She, though, hardly had the grace to thank them, much less fall into conversation which Charlie thought was bad enough. But it was as Rosie turned away, having tried to make small talk and maybe having gabbled on, a little inanely knowing Rosie, he caught a brief, contemptuous curl of that complimented bride's lip behind Rosie's back.

It set him to disliking the girl even more, though he kept his thoughts to himself for Frank's sake, hoping Frank would be blind enough never to realize what went on inside that girl's head.

'How did it go?' was Elsie's first words when he went to see her a couple of weeks later.

'It went quite well,' Charlie offered, but Elsie had more to say.

'I must say it was unfortunate choosing such a date to get married. Rosie told me she's a strange girl. She said she wonders what Frank sees in her. Says she was quite rude to Rosie, hardly spoke to her, never even said thanks for her and Arthur's present, though Frank did. Eileen was a bit taken aback by her too. What did you think of her, Charles?'

'I found her OK,' he said carefully. The last thing he was going to do was relate the look of contempt he'd seen on Lorna's face that Rosie had luckily missed. She'd have been so hurt.

He still felt angered by it. Had the woman married Frank as a last desperate resort – *using him*, he guessed the words were? But to voice his thoughts to Elsie would be to have it go straight around the family, getting back to Frank's ears, and he wasn't prepared to make an enemy of him. Maybe in time he would find out for himself the woman he'd married. Yet maybe he never would. In a way he hoped not.

Elsie had changed the subject but not the idea of companionship. 'Now Frank's married and happy again, isn't it time you started thinking of settling down again, Charles?'

He evaded the question by making a thing of finishing the rest of the cup of tea she'd given him. From the kitchen the aroma of the Sunday roast filled the air. He looked forward to his dinner but he wasn't eager to be pumped for the rest of the afternoon on the subject of finding a nice young lady.

Elsie's stock in trade was badgering. Thankfully she no longer badgered him over the project to build that block of flats. The topic seemed to have died a natural death since hearing that everyone would be expected to contribute a small fortune towards the building of them.

The land in Stratford had begun to bug him. The date for expiry of planning permission was drawing ever closer. Before long he'd either have to reapply or find the money to start on the building. And he didn't have that sort of money, not to throw around anyway.

The outlay for architects had been more than he'd anticipated and coupled with quite a few other costs to be considered, even before the first bricks were laid – drainage, water, gas and electricity, telephones and a host of other outlays – it promised to become an exorbitant drain on his finances.

Worse, a couple of his investments had lately taken a dive leaving him well down financially. The only solution was to sell on the whole project as it stood with planning permission and architectural plans.

It was becoming a nightmare, a chain around his neck. He no longer cared what the rest of the family thought, though he doubted they would say anything, only too glad not to be asked to fork out. But if they expected to get any money from his selling of his own land, they were going to be very disappointed.

Acting on instinct, he put the entire project in the hands of an agent and damn what the family thought. In the space of a couple of weeks a large building company had made him a surprisingly fine offer, which he accepted with a sigh of relief.

It no longer felt like a place where his parents had once lived anyway. He would not go back to watch the flats being erected. He would never go back there again.

From the family there wasn't a peep. He knew word would go round after telling Elsie, maybe a few scathing remarks, but none of it reached his ears, for which he was glad.

Putting his previous investment losses behind him he took a chance using half the money from the sale on a gamble, buying shares in a new Australian mining project whose explorations he'd been following for some time. If the results proved poor he could stand to lose a hell of a lot. This time the waiting was fraught, fearing losing any of the money he'd made on selling that land.

For the next few weeks he scanned the *Financial Times*, growing more concerned as nothing seemed to be coming out of the ground, cursing himself for having taken such a gamble, his luck having obviously run out.

Two weeks later, hardly able to breathe, he was staring at the results of the survey looking back up at him from one of the finance columns. Minutes later he was on the phone to his bank, his heart thumping fit to burst through his chest wall.

He might have waited but something said he should strike now, no matter that they might go up even further, the survey having proved more than promising. The following week his hunch was proved right. Yes, the price of the company's shares had gone up a fraction after he'd sold his, but with investors leaping on the band wagon they'd levelled off and had even fallen a little. But those who, like him, had sold had already doubled their money. Luck had smiled on him again. If only he had someone to share it with.

He'd never felt this way before. Sitting in his house in Dartford, a nice car in the driveway, money in the bank, no worry about finances, but one thing was missing, one thing he couldn't order up. Yes, he could have gone to someone, been given a good time, he had the money for many good times. But it would be transient; it wouldn't mean a thing and it didn't interest him anyway. It wasn't what he needed. He needed stability. He needed love. And thinking of it as he sat in his nice little house he felt suddenly, desperately lonely and there was nothing he could do about it.

Thirty

Elsie's face shone with hope as she gazed at Charlie after having cleared away and washed up the remains of a sumptuous Christmas dinner.

'I was reading in a local newspaper the other day of a lonely hearts club and I thought of you.'

It had been a nice Christmas. Vic's brother and sister and their families had spent it with them and young Victor had brought his young lady to have tea with his family – quite a gathering. They'd watched the Queen's speech and now a comedy was on but no one was watching it, either chatting quietly as they digested their fine dinner or half dozing it off.

Elsie had already torn the piece she was referring to from the paper and now held it out to him. Sighing, Charlie took it from her and read it without interest but trying to be polite.

It had an account of a coach ride somewhere for an evening meal and a future organized outing to the seaside to take place in the spring.

'What do you think?' she taxed as he handed it back to her.

He shrugged. 'It's in Romford. Nice thought, Else, but how would I get all that way from Dartford? I wouldn't be home until the small hours.'

'It's only once a week and you don't have to go every week. They hold dances. You used to like dancing. You were a good dancer.'

'I'm past dancing,' he told her.

'But you can see they do other things, bingo, whist, going out to dinner, and outings like the one you've just read about taking place next year.'

It sounded the most boring thing he could ever do, but she wasn't finished. 'You could always stay here the night and go home next morning.'

'I don't think so, Else. But thanks very much.'

Later on, as Elsie made tea and sandwiches in the kitchen,

leaving her husband and brother alone, the other guests already having left to make their way home, Vic lit a cigarette and turned to Charlie, 'She's always talking about you, you know. She worries you're too much on your own. To tell you the truth, Charles, I tend to agree with her. I know she can be interfering at times but she does have your welfare at heart.'

He wouldn't have thought so at one time. There was a time he'd seen her as his bitterest enemy. How things change.

'I'm not ready to go looking for someone to settle down with,' he said. 'I know Ethel's been gone some time now, but to me it can sometimes seem like only yesterday.'

'I can guess,' said Vic, turning away a little to draw a deep lungful of smoke. 'Your sister can drive me to drink cold tea sometimes, but I wouldn't want to be without her. I often wonder how I'd be if anything happened to her. But I suppose we do have to move on or get all crabbed up inside, no use to anyone.'

Silence fell between them for a while and from the kitchen came the sound of food being prepared. Vic took a last puff of his cigarette and began to stub it out in an ashtray on the coffee table.

'Look, Charles, I don't want to interfere, but it might stop Elsie from nagging you if you just tried that club in Romford, just to see what you think. You know, she'll never leave you alone if you don't. I know her by now. She'll nag and nag at you and you'll stop coming, and I do enjoy your company.'

He was still putting out the now massacred cigarette end, not looking at Charlie as he went on: 'You're quite a card, Charles, you light this place up when you come here and Lord knows, it needs lightening up sometimes. Elsie can be so intense, I could throttle her sometimes. I look forward to you coming. Why not give it a try?'

From the open door issued golden light and waltz music. As he stood there in the cold, two women well wrapped up in warm coats passed him, hurrying on into the beckoning warmth of the hall, their chatter trailing behind them.

What was he doing here? Why on earth had he let Elsie talk him into this? This wasn't his scene. He'd tell Elsie something or other to make it look good. At least he had come.

Making up his mind, he turned to leave. Another man had come to stand not far away, hovering more like. Seeing Charlie about to move off, he stepped quickly towards him, barring his way.

'Not going in there then, mate?'

The voice was coarse, threatening it felt. Forced to halt, the man now positioned directly in front of him, he braced himself to sidestep if things turned violent. He wasn't tall but he was broad-chested and strong from lifting heavy scrap iron and managing a smallholding, strong enough to floor this skinnier chap, which he was well prepared to do if need be.

'Why?' he asked tersely.

'Well, I was goin' ter go in there too,' the man answered. 'But not on me own. I need . . . well, you know, someone else ter come in wiv me, if yer know what I mean.'

Charlie relaxed. Yes he knew exactly what he meant.

'Me name's Bob,' the man went on. 'Bob 'Ollins. Bin on me own fer five years and I'm sick of it! Wife left me, took the kids. I was gutted. We're divorced now. 'Ardly see the kids. Two I've got. 'Ardly see 'em. Someone told me about this place so I thought I'd come along and 'ave a dekko. But . . .'

He shrugged, his voice fading away. Seeing the thin, forlorn features Charlie felt sympathy with him; suddenly felt a need to help the man.

'Perhaps if we go in together,' he suggested and saw the face light up.

'Great!' Bob hesitated then said, 'You first. What's yer name?'

Encouraged, Charlie told him then turned to lead the way, the warm air of the place and the beat of a quickstep hitting them as they entered.

Hooking their coats and scarves on pegs in the cloakroom, they made their way together into the noisy hall to stand on the perimeter of the small dance floor. Watching the couples, they saw only a sprinkling of men, most women dancing together, women of all ages from somewhere around thirty to heaven knows what age, all in nice flowery dresses, faces made up, hair carefully combed in their favourite style, each one in dance shoes, open toed, thin heeled, silver, gold or black studded with diamanté.

By contrast the men wore ordinary suits. Charlie glanced down at his, glad not to have got too dressed up but noticed the slight fray of the cuffs of his shirt sleeves protruding below those of his jacket. Too late to do anything about that, but did it matter? None of the women would even glance his way, though some were about his own age, some maybe older, some younger.

He took another glance at the frayed edges. Ethel would have had a fit. She had always seen to it that he was neat and tidy. On his own he didn't care. They used to dance together. Those days he'd have worn an evening suit. Now it didn't seem to matter. How would she have viewed things now? He could see him and her dancing like one person. She had been such a wonderful dancer. He hadn't danced for years. What the hell was he doing here?

He turned to Bob Hollins to say he was thinking of leaving to find he was no longer there. Throwing his glance further a-field he saw him, already on the dance floor whirling a rather thin, plain-faced lady around in a waltz, chatting away as if he'd known her for years.

Fast worker, came the thought, but he wasn't as ready as that. Yet how could he just walk out? He could pretend to be going off to the toilet. Yet he remained standing here, his mind in turmoil. If he stayed here would he have to look willing and find someone to dance with? But who?

Across the hall a group of four women were talking, three sitting at a table, the fourth standing, laughing at something that had been said. He saw her glance sweep the dance floor then lift, settling directly on him to linger for an instant before moving on. From where he stood, she really looked as if she was longing for someone to dance with but no one had gone over to her.

Why he did it, he couldn't say, but in that moment he moved forward. Having done so, he could hardly step back again. He'd almost reached her when it came to him that perhaps she didn't dance or didn't want to after all. How embarrassing if she shook her head. But he was here now.

'Excuse me,' he began. 'Do you dance?'

Her reply was instant. 'Yes I do.'

'Then shall we . . .' He broke off as she plonked her handbag on the table where the other three were sitting. Seconds later he was whisking her off into the moving throng.

Wondering if introductions should be in order, he quickly told her his name, making an attempt at a joke, 'A proper Charlie,' relieved to hear her laugh with him, saying, 'Hullo Charlie, I'm Marion.'

The waltz had already been playing some time when he had asked her to dance. Now he just had time to ask how long she'd been coming, being told it had been only a few months when the music ended and he escorted her back to her table to leave her there, knowing hardly anything about her.

She'd proved a really good dancer and they'd immediately fallen into step, him not once treading on her toes nor she on his. She had been like a feather in his arms, and though not slim, was trim. He took her to be in her early thirties. Her perfume still lingered as he went back to stand with Bob. Feeling much more at ease, he contemplated getting himself something to drink at the small bar before going over to ask her for another dance.

'How did you get on,' he asked Bob, who grinned broadly.

'Smashing!' Bob looked a different man to the one he'd come in with. 'Got meself a date – wants ter come out with me tomorrer to the pub.'

'That was quick work,' Charlie commented, blinking.

Bob's big grin broadened still more. 'No point standin' in cere-mony. She's divorced like me. So we're a pair well matched. Right,' he said sharply as a quickstep struck up. 'I'm off! See yer later!'

Charlie watched him make off across the floor to the woman he had found, and wondered if he had the courage enough to try the young woman he too had asked to dance previously.

This time she was sitting with the other three, two quite young, quite jolly, the other tight faced and glum-looking. As he approached they looked up but he kept his eyes on the small, bright-faced one who'd called herself Marion. He didn't need to ask, she was on her feet saying, 'Thank you.'

She proved as good at a quickstep as she had been with a waltz and later proved herself thoroughly adept at one of the hardest dances to do properly, the foxtrot. In fact, it turned out she knew more steps than he did.

'My husband was a wonderful dancer,' she said lightly. 'In fact we met each other at a school of dancing. But we were only married for four years. That was thirteen years ago now.'

'You're divorced?' he assumed, though a quick calculation of her age made him doubt the result he came to. Four years of marriage plus thirteen would have made her thirteen when she married. That couldn't be right.

She was shaking her head. 'No, he was killed at work.'

'I'm so sorry,' he said quickly, still worried by his sums that surely had to be wrong. 'You must have been very young when you married.'

He heard her give a little laugh. 'That's if you want to call twenty-one being very young! We already had a little girl and I was carrying our son when I lost my husband.'

'I'm so sorry,' he said again, making yet another rapid calculation. She was forty! Yet she looked thirty. 'So you've two children,' he said.

'Yes,' she returned, then, 'Are you divorced?'

'I lost my wife eight years ago,' he enlightened. 'She had cancer.'

It was her turn to say sorry. 'Have you got children?' she asked softly.

'No.' He'd not meant to sound so abrupt; for all it was a sore point and they fell silent, concentrating on a few rather exacting steps of the foxtrot, negotiating it better than they'd expected. Her light laugh at their success eased him immediately and he laughed too.

The number ending, he took her back to her table, determined to have as many dances as she would oblige him with. But it was only the traditional last waltz of the evening that he finally found courage enough to ask what had been on his mind ever since that second dance.

In two weeks' time his lodge was holding its annual ladies' night. When Ethel had been alive they'd always attended as a matter of course. But he'd not done so since losing her. Now had come this thought and with it fear that he'd be seen too forward should he ask, maybe even receive a blank stare, she not knowing what he was talking about. Drawing on his courage he decided to risk it.

'I hope you don't mind if I ask you something,' he began hesitantly. 'The thing is, I'm a member of a . . . a sort of club – Masonic . . .' he paused. She probably didn't know what he was talking about.

'The thing is,' he went on, 'there's a dinner-dance each year but to attend you have to take a lady. It's called a . . .'

'A ladies' night!' she burst out before he could finish.

'You know about that?' he asked, astonished, and she laughed.

'My husband's brothers are freemasons. I go with them and my sisters-in-law – you *are* allowed to take two ladies. They're a great family, they won't even let me pay for my own ticket. As I said, my husband has been dead thirteen years and they've never allowed me to drift away. I'm asked to every one of their do's, Christmas parties, outings, weddings, ladies' nights, everything. They really are wonderful. They always asked my mum and dad along too, though I lost my dad only a few weeks ago.'

Her voice had dropped as she said it and he was obliged again to offer condolence. Her long explanation of her late husband's family hadn't given him a chance to finish the question he was aching to ask. Now as she fell silent he leapt in, aware that any minute the waltz would end, he having to return her to her friends who'd be all ears to his request; might even giggle.

'The thing is,' he leapt in, 'I never go because I haven't a partner and you can't just ask anybody. So . . .' He paused. What if she said no after all this?

'So I wondered,' he continued doggedly, 'if you might care to go with me. It's in Aldwych, just off the Strand. But I don't want to sound forward or anything and if you don't want to go, I'll understand. It's purely—'

'No, I'd love to,' she broke in. 'I really would.'

Such an immediate acceptance took him by surprise. She didn't know anything about him, yet she was accepting his invitation without question.

'Only one thing,' she added as if she had read his mind, 'I don't want you to think I come here looking for dates. I'm pretty self-sufficient. I have a car so I'm very independent – not looking to be taken out here, there and everywhere. But to me you seem different to some who are looking for dates.'

The dance was winding down. Becoming aware of it she had begun to talk faster. 'I rather enjoy coming here. It's a chance to go out. I work in London, come home, spend my evenings with my two youngsters but they're almost teenagers and I began to find myself being left on my own. You know what kids are like.'

No, he didn't know what kids were like.

'They grow up,' she went on, unaware of his thoughts. 'Grow away from you. It's to be expected. It's only natural and I don't want to stop them just because I feel lonely. That wouldn't be right.

'Then last year,' she continued, 'someone suggested I come here with her for a bit of company and I've been coming ever since but not to look for anyone – just for something to do with myself one evening a week, you know what I mean?'

Yes, he knew, only too well.

'But if you need someone to go with you on your ladies' night, I would really enjoy that. I just hope you don't think I'm making a grab at you.'

'I don't think that at all,' he said quickly as the waltz tune ended with a flourish, a rattle of sticks on a side-drum, the clash of a symbol ending with a single drum beat.

The dancers briefly applauded and began dispersing, filling the now quieter hall with the low hum of multiple conversations. He and Marion had remained where they were in the centre of the dance floor.

'So you'll come,' he said and she nodded.

'When is it?'

'It's Saturday week. It's formal evening dress.' But she'd know that. It was a relief not to have to explain. 'Can I pick you up around six? I'll need to know where you live of course.'

Told the address and her phone number, he made a mental note of it. People were making towards the cloakrooms. Her friends had already gone.

'Now isn't that just perfect!' she exclaimed as they reached the empty table. 'They've walked off leaving my handbag here – all on its own!'

But she didn't seem too put out as she searched it for a piece of paper on which to scribble her details while he wrote his address in Dartford, she surprised at the distance he had come.

'I was thinking,' he said as she made to follow the dwindling flow of the homeward-bound, 'it might be a good idea if perhaps we met for a proper chat beforehand, get to find out a bit more about each other beforehand. I could meet you here next Saturday and we could go for a quiet drink instead of coming here. What do you say?'

'I think it's a good idea,' she said without hesitation. 'But I have to go now. I don't want to be late. My youngsters will be home by now.'

'Yes, of course,' he said as she moved off. 'Till next Saturday then,'

'Till next Saturday,' she echoed brightly. 'Here at eight o'clock.'

Thirty-One

The ladies' night had been one of the happiest evenings he could remember. He'd been to many with Ethel but, whether his memory of them had faded, he couldn't recall any being as enjoyable as this one had been.

The previous Saturday they had gone to the pub for a drink so as to get to know each other better. He'd told her about Ethel and her fear of childbearing and that he had respected her fears, and she had told him of the trauma of her husband having been killed at work while she'd been carrying their second child, and while everyone had thought how terrible that was, to her, carrying that baby had virtually been her salvation.

The sight of her in a beautiful evening dress on ladies' night had taken his breath away. Since then they'd met every Saturday evening, he coming over from Dartford and staying at Elsie's so as not to have to go home in the early hours.

Elsie was thrilled out of her skin, bombarding him with endless questions about *his* young lady, until he had to give up staying with Elsie and get all the way back home to Dartford in the early hours to avoid being quizzed.

He could hardly believe he'd been seeing Marion for six weeks. There were times he still thought of Ethel but Marion was mostly in his thoughts these days.

She had a semi-detached house in Chadwell Heath near Romford, had a good job as PA to the chairman and the managing director of a chain of supermarkets and, exactly as she'd once said, was proving herself quite an independent sort of person, making up her own mind on an instant without need of consultation. In a way it was quite refreshing. So different from Ethel who had relied on him to make decisions, sitting back while he did much of the housework, the decorating, maintenance, paying of bills.

He discovered that prior to meeting him she'd redecorated the living room, wallpapering and painting.

'I was shown how to by a professional interior decorator,' she told him. 'He was a neighbour of mine where I used to live. But I couldn't have him keep coming in to do it for me, especially when he wouldn't let me pay him. So I asked him to show me how.'

She'd even been up ladders painting the upper window frames before now. He'd never known a person like her and she intrigued him.

'You learn to manage for yourself when there's no man around,' she explained. But her previous in-laws were a very caring, supportive crowd, the brothers-in-law quite willing to help her should she need them.

'I don't like relying on others too much,' she said when he pointed it out and he silently commended and admired her resourcefulness, in fact realized that what he felt for her was more than admiration, even felt a little jealous of that helpful neighbour whom she'd had to rely on in earlier years.

He wished he could see her more often but living in Dartford made it a long and tedious journey getting there and back all in one day. It was Marion who came up with the solution.

'Why don't you stay here on a Saturday and go home Sunday night? That gives us a full weekend without you having to worry.'

'I can't do that!' he told her. 'What about your neighbours. What will they have to say?'

Her tone was slightly disparaging. 'I don't live with my neighbours. They can mind their own business. I'm friendly with next door but she's a real chatterbox and I hate going out in the garden when she's out there because she won't stop talking. Her husband's nice but if he talks to me, she's out there straight away. I can't get away from them.'

'But what will she think?' he asked.

She gave a laugh. 'I don't care. We'll not be doing anything improper.'

It was as good a warning as any to keep his place. He now stayed weekends, using the sofa. With her youngsters sleeping upstairs it wouldn't have been right had things begun to get more intimate. But it made him wonder if she saw him only as company. Perhaps she didn't have anything more in mind, certainly not marriage.

Her two, Janet and John, like in the children's books, were more or less off hand, her daughter sixteen, the brother thirteen. Even so, she'd balk at going up to London to a theatre, deeming that it made it late getting home, not wanting to leave them alone for too long at night.

'They're only just in their teens,' she maintained firmly. 'I don't like them staying out too late. You never know what they might be up to. Any parent will know what I mean.'

It wasn't meant to be aimed at him and it wasn't her fault that the words bit home. But he saw her point and guessed he'd have been the same if he had children of his own.

'I've had to be mother and father to them two for thirteen years,' she said in case he thought she was being too protective. 'I've had to be a bit on the strict side with them but without a dad's hand I needed to keep them reined in to some degree. So I can't just go waltzing off whenever I feel like it. I need to set an example even if it inconveniences me.'

He admired that in her. It seemed to him that she had succeeded. They were well behaved and had taken to him from the start and him to them. Were he to marry her he would acquire two ready made children. They would never truly be his but it was the nearest he would ever get to having children. He was fifty-two and she was forty. If they were to get married it would be too late to hope for a child of his own.

He was thinking more and more along the lines of marriage but the memory of Ethel stopped him broaching the subject. Yet when they came back to her house and she'd sit next to him on the sofa, things were starting to become more intense, but knowing her children were upstairs in their beds they were both beginning to become concerned by it.

'This isn't right,' she said one evening quite suddenly. 'You've never once said how you feel about me.'

He found himself dodging the question, wanting to reply yet not knowing how to start. It had been so different when he was first courting. Things had developed naturally, a kiss and a cuddle between two young people, moving on from there until by some mutual consent it was understood that they would be married; after that the excitement of making arrangements for the wedding day, the buying of the proper gear, the booking of the church, the bans, the guest list – he couldn't remember if he had actually proposed in the romantic way or not. Now he was being asked to declare his feelings. He needed to take the first step, but somehow he felt that if he did he would almost be mocking his dead wife's image. But Ethel was gone. The women he held in his arms now was his future, and yes, he was in love with her, yet it was hard to say.

'Do you love me, Charlie?' she challenged suddenly, taking him off his guard.

Utterly confused all he could say was, 'Yes.' Not a bit romantic.

'Then will you marry me?' Her tone was dead serious, his confusion ignored. 'It is leap year,' she went on. 'The lady has the right to propose to a man on a leap year, did you know that? So I'm doing the proposing. Will you marry me, Charlie?'

For a moment he gazed at her not sure how to deal with this. Yet he knew what he wanted to say. Very slowly he said it. And this time he was certain.

'Yes,' he said slowly, all else in his past flew from his mind. This was what he wanted.

For a second they stared at each other, then suddenly both of them burst into laughter.

'Ssh!' she hissed, she the first to recover. 'We'll wake the kids.'

'Mustn't do that,' he whispered, instantly becoming aware of his position here, and gently he kissed her, she melting into his arms as if they were already married.

That night he did not stay until the next morning but drove home as dawn was breaking. Somehow it didn't feel comfortable staying over the Sunday, the two of them not quite knowing what to say to each other.

As he left, turning in the driver's seat to wave goodbye to her with a promise to see her next Saturday, from the corner of his eye he saw next door's bedroom curtains twitch and smiled to himself as he turned and moved off down the road.

On Thursday afternoon there was a phone call from Marion, her voice sounding irate as he picked up the receiver to say 'Hello.'

'Charlie! I've just had to phone you,' she said without replying to him. 'I'm mad! I'm fuming mad!'

'What's the matter?' he asked, making his own voice calm but she gave him no chance to think any thoughts.

'It's that bitch of a woman next door! She's just had a go at me.'

'What's she done?'

'She called me a slut, a loose woman or words to that effect.'

Before he could say anything he was listening to a tirade of what had transpired. It seemed the previous evening some of her daughter's friends, girls and boys, had come back for a cuppa, parking one of their cars outside her house, the other outside her neighbour's. This morning the woman had confronted her complaining of oil marks in the curb outside her house, going on to remark that she didn't know what it must be like in that house, the daughter entertaining young men all times of the evening and she allowing a man to stay all night, that it was a scandal in a nice road like this!

Charlie tried not to smile as he listened. He knew by now that no one upsets her and gets away with it and he silently commended and admired her, imagining how little the complaining woman had been made to feel.

'I told her to watch her own evil-minded business! What I do in my own house is nothing to do with her and if she thinks she can play the madam with me she's got another think coming. I don't suppose we'll be on speaking terms again. Nor do I want to.'

It seemed that the husband had tried to calm things. But Marion's mind was made up. 'I know this is a funny time to say this over the phone, Charlie, but I have to ask, do you still want to marry me?'

This time his reply was immediate. 'More than anything,' he heard himself say.

'Then I think, the way things are,' she said, 'it'd be a good idea if we got married as soon as possible under the circumstances. Not only to clip up wagging tongues – I don't care about them anyway, I love you, Charlie – but so that we can be together all the time. What do you say?'

'I say, yes, definitely. I'll start the ball rolling this very week.' He could hardly believe he was saying all this so firmly.

He had meant to say goodbye as the time came to do so but

instead all he could say was, 'I love you, very, very much. I really do.'

Putting the phone down he felt his blood tingling, his heart racing. By the following Saturday he had booked the date of the wedding with his good friend James Fox, canon of Stratford Church who said he'd have the hall due for redecoration to be done earlier so as to be in time for the reception.

'All we have to do now,' he told Marion that day, 'is to arrange the cars, the caterers and do the invitations. What do you say to August?'

'I say that's wonderful,' she told him.

Everything was falling into line as if in great haste to be done. The following week they went out to choose an engagement ring. He watched her remove the wedding ring she had worn constantly from her first marriage and put it tenderly in a box in one of the drawers of her dressing table, closing the draw gently, almost reverently.

Somehow the action had a significant feel to it and he realized that she would never forget her first marriage, nor would he his, but now they both had an easier mind. He found himself slowly taking charge of arrangements, surprised that she was letting him do so, as if glad to be relieved of responsibility she'd taken on her shoulders all those years as a widow.

He was happy too that her children were thrilled by the news, and he had been welcomed by her first husband's family as if he was about to become a new brother-in-law. It confused him at first until she explained this was what they wanted, confirmed by one of the brothers-in-law in that family.

'Thirteen years since our John went,' he said to him. 'It's time she got on with her life and the kids need a dad.'

Thirty-Two

Stratford Church was filled to bursting, not only with her immediate family, but her previous in-laws – a huge family; dozens of
friends, a host of colleagues where she worked, including her
immediate bosses. There was his family of course, which wasn't
small, and an army of friends from his lodge – a wedding never
to be forgotten.

The cost of it all hadn't mattered. His Australian investments
were still standing him in good stead and always would, so long
as he kept an eye on them. He also now planned to sell his house
in Dartford. He'd suggested they live there but she had said no.
It was the one thing he'd seen her show any real reluctance on.
In all other matters she seemed happy to fall in with him.

'I can't go right over there, it's too far from my mother,' she
said. 'Having lost my dad, she'd be all on her own.'

'She could come and live with us,' he had suggested, he still
loath to get rid of the house in which Ethel had spent her last
years.

'Mum wouldn't have that,' Marion had said firmly. 'She likes
to keep her independence, keep her own home, so if we move
it can't be too far away.' He knew how she felt. He had felt the
same way about his mother.

The honeymoon was in Cornwall. Visiting the same places
where he and Ethel had gone on theirs no longer seemed to
have any nostalgic echoes. He was glad, and relieved. There was
nothing to be gained looking back over the past. He had a new
life now. He was in love with his new wife.

True she could be fiery but was usually reluctant to speak her
mind outright unless provoked.

'You can't go around hurting people's feelings just as you please,'
she said and he understood that – he was of the same sentiment
– but her point would eventually come across if pushed too far.
He thought it could be called diplomacy and perhaps that's what
he'd practised himself all his life.

'Do you really miss not having children of your own?' she asked on the second day of the honeymoon as she snuggled next to him. That *was* forthright and it took him by surprise.

'I suppose I did in a way, once,' he admitted, adding hurriedly, 'but maybe not any more,' trying to sound unconcerned, reluctant to betray the emptiness that had lingered in him all these years and still did.

He now had her children to play father to of course, but it wasn't the same as being his very own, they more or less grown up. But she seemed to divine the hollowness in his non-committal tone.

'You could still have one, you know,' she said quietly, and when he remained silent, she went on, 'Would you like a little one of your own? Because you could, you know.'

Lying beside her he felt stunned, almost unable to give a reply, finally saying, 'I couldn't ask that of you.'

'Why not?'

'Well . . . you're forty.'

'So?'

'No – it wouldn't be right.'

'Let me be the judge of what's right or not in that field,' she said quietly. 'It'll be me having your child. That is if you want one. Do you?'

He had no idea how to reply. Finally he said, 'Yes, but my . . .'

He stopped, confused, aware that he'd only be inanely repeating what he'd already told her about Ethel and suddenly he didn't want to bring up the name again. It was gone, locked in the deep, darkest recesses of his brain, tucked away from the world as it should be, away even from himself so that he could enjoy a life once more. Marion was his wife now and he was happy but for this one failing.

'I tell you what, love,' she broke into his thoughts, her tone lightly humorous. 'Let's play it by ear. See what happens.'

The honeymoon was the most wonderful time he thought he'd ever spent in his life. He seemed to be a new man, not only in his mind but in all he did, making love an entirely new voyage for him with no restrictions, no sense of embarrassment, awkwardness, fear of sudden repulse, it became fun. They laughed together until finally growing serious and afterwards lay easily in each other's arms, content and fulfilled. He thought of how it had always been with Ethel – that dread of hers that had driven him to leave her in peace, but he couldn't quite recollect any more exactly how it had been and so forgot to think back on it. This was a new life.

Once back home, he put his house in Dartford on the market, selling it within a few weeks. Marion too had hers up for sale, they seeing it as far too small for them and the children.

They were already scanning brochures, today driving along the A127 towards Southend-on-Sea armed with a small bundle of them, one in particular having taken their fancy. It was out in the country, room to stretch their legs as he put it. 'I think I'd rather live in the countryside,' she had said, excited by the new venture. 'When my dad was alive I'd drive the kids and my parents all the way to Wales sometimes over a weekend. Coming back to a built up area always felt a bit sad.'

Now she gazed at the road ahead. They were nearing a turn-off signposted to Brentwood with a couple of properties showing in the area.

'This is our turn off,' she directed, and as they negotiated the narrow lanes she leaned forward with anticipation.

It wasn't until they'd come to the last one that either of them found any enthusiasm. It wasn't the best by a long chalk but had three acres of flat land, sat well back from the road and something about it caught their interest immediately. It was a bungalow that sat isolated from the few other properties nearby and straightaway Charlie could see it had potential for enlargement.

'This place looks promising,' he said, his instinct to see a worthwhile project kicking in. This he could work exactly how he wanted, while carrying on studying his investments, just like in Newhaven.

Outside a sign said, 'Dunton Nursery and Garden Centre', but the gate was half closed with not a sign of any activity.

'It doesn't look very busy,' Marion remarked. 'Not a car or customer in sight.' But she didn't seem disappointed.

'We could do a lot with this,' he replied firmly, making her smile.

The owner turned out to be a disgruntled sort of man with a scowl enough to turn any customer away, but he brightened up by the time his buyers decided the property was what they were after. By the autumn they had moved in, Marion's house now empty with a buyer in tow.

Charlie had said that after settling up the mortgage people, what was left from the sale of her house was hers. 'If I can't buy us a place of our own with my own cash I'm not much of a husband. That's your money.'

Again he saw that smile. It was a sort of secret, self-satisfied smile which he took for her being pleased that he'd not expected her help towards buying the place as some might.

'So long as you don't squander it,' he warned in mock severity, though it was going to take quite a few months before the buyers could complete.

'Tree Lea' as they had now renamed the place had cost eight and a half grand. Marion's house had gone for five and a half, so this place with its whole three acres had been quite a snip in his estimation. But it was going to take quite a few more thousand to enlarge the bungalow and bring the business up to scratch. He got himself an architect and with quite a lot of wheeling and dealing had succeeded in getting planning permission quicker than hoped, though it would probably take a few years to complete.

Meantime Marion's smile had become even more secretive as autumn moved on, always saying how happy she was here as she mucked in with redecorating and getting rid of the rubbish they'd found strewn around.

Lately she'd been gaining a little weight but it suited her. It was a sign of contentment, far better than the strained look she'd once had when she'd been at work.

Then about mid November she began helping less and less, spending afternoons with her feet up. When asked if she was not feeling well, she'd give that quiet smile and say she was fine, just a little tired. But at times she didn't look fine, especially first thing in the mornings. He thought of Ethel, how she had suddenly begun to go down, and he felt alarmed.

'I'd like you to go and see a doctor,' he said. 'It could be serious.'

'I have,' she told him, giving him a sly look. 'And he told me to tell you that you're going to be a father by late June, early July.'

Outwardly he was calm, seeming to take it all in his stride. Some might have even said indifferent. Inside he was a seething mass of fear, for her, for himself. He had never been in this situation before; getting on for fifty-three, an expectant father for the first time and he had no idea how to deal with it.

Even as spring arrived she remained strong and healthy. Ethel too had been strong in her own way. Then without warning her strength had left her, her health failing her completely. What if the same happened to Marion? Forty was a dangerous time for a woman to have a baby, especially after a lapse of fourteen years since her last child. If he lost her his life would be over. He couldn't go through that sort of grief twice in a lifetime. And what would happen to her children? How could he cope with them, the memory of her ever present in their faces?

Something very near terror gripped his insides even as he presented an unruffled face to her steadily growing stomach, while he worked to develop their garden centre, buying in hundreds of boxes of flower seedlings, shrubs, rose bushes, replacing broken panes on the two existing greenhouses, the other two having collapsed in on themselves. He needed to keep his mind on work so as to help dull the dread seething in his heart.

The nursery was doing well. Customers, hearing that it had reopened under new management, were coming in droves to buy spring bedding, shrubs, trees, tubs, fertilizers, garden tools. He had his work cut out dealing with it all, as once he'd hauled huge heavy piles of metal, he now shouldered hundredweight sacks of potting compost to load into their cars, compost he made himself and which his customers seemed not to get enough of.

Summer was already arriving and with it business stepping up. The enlarging of their bungalow had been put on hold, and even in her developing condition Marion would work alongside him, pricking out seedlings by the hour, serving customers, watering shrubs, all despite his telling her to rest.

Now in early June, hot and sticky, it was discovered that her blood pressure was far too high. He was told it could be quite dangerous at this stage of pregnancy and the hospital had ordered her to rest with her feet raised. She would sit in the back garden, feet up, as ordered, trying not to fret at her idleness and the pressure she knew he was under as customers continued to flood in.

It was nine o'clock in the morning on the second of July. Charlie sat in his car trying to fit the key in the lock, the nursery gates closed. He'd already been up two hours and going about opening up the nursery when he heard the phone ringing distantly through the open door of the bungalow. It had been a call from the hospital and now his hands shook as he inserted the car key.

Driving like the wind, careless of any police car spotting him, he made it to the Gidea Park Hospital near Romford in twenty minutes flat, leaping out of the vehicle in the car park and running at top speed to the hospital's anti-natal wing.

He had brought her here yesterday for her usual check-up. She was very near her time and had been having bad dreams about going into labour while he messed about serving a customer! He had laughed and said that would never happen but he knew she hadn't believed him.

So when the nurse examining her said it was only a matter of a few hours before she gave birth, she had opted to stay while he went home. When he had telephoned that evening they had said she was comfortable and doing well, but the baby would probably not be born until the next morning. He'd left her there feeling fine but was still worried.

And now he was standing facing them, they telling him that he had a lovely little daughter, that the mother was doing well, and did he want to go in and see the two of them?

Did he want to? Good God, of course he did!

Marion was lying back on her pillows in a fresh clean private ward, looking absolutely wonderful, her face bright and flushed, her brown eyes twinkling as he came in. Beside her stood a cot and in it the white covers seemed to be wriggling with surprising energy.

'She's a girl,' she announced, and he nodded.

'They told me,' he replied coming forward to bend over and kiss his wife. 'How are you feeling?'

'Wonderful,' she said. She looked radiant.

'It all happened so fast this morning. I hardly had time to breath. And she's perfect. How have you been?'

'Worried,' he said quietly. He wanted to add 'sick', but left it at that.

'Would you like to hold her?'

'Can I?' He tried not to betray alarm. He'd never held a newborn.

'Of course,' she laughed. 'She won't break. And you won't drop her.'

So much had changed. He could hardly believe it as the tiny bundle was given to him to hold. He held it awkwardly, gazing down at the perfect little face. His daughter, his child. Marion was looking up at him, smiling.

'What do you think of her?' He couldn't answer.

'Let's call her Clare,' she suggested.

Still he didn't answer except to nod agreement. The baby was getting easier to hold, he gaining confidence by the minute. This tiny little bit of humanity he held was his, his own flesh and blood. Life was complete and there were years and years ahead of them both – a little family of his own, something he never ever dreamed he would ever have. God's gift for all those years of yearning he'd kept bottled within him.

His gaze went from Marion, his wonderful wife, to his tiny daughter, perfect in every way.

Tears misted his eyes. 'Never in my whole life did I ever dream I'd ever be a father,' he said quietly, reverently, almost like a prayer. Here he was, at fifty-two, a father, deeply in love and his life utterly complete.

Marion gazing up at him from her pillow, full of love and joy for his happiness saw the emotion churning in him and knew that what she had done for him was not only her reward, but his.